Second Ch...

An Oceans Apart Novel

Hattie Wells

ISBN: 9798595129336

DEDICATION

To my wonderful family for always being there.

I wouldn't be anything without you.

To my readers. Without you, there would be no point in writing.

CHAPTER 1

The sun was beating down from above me as I stood in the street. The sound of the crash had been awful drawing attention from all around and the vehicle was still smoking. Suddenly the driver flung the door open and stumbled out into the road, making off as fast as he could despite the fact he seemed to have hurt his leg and was dragging it behind him. Sweat and blood dripped down his face as he ran, pedestrians stopping in shock as they watched the scene unfold before them. I could hear a siren approaching in the distance and soon I could see the car approaching fast, it screeched to a halt behind the wreckage before two men exited it and began to give chase. It was clear from his speed that the first man was indeed injured, but he showed no signs of giving up the chase, turning to fire a gun out towards the officers with no care for the innocent bystanders. The first officer called out a warning as he pulled out his gun, stopping to take aim. More back up was arriving and the tension was rising, I could feel it in the air, even though I was some distance from the danger itself. People were trying to take cover and I could hear their cries of distress. I'd never felt so on edge, and there was nothing I could do. I took a breath my eyes focused only on one person, the officer holding the gun. He shouted again and was about to pull the trigger when I heard someone from behind me shout, "Cut!"

Sometimes the drama drew me in. Sometimes I found it a little hard to remember that I was just a normal girl who just happened to be involved in the filming of a TV programme, and all the drama and action wasn't real. It often looked and felt real. Most days I feel like I'm living a fantastic dream and although it sounds stupid, I worry that when I wake up, I won't remember the details. Getting a job at the 'LA Rescue' studio was not on my list of things to do, it never had been, but luck had stepped in and that was where I worked now. Granted, I had trained as a make-up artist, and I know most days that I'm a pretty good one, but given that I had travelled a lot and struggled to stay in one place for a long time meant I had no plans to try to land such a prestigious job. Being in the right place at the right time seemed to be something that in this case at least, really helped out. Of course, having a best friend already on the crew and running the wardrobe department helped too, as not only had Nicole found out about the job well before anyone else had and told me about it, but she also gave me a recommendation that got me through the door to meet the right people.

In honesty though, accepting this job was way out of my comfort zone. Everything about it was. The fact that I'd be head of my department, the fact that it was the biggest set I'd ever seen, let alone worked on, the fact that I'd be working with really well known and recognisable actors… In many ways, it was a dream job, and I was so grateful, but it was scary too and each day began with butterflies and me feeling nervous. When I accepted the position, I knew I'd be under pressure, but this was no basic television make-up work, there was a wide array of special effects too, and the thought of that was exciting and far too good an opportunity to pass up. Each day was different and fun, and it felt good to be part of such a great team. If it wasn't for Nicole pushing me, I probably would have turned it down, and regretted it in the future, but Nic had said, 'fake it 'till you make it', and so I decided I would try to. What was the worst that could happen? Well, I smiled to myself, thinking of how many times I'd made an utter fool of myself in front of one of the extremely good looking male stars of the show on an almost daily basis.

I watched as Jackson Stone sauntered off the set, he didn't have a swagger as such, but it was clear he was comfortable in his own skin and he chatted with some of the crew as he went. He was hot. I hated to admit it, I'd have preferred him to be completely unattractive, but as one of the two leads of the show, that was unlikely. He played a police detective, while his co-star Mason Delaney played a fire fighter. Seeing him made me remember the first time I had seen the cast of the show in the flesh. I had never expected to enjoy working with the 'beautiful people', including the two male co-stars and had wondered before I met them if I might be star-struck by them. The thought of not being able to look at them or speak to them was terrifying. In reality though it was okay, even though they were both clearly handsome, looking as if they'd stepped off the page of a magazine. I also wondered if they would be superficial, but although of the two of them, one was far more approachable than the other, they both seemed grounded and for want of a better word, really normal. Mason at least seemed to enjoy my company, I got on well with him which made it harder to understand his co-star. I couldn't put her finger on what it was, but Jackson, well Jackson gives me butterflies at the same time as making me quiver with nerves. He was handsome, they both were, and tall and muscular, but again, they both were. There wasn't particularly one thing about him, but the whole package, from his soft brown hair to his intense blue-green eyes. Of course, I'd only imagined his hair was soft, it certainly looked it, but I'm not in the habit of touching men's hair without invitation. All I knew is that I went a bit to pieces when I was around Jackson, and I hated it, but of course knowing he made me nervous only made it worse. I couldn't avoid him, rather as I was responsible for his make up, I had to be close to him and touch him. It was torture, but he barely even noticed I was there for the most part. My only plan was to try and push through. I hoped that if I carried on doing only what I was supposed to be doing that my feelings would eventually die down, and maybe I'd one day be able to act normally around him. I hoped facing up to my troubles would somehow desensitise me. It seemed like he didn't even like me anyway, and I don't even mean in a romantic way, he barely even spoke to me, and just a few times I've turned and caught him watching me, with a frown on his face, it makes me feel like I've done something wrong. I've tried to be friendly; I've done all I feel I can, but I just can't break that wall down, so I've decided to just give Jackson space. I'd be polite, but not too familiar, if he didn't want to talk to me, he didn't have to.

As the end of the working day edged nearer, I began to make my way back to my makeup trailer in the parking area of the studio. This was my base on the set and where I did the majority of my work. It was large enough to have two stations for hair and beauty, but also a sofa running along the back wall. When I was working on one actor, others often relaxed there, chatting things through. With my role came plenty of freedom which I loved, not just in the way I could tackle my work, but also in making the space my own. It had been mine for two months or so now, and I'd added little touches like plants and a few photos of the team to make it more homely. Now the filming was finished for the day the actors would be making their way back too, ready for me to clean them up before I could go home.

The sun was still hot, living in California with the almost ever-present sun was something I was still getting used to. Without thinking about work, it felt almost like being on holiday permanently, although it felt too hot sometimes, and I ran my hands through my long hair twisting it into a makeshift ponytail for a moment to let the air get to the back of my neck in an attempt to cool myself down a little. Despite the heat I found the sun definitely improved my mood. Even getting stuck in early morning traffic felt better than it had done back home where rain had been a lot more frequent. Each day flew by in a whirl, there were many costume changes and wardrobe rotations, and often this meant at the very least make up touch ups, but also depending on the scene, sometimes it was much more complicated. LA Rescue was an action show, a drama based on two brothers working in different rescue services having to deal with challenging situations on a weekly basis. The crew were skilled and tight knit, they were a supportive bunch to work with, and when filming was underway I often stood on the sidelines watching. I liked to be nearby in case I was needed. As the key make-up artist for the show I was in charge of looking after the two lead roles as well as overseeing a small team who worked on the rest of the cast.

There was also a lot of planning to do, checking that looks fitted the scenes and then making sure there was continuity between the scenes. It was interesting and kept me on my toes, I just still couldn't shake the feeling that I should be doing something more to settle things down between me and Jackson. Although I hated to admit it, I knew that I was more than a little attracted to him, and while I was sure I could work through it, it confused me as to why he couldn't do the same. It's not like I've done anything to make it obvious about the way I feel and it just doesn't make sense that he's being so weird. The doubt springing up in my mind reminded me of the many times I've been told I'm oversensitive, so in all likelihood, maybe it's just me imagining things that aren't there.

"I'll see you tomorrow Imogen." Mason said raking a hand through his shaggy brown hair and waving at me. He was tall, towering over me, but there was a gentleness to him, a gentle giant, I thought as I replied.
"Night Mason." They got on well, it was comfortable without being too comfortable, easy without being too relaxed. I waved back and continued wiping down the counter that I'd been working on that day. Jackson stood then too, and moved towards the trailer door. He was much taller than me too, and broad across the shoulders making his presence a little imposing. I think because I can't work the man out, I always feel a little on edge around him.
"Night Jackson." I said, knowing that my eyes had not quite managed to meet his.
"Goodnight Imogen." He replied reaching for his jacket which was hanging near the door.

"Actually, Jackson?" I said nervously. I'd been working up the courage to talk to him, to ask him if there was anything I could do to make our working situation easier and it had seemed a good idea, but now he was here, in front of me, it was so much harder. It was like the words had jumped out of my mouth and now I had no idea about what I wanted to say.

"Yeah?" He stopped and turned back to face me, his face gave nothing away, he was impossible to read.

"Do you have a minute?" I bit my lip, feeling incredibly nervous, and beginning to wonder if I was just going to make matters a whole lot worse.

"Of course. What's up?" He hadn't come any closer, just stayed where he was, and I struggled to look at him, feeling like a rabbit in headlights.

"I, um." I stopped, "Look, I'm not sure what it is that I've done..." I trailed off. I just wanted him to somehow mind read what I was thinking.

"What do you mean?" If I'd have looked up, I would have seen he looked confused but I couldn't bring myself to. In fact, I would have preferred the ground to open up and swallow me, but of course, the chances of that happening were slim to none. There was no way out of the situation I had just created, and slowly, nervously I ran my tongue across my lips, nerves made my mouth feel so dry.

"Well, I just don't know what it is that I've done to offend you, but if you tell me what it is, I'll try not to do it anymore. I really just want to do my job and get on with everyone." I looked down at my feet, unable to make eye contact. I didn't want to feel in awe of him, but just being this close to him was difficult, and I felt so nervous. Well, not even nervous, just a little on edge.

"You haven't offended me." He replied, breaking my thoughts, his voice gruff.

"Oh okay. Good." I let out a huge breath that I didn't even realise I'd been holding. "That's good." I was no further forward but I had no idea what else to say to him. If he said things were okay, then I'd just have to take his word for it. I reached down and grabbed my bag from the floor beside my workstation swinging it up and onto my shoulder, wrapping my fingers around the strap and looking anywhere but up at him. I hated feeling wrong-footed, but that was all he seemed to do to me and he didn't even seem to be trying. "Well, I'm sorry to have stopped you, I need to get off now. It's my turn to cook tonight!" I added, trying to smile, still without eye contact as I moved towards the door of the trailer.

"Imogen?" He reached out and caught my arm, making me gasp. His grip was firm but not hard, and I held my breath, unsure of what to do. I suddenly felt incredibly awkward and wished I had never tried to address the situation between us, I probably should have just ignored it.

"Yes?" My voice sounded odd; it didn't even seem to come out of my mouth.

"You can look at me you know." He said, and I could hear the smile in his voice.

"I, er, I'm sorry." I murmured, he literally seemed to stop me functioning properly. "I, well you make me a little bit nervous." He released my arm as I spoke, but I finally managed to look up at him.

"I make you nervous?" He said sounding shocked and taking a step backwards, clearly putting distance between us. He sounded almost wounded by my comment and I immediately wished I could take my words back. Things often didn't seem to come out of my mouth quite as I'd want them to.

"Not in a bad way." I said quickly, watching as he sank down so he was sitting on the edge of the countertop. It reduced his height, but he was still much taller than me. Slowly he crossed his arms across his chest and looked back at me, clearly waiting for me to continue. "Well, I don't know. You're just you! You know?" I looked down at my feet again, they seemed to be particularly fascinating tonight, especially when I felt this shockingly embarrassed. I wished words would stop falling out of my mouth. Especially when they didn't really make sense.

"What, because I'm on the TV?" He raised an eyebrow, "Because Mason's on TV too and you seem fine chatting with him." He'd gone from sounding put out to slightly upset.

"No, it's not that, it's just…" I stopped, unsure of how to finish the sentence, without saying the words, 'because I'm attracted to you and every time I'm close to you, my mind wanders'.

"Well, what then?"

"Jackson, I'm sorry, I shouldn't have said anything. I just seem to lose my ability to think straight when I'm around you…" I offered, being more honest than I would have liked. Taking a deep breath I added, "Can we just pretend that this conversation didn't happen?" I looked at him, "Please?" Jackson frowned as though he was trying to work me out. "I should go." I added, gesturing to the door.

"Okay." He nodded slightly, not moving from his perch on the counter, the frown never leaving his face.

"I'll see you tomorrow, I guess?" I added, directing the words somewhere between his shoulder and elbow, and looking down I walked out towards the door.

10

'What a complete idiot!' I thought to myself as I walked through the maze of buildings and out to the car park. I pulled my sunglasses down as I screwed up my face in disgust at myself before remembering that other people could still see me so quickly stopped. It was late evening, and so quiet thankfully. Nicole would probably have been home and gone out again already by the time I got home. I was under the impression that she had been seeing someone, or maybe a few someones, but as she hadn't said anything yet, I knew it was early days. We were best friends and very close, but we still had our secrets. When it was serious Nicole would be sure to tell me, but until then I felt it wasn't my business.

I always parked at the far end of the car park, away from the nice shiny, new cars. I wasn't trying to hide it exactly, well maybe a little, it was old, rusty and not that reliable, so I just felt better when it was slightly further away. Lately it had been playing up more and more, only really starting when it felt like it, but it was difficult because until this job I hadn't settled anywhere for long enough to spend enough money on a car that would last, and until now, it had been doing it's job. It seemed pointless to spend more money on something better and the last thing I wanted to do was have my money tied up if I needed to get away. It made getting away difficult when things no longer worked out. Nicole often offered to drive, but as much as I valued her as a friend and wanted her support, I didn't want to alienate the rest of the team by making it look like I was only in my job because my friend was the head of wardrobe. My most successful long-term relationship was the one I had with my best friend. Nicole and I had known each other for years, and in between other things we had travelled a lot, seeing and sharing everything together, until one day, when Nicole decided to settle in LA. So for a while I carried on by myself, eventually coming back to stay with Nicole for a while. Before long this job came up, and it was just too good to say no to. Strangely, for the first time in years, I felt settled. Not in my home maybe, that was just temporary and a little small for the two of us, but in the place certainly. It seemed like I could make a life here, and I could definitely see why Nicole had stayed.

I virtually kicked myself again as I remembered the conversation with Jackson and hoped things wouldn't be too awkward going forward. Cringing at the memory, I was grateful to open the door and sink into the seat, hoping he would let it go. Maybe he'd joke about the crazy English girl, but leave it at that. It didn't help that he was so attractive, but then, it should have been no surprise, he was an actor. Mason was different though, he seemed like a big brother figure almost instantly. He was clearly attractive, but there was nothing there, just friendship. That at least was a relief.

Pushing the keys into the ignition I turned the car over but there was nothing. Groaning I tried again. It was temperamental at times, but until now, I'd been able to limp it along. I hit the steering wheel in frustration, trying once more and the engine chugged into life, giving me a moment's hope before it coughed and died. Letting out a moan, I pushed the door open again and climbed out. I know nothing about engines, but I also know that cars don't tend to fix themselves so I popped the bonnet and looked underneath. Nothing seemed to be out of place, I had hoped maybe the battery had become disconnected and an easy fix would sort it, but it looked like it might be more than that. Hearing a car, I bent over, trying to make it look like I was tweaking something in the engine bay. The last thing I wanted was to look like I needed help, I hate relying on anyone. It reminds me too much of the past. The car carried on past, and once the noise passed I returned to the driver's seat for my bag. I'd have to search for a breakdown service and get it towed to a garage. It was going to be expensive, but it was probably the only option.

"Car trouble?" Jackson's voice made me jump literally out of my skin. I hadn't heard him coming and I swore lightly under my breath. "Hey, sorry! I thought you saw me coming!" He added with a smile.

"It's okay, no I didn't, I was trying to think of who to call for help." I replied, giving him a small smile. I nodded to the car, "Bloody thing won't start."

"It should probably be in a museum, rather than on the road, shouldn't it? Did it get day release? Do they let it out for special occasions?" He spoke as he moved past me and looked under the engine. He seemed to be acting more relaxed than usual which was surprising, and I wondered for a moment if maybe the chat had worked? Maybe it had been worth the embarrassment.

"Oh, ha ha. Yeah, I know. I should get a new one. I just haven't got round to it yet. It normally does the job."

"Well, I can't see anything obvious." He stopped, "Why don't I give you a ride home? Calling a mechanic in the day will be a lot faster and cheaper than calling someone now." He said, dropping the bonnet back down and securing it.

"It's okay, you don't have to do that. I wouldn't want to put you out." I replied uncertainly.

"You're not. I offered." He said looking down at me, pushing his hands into his pockets, then smiling he added, "Unless of course, I make you too nervous?"

"Are you laughing at me?" I frowned at him, trying to hide the smile I felt. He didn't reply but held up his hand, motioning just a little with his fingers. I shook my head at him in disbelief. "Well only if you are sure, I don't want..."

"Stop it." He interrupted me, gesturing towards a shiny black SUV parked a little way away. "C'mon, what's the worst that could happen?" He grinned again, and my stomach did a little somersault. How was it possible for one expression to make someone feel so special?

"Here you go," Jackson opened the passenger door for me and shut it again once I was settled.

"Thank you." I told him once he had climbed in next to me.

"It's no problem. You're going to have to tell me where you live though." He added, and once I did, we quiet fell for a moment.

"This car is massive." I commented after Jackson had exited the studio complex. The car was top of the range, with leather seats and just about every gadget under the sun. It felt like pure luxury, and the complete opposite of my own car. It was everything I usually avoided, and yet it didn't seem like it was for show. My ex had driven a Porsche. It was small, but expensive and flashy; he drove it to be noticed.

"Well, you may not have noticed, but I'm not exactly a small guy." He said with a grin in my direction.

"Of course I had noticed. Both of you are tall. You and Mason I mean. I'd never thought of myself short before I worked with you two!"

"You should meet my brother. He's taller." I laughed.

"Really?"

"Not by a lot, but enough to make me remember I'm the 'little' brother." He laughed too.

"Is it just the two of you?"

"No, I have a younger sister too, she isn't taller than me thank God!" I smiled, realising how weird it was to be having such a normal conversation with Jackson. It might not have been his innermost thoughts and feelings, but it was by far the most he had ever talked to me. "So." Jackson said, breaking the silence and glancing over towards me once more. I looked back towards him expectantly. "It's getting late. Shall we stop and get something to eat on the way?"

"Oh, I'm not sure." I felt awkward. It was strange sitting in such close proximity to him, he seemed to have softened from the exterior I normally saw at work and that made me feel even more unsure of myself.

"Well, are you hungry?" He said grinning again. He had a beautiful smile, and when it was directed at me it made my tummy flutter a little.

"Well, yeah I am, but don't you need to be anywhere?"

"No, I was just going to grab something on my way home, but company would be nice. I know a place just around the corner." He shifted lanes, checking his mirrors as he did so. "Did you say you were supposed to be eating with someone though? Your roommate? Or is it your partner?" I wondered why it sounded like he actually cared who it was.

"I don't have a boyfriend." I started, just wanting to make that perfectly clear, before adding, "I did say that I was eating with my roommate, but it was a bit of an exaggeration, she probably isn't even home." I replied sheepishly, "It was just the first reason I could think of to get away earlier. It was pretty awkward." Jackson laughed and looked across at me.

"And now you're stuck in my car with me. Do you still find me intimidating?"

"I didn't explain it very well." I answered, "I'm sorry. I didn't mean to... Ah, I don't know. It's hard. I just feel a bit on edge around you normally. I feel like I piss you off a bit."

"You don't." He said softly, slowing the car and swinging into a parking space. "You don't." He repeated as he turned the engine off and turned in his seat to look at me. "Not at all."

"Okay." I nodded still feeling doubtful. Biting my lip, I looked up at him. "I'm sorry."

"You have nothing to be sorry for. In fact, I should be the one apologising if I've been making you feel awkward. I really didn't mean to make you feel that way." His voice was low, and it seemed like he really meant what he was saying. "Maybe if you have dinner with me, it'll clear the air and you'll see I'm not so bad?" He said and there was a pause before he asked, "Do you like steak? This is one of my favourite places." He gestured to the restaurant they'd parked in front of. It looked expensive.

"I do."

"Good, come on then."

* * *

"So, I want to understand." Jackson said, putting his beer down on the table after taking a drink. We'd been shown to a secluded table where the waiter had taken our orders, and brought drinks. Now we were just waiting for our food. I was surprised at how comfortable I felt in Jackson's company. Soft music played, and there was a low hum of conversation from the other tables. Jackson sat across from me, leaning back in his chair, arms outstretched, he looked the most relaxed that I had ever seen. "Understand what?"

"What it is about me that makes you nervous?"

"It isn't nervous so much," I paused and took a sip of my wine. "I just feel like you're on edge around me, and that makes me feel on edge. It's like I'm doing something wrong, but I'm not sure what. Mason seems to be okay with me, so it confuses me more, like I just don't know what I'm getting wrong. Some days you barely speak to me at all, and it just makes me panic. That's why I said something earlier. I don't want to get fired, at least not without having had a chance to fix whatever it is I'm doing wrong."

"Okay, so number one, Imogen you are not getting fired." He leaned forward a little catching my gaze, maintaining our eye contact. His blue eyes twinkled. "You are great at your job, and you fit right in with the whole team, okay?" I nodded, grateful for the compliment, but embarrassed at the same time. "Number two." He stopped, raising his bottle once more to his lips, and took another mouthful of beer. "I probably have been a little weird around you, and for that I'm sorry. Being really honest, the reason is that I find you very attractive." He put the bottle down and I focused on it, wondering if I had heard him right. Seeming to guess the doubt in my mind, he continued, "I was very aware that I could make things awkward if I was to try anything on with you, so I thought I'd try to ignore it. But, it seems, I have made things worse. Maybe I should have just asked you out that first day I met you?"

"Are you joking?" I asked looking up at him, trying to work out from his expression whether he was serious or not. "Or is this just some set up, is a camera crew going to pop out in a minute to catch my reaction and give everyone a good laugh?"

"No!" Jackson actually sounded a little hurt, and I bit my lip unsure of how to respond. "Can you just take what I am saying at face value please? I don't play games. I've been on the receiving end of them too many times. I'm just trying to be honest."

"Really?" I asked, puzzled, but holding his gaze, I knew I was frowning but couldn't help it. He was impossible to read, his eyes looked genuine, but in fairness I didn't know him well enough to know if it was just an act. It made me feel awkward, and knowing he acted for a job made it worse.

"Yes really. Man, this is so much easier when I have a script. It all goes smoothly, and then the girl just falls into my arms or my bed."

"I'm not going to fall into your bed. Not tonight anyway." I said, my face far more serious than my mood. Inside I felt flattered that he would even suggest such a thing.

"I didn't think for a moment you would, and I respect you for it." His eyes didn't leave mine, but he stopped speaking as the waiter approached, carrying our food before gracefully placing it down in front of each of us. We'd both ordered the same, steaks with fries and salad. He smiled at me again, "I love that you ordered proper food. I can't stand it when girls pretend that salad leaves are enough."

"Salad is great, but life is too short to miss out on steak." I said appreciatively as I picked up my knife and fork. "This looks amazing."

"It does. Well, enjoy!"

Things were quiet for a few minutes as we ate. I hadn't realised how hungry I was, and I was still trying to process the things Jackson had said. Much as I wanted to believe him, I couldn't imagine for a moment that he was serious. It all seemed too much.

"What are you smiling about?" He asked, breaking my thoughts.

"I hadn't realised I was." I smiled then, wrinkling my nose a little as I looked up at him, his eyes seeming more blue than green and twinkling in the light. Tall, dark and handsome, an actor, it made no sense that he would be interested in me. "I was just thinking about what you said and trying to work out whether you were having me on or not."

"Oh Imogen, I'm not joking. Do you really think I would joke about something like this?" He looked sincere and I wrestled with my thoughts. Trust was not something that came easily to me, and I often doubted the intentions of others.

"I don't really know you, but generally guys like you don't go for girls like me." I said quietly.

"Guys like me? Don't be so judgemental."

"It's not necessarily a bad thing, you just must know so many beautiful women. Why would you be interested in me?"

"Yes, you're right, I do know a lot of beautiful women." He said seriously, "I'm sitting opposite one right now Imogen. I might be in the public eye and have a bit more money than the average man, but other than that, I am just a normal guy. I want normal things, you know? I want to settle down one day, I want someone real, who wants me for me, rather than my job or for who I know. It's really hard to meet girls that are genuine, and when I met you something just clicked. Well, it did for me at least." He smiled at me again. "You are funny, kind, beautiful and way more natural

19

than most of the girls I get to meet. That just makes me want to get to know you better. Is that really so hard to believe?"

"A little." I said managing not to look away. "I mean, of course, I want to believe that what you're saying is true, I'm just afraid I'll look like a fool and everyone will laugh at me." In my head I added, *'and it's hard to trust when you've been burned by a relationship before'*.

"I wouldn't have told you any of this to be honest, but you said something earlier that made me wonder if you were interested in me too." He said softly.

"What did I say?"

"I can't remember word for word, but it was enough to give me a glimmer of hope. Was I right?"

"You might be." I said shyly, a small smile playing on my lips.

"So you're telling me I need to work to prove to you I'm serious?" He said slowly, "You need me to show you I'm not playing around?" I nodded, "Okay, I can do that. I can be a patient man. Just tell me I have a chance and I'll be as patient as you want."

"You have a chance Jackson." I said softly, looking down as I felt heat creep up my face. I dreaded to think the colour my face must be, but I was sure it would be close to beetroot.

"Don't be embarrassed." He reached out and covered my hand with his own. It was warm and safe and made mine feel tiny. The contact made my tummy flutter, and I drew in a breath.

Later that evening as Jackson drove me home, I went over and over the last few weeks in my head. How could I have got him so wrong? Or had I? It was so hard to work out. Over the course of the evening I'd found out a lot more about him, only small things, but things I wouldn't otherwise have known, like he enjoyed working out in the gym most mornings before work. He told me it burned off nervous energy before he went to work. He seemed genuinely interested in me too, and asked me what I liked to do outside of work. He even listened when I told him I was really into photography. For me it had never been a professional thing, but something I enjoyed as a hobby, especially over the time I had been travelling and it was nice to be able to tell someone about it. My thoughts were broken as he asked for directions, and eventually they pulled up outside my building.

"This one?" He asked, pointing.

"Yeah. Up on the third floor. It isn't much, but it's nice enough. The best we could afford. It's a balance trying to get something big enough and in a nice enough area." I said knowing it wasn't the biggest or best apartment, and certainly, I could be sure it wasn't up to the standards of the home he had for himself.

"I wasn't judging." He said, holding his hands up in defence.

"Just asking so I knew." He smiled again, "So you said you had a roommate? Is it two of you who share?"

"Yeah. You know Nicole don't you?"

"Nicole?" He looked blank. "The only Nicole I know is Wardrobe Nicole."

"Wardrobe Nicole? She'd love to know you call her that." I smiled, "But, yeah. That's her."

"Huh, I didn't know that. How did that happen?" He asked.

"Well, we've been friends for years. We went to school together, we travelled together, and she ended up settling here, so when I eventually got bored of being nomadic, I came too. She told me about the job and put in a good word for me at the studio."

"Ah I see. You deserve to be there though, don't think you're there because of favours. You're really good at what you do." He smiled at me and unbuckled his seatbelt. "Can I walk you to your door?"

"What if someone sees?"

"Who cares? Unless you don't want to be seen with me?" He grinned.

"Ah, you hit the nail on the head." I shook my head at him. "Come on then."

It was much later now and the streetlights and passing cars were the only thing lighting our way. Jackson walked so close to me that although we weren't touching it felt like I could almost feel him. It made me tingle.

"Well, this is me." I stopped, digging around in my shoulder bag for my keys.

"What time shall I pick you up?" Jackson asked, standing in front of me, hands in pockets. I'd noticed he seemed to do that when he was unsure of something.

"What? When?" I asked puzzled.

"In the morning? You left your car at work remember?" He grinned, "Unless you want to walk?"

"That's kind of you, but I don't want to put you out." He stopped me from speaking by placing his index finger on my lips. It was such a simple thing, and yet it felt so intimate.

"You worry a lot don't you?" He said smiling and I nodded. "I offered; I wouldn't have done if it was a problem."

"Okay." I replied as he moved his finger away, "Thank you, that would be good." He smiled down at me.

"8am okay?"

"Perfect."

"Okay, I'll be here."

"Thanks Jackson." I smiled back at him, brushing my hair back behind my ear.

"It's no problem. Thank you for tonight, it's been lovely getting to know you a little better." He leaned down, and gently brushed his lips against my cheek, "I'm going to convince you I'm genuine. I don't give up on things I want. Not easily, anyway." He took a step backward, creating space between them. "Goodnight Imogen."

"Goodnight Jackson." I replied, standing in the doorway and watching as he walked back to the car. As he pulled away I waved to him, and he smiled back at me, looking like he'd won first place in a competition.

I didn't sleep well. Relationships had never been my strong point. I struggled to pick the right men and even when I did get a good one things got so complicated that it was exhausting. My last relationship had been long term, and leaving it, and him, had left me far more scarred than I'd ever realised. While I didn't regret it, I hated how wary it had made me. I tended to second guess everything nowadays. My mind whirred as I tried to sleep but try as I might, I couldn't get rid of the butterflies I felt every time I thought about Jackson or the memory of him leaning in to kiss me.

I really wanted to talk to Nicole, to ask her opinion and see what she thought about it, but then I realised that the last thing I wanted to do was talk to anyone. It was too new, too personal and I was still worried that I would be the laughing stock or the butt of a joke if I took anything Jackson said too seriously. But, if he wanted to show me how he felt, I decided I would let him. If things worked out, then that would be amazing, but I couldn't imagine for a minute that it would. What on earth could he really see in me?

CHAPTER 2

"What are you smiling about?" Nicole asked as they moved about the kitchen, making coffee and eating toast.

"Nothing." I replied, smiling even more.

"Nothing my arse." Nicole replied. She'd lived in America for so long now that her accent was faded to almost nothing, but her phrases were still as English as ever.

"It's nothing. I was just thinking about something I saw on TV." I said slowly, hoping my awful lie wasn't too obvious.

"Whatever." Nicole shrugged, "I am sure you'll tell me when you're ready."

"You know I will."

"In the meantime, I won't tell you who I was with last night." Nicole smiled, knowing the suspense would be too much for me.

"Oh really? A someone?" I asked raising an eyebrow and Nicole nodded. "I thought you were out late last night."

"Well, I did think about staying over, but I then I thought you might wonder where I was." We had always had an agreement to look out for one another, it came from so much time spent travelling and exploring together.

"You know I would have done." I looked at my watch. Nicole always left before I did, she liked to be on set earlier, but she was cutting it fine today and I hoped she'd be gone before Jackson arrived. I wasn't sure I was up to explaining anything today, especially to my best friend. The more I thought about it, the more I thought there wasn't really anything to explain anyway, the night had only really been a conversation and a small kiss goodnight. And then there was the subject of my car. I didn't want Nicole leaving as I did and wondering where it was, although to be honest, she'd probably see it in the car park when she got to work. It was hard keeping up with secrets and mine weren't even that big!

Thoughts whirred around in my head and suddenly Nicole was shouting goodbye over her shoulder, rushing out the door with a coffee in her hand. It was annoying at how Nic seemed to be able to roll out of bed looking fabulous. Her hair seemed to fall into place with little help, and she wore little make up. I'm not jealous of her, I just wish I had her ability to look so good with so little work, she really had a way of harnessing her natural beauty and using it to her advantage. We're very different, and while I don't feel like I'm in her shadow it does take me a lot more effort than her to look so natural, and like I hadn't tried. The other thing that was playing on my mind was that I didn't want to go making a huge effort now, it be obvious, and Jackson think I was only doing it in response to his attention. After a lot of contemplation, I decided to keep it simple, and pulled on a pair of denim shorts and a loose t-shirt. Looking in the mirror I decided that I looked okay. Not bad, not stunning, but then it was only work, and after brushing my hair one final time I went to the window overlooking the street and peered out to see if Jackson had arrived. It was almost 8am, and I didn't want to keep him waiting. Not knowing him that well didn't help my nerves and I didn't think it was fair to keep him waiting for me when he was doing me a favour. I was watching the road when I saw his SUV approach, swinging into a space outside near to where he had parked the night before. I noticed the butterflies were back, it had been a long while since I'd had this sort of anticipation of seeing someone. It made me feel nervous, and yet underneath it all I felt excited to see him too. Grabbing my bag, I ran down to meet him.

"Good morning." Jackson walked towards me as I closed the front door. He was holding two cups of coffee and as he reached me he smiled and passed one to me, "I hope you like coffee? I kept it simple, because I wasn't sure."

"Thank you, that's so kind. I wasn't expecting this!" I hadn't expected him to be so thoughtful, and I returned the smile as I took it from him, "I do like coffee, although as I'm English, tea is still my preference in the morning, I'll have to educate you on it."

"Okay, I'll remember that, and I'll look forward to it." He grinned, and nodded to the car, "Shall we?"

Once again he opened the door for me and shut it behind it me once I was in. I watched him swiftly move around the front of the truck to the driver's side and climb into the seat beside me. Starting up the engine, he moved out of the space, slowly joining the traffic on the road.

"I can't work you out." I said after a little while. I was feeling more comfortable in looking at him now, not quite so intimidated, although to be honest, I hadn't managed to relax fully yet either.

"What's to work out?" He asked turning to me and I saw a frown playing on his brow.

"Only, well, you'd barely spoken to me, and now you're driving me around and buying me coffee. You seem different to how you've been at work."

"Different in a good way?" He asked, and I nodded.

"Of course in a good way. I always prefer someone to talk to me that to ignore me." I smiled.

"I didn't mean to ignore you. I was just trying to avoid making things awkward. I screwed that up didn't I?"

"No." His honesty made me giggle a little, "It's just nice to know you don't hate me."

"Oh no, far from it."

"Thank you for the coffee." I said taking a sip.

"No problem."

"And the lift."

"Anytime." He replied, "It's been nice just being able to talk to you, without everyone one else, you know?"

"Yeah."

"But Imogen," He said seriously, and I turned to him cautiously wondering what the problem was, "I think you need to buy a new car."

"I think you're probably right." It was a relief that was what he was talking about. "I just put it off. It's been a long time since I stopped in one place for any length of time."

"Really? How long?

"I'm not really sure. A little over a year and a half guess, no, maybe two years actually."

"And then you travelled until you came here?" I nodded, "Where did you live before that?"

"In London, with my, er, my ex." I said awkwardly before trying to change the subject away from that a little, my past wasn't something I was that comfortable talking about. It was too complicated. "I'd always loved travelling, Nicole and I used to go away whenever we could and when I was single again, I just started travelling more. Nicole ended up here, so I thought I'd come and see her for a while, maybe try to convince her to come exploring with me, but she convinced me to stay instead. She told me about my job and let me move in with her, until we got our place." I felt like the words were tumbling out of my mouth as I struggled to explain myself, I wanted to tell him about myself, but I didn't want to scare him off with too much information.

"What are your plans now? Are you planning on staying?" He asked momentarily taking his eyes from the road to look over at me.

"I might." I smiled. "I've stayed far longer than I planned already, and I like my job, but it depends on how things work out really."

"I hope you do." He said and I looked over at him. Suddenly it seemed, if he was serious and as genuine as he seemed, I'd have a really good reason to stay.

CHAPTER 3

I couldn't get over how quickly things seemed to change. I was still doing the same job, at the same place, with the same people, but only the day before I had felt on edge whenever Jackson was around and now each time I saw him he smiled at me. It made me feel special to catch the little knowing looks he cast my way and while I was cautious, the last thing I wanted was to give myself away to the rest of the team I found it hard to keep my distance. I could already feel myself melting, and it was far too soon. I kept having to remind myself that I wasn't ready, and that he might not even be as serious as he seemed.

That morning when we'd pulled into the carpark I noticed my car was missing which made me panic. Jackson leaned over, gently taking my hand and told me he had had it towed to a repair shop for me. I couldn't get over him doing that for me. It was so unexpected and so kind. He told me that as soon as it was running again, it would be returned. Since my last breakup, I had really tried to focus on making myself self-reliant, independent and I didn't want to fall back into that trap but annoyingly, in a weird way it was nice to be looked after a little bit. I didn't want to come to rely on Jackson, certainly not in the way I'd relied on Adam, but that had been different. Right from the start Adam had taken charge, he had pushed and smothered, but only ever because he cared, according to him. Breaking free had been a breath of fresh air, and much as I liked Jackson, I didn't want to fall into a similar trap. Or a worse one. I couldn't help but worry too that others might see this thing blossoming between me and Jackson and think the worst, maybe judge me or think I was a gold digger. That worried me and played on my mind a lot, so I was careful to tell him that I wanted to keep things professional at work. He'd nodded and agreed and seemed to understand why I asked that of him.

"Do you have plans tonight?" Jackson asked, his voice low as he slid into one of the seats near my work station. The end of the day neared, and it was quiet but I still glanced around to check that no one was nearby. "It's okay, the coast is clear, there's no one here but us." He smiled at me, the smile that never failed to make my tummy flutter, and I pressed my lips together hard to stop myself biting my bottom one, I knew it was a bad habit. He seemed to make me do it a lot.

"No I don't. Why?"

"Ah just wondering is all." He said deadpan, and I glared at him.

"You tease!"

"Hey, I'm kidding!"

"Hmmm." I fake frowned at him, loving that he felt able to relax and joke with me.

"I was!" He shook his head, running his hand through his hair and tousling it a little. "Well, your car isn't back yet, so I could drive you home, and if you wanted, we could grab some dinner? Or I could cook?" He spoke quickly which made me wonder for a split second if he was nervous, but I soon shook the thought off. What did he have to be nervous about?

"You cook?" I stopped what I was doing and just looked at him.

"I'm an actor Imogen, not stupid." He offered shrugging. "I've lived alone for a while, it's either cook or get someone to cook, and I'm not great with having people do everything for me."

"You're full of surprises!"

"Just keeping it interesting." He shrugged again, "In the interests of transparency, I do have staff, well a housekeeper, she cooks sometimes for me, and a grounds man who looks after the outside space, but I like feeling I live in my own home, rather than a hotel."

"I can understand that." I said with a little nod, I wasn't going to admit right now to him that I knew exactly what it was like to have staff, security, well pretty much a whole entourage. It had affected me, but it had been Adam's world and I'd left it behind when I left him. I leaned back on the bench in front of Jackson, for once looking down at him, although admittedly not by a lot. "I don't want to rush things; I've done that before and it seldom works out. If we're getting to know each other, that's what I want to do if that's okay? I meant it when I said I'm not going to jump into bed with you straight away."

"Hey, I'm not asking you to Imogen, that isn't what I meant." He reached out and took hold of my hand. He really seemed so genuine and so gentle it made me wonder why he wasn't already spoken for. "I really did just mean dinner, but if coming home with me is too much right now, then let me take you out again? I meant it when I said I liked you and I'm not trying to rush you. I know it's new, but I don't want to wreck this thing we have, whatever it is."

"Thank you. That means a lot." I said softly, unable to stop myself chewing my bottom lip.

"It's very cute when you do that." He said with a smile.

"It's a bad habit. I'm trying to stop myself, but I forget I'm doing it."

"Well don't stop on my account." There was a pause before he said thoughtfully, "You know, sometimes, when you reach up for something and your top lifts a little, I can see what looks like a tattoo near your waist." I nodded, it made sense he'd seen it although I tried to cover it as much as I could, especially at work. "I haven't worked out what it is yet, but it is intriguing, and I want to see it."

"You want to see my tattoo?" I smiled raising an eyebrow at him.

"Yeah, it's tempting as hell. Like, on the outside, you're all respectable girl next door, and yet I think that maybe you've got this hidden side. I want to see that side."

"It's not so small." I told him, as I began sorting through my brushes on the counter, replacing lids on pots and generally tidying.

"What your tattoo or your hidden side?" He grinned.

"My tattoo." I batted his arm.

"Isn't it?" He looked at me questioningly. "You didn't strike me as a big tattoo girl." I laughed.

"No? Is it only biker girls who have big tattoos? I thought you told me not to be judgemental?"

"True - I don't know. I just don't know many girls with big tattoos. Lots of them maybe, but they're all small if you see what I mean?"

"Well, I suppose mine is like lots of little ones, but all together. It just covers a fairly big area. It's from a time when I was a different person." I wasn't ready to tell him just yet about my life in London. It was hard to explain, and I had the feeling it would scare him off. I didn't want to do that straightaway.

"You're not going to let me see it are you?" He was still sitting in the chair, spinning around so he could watch me as I moved around the room. "I'm even more intrigued now."

"I'm not generally in the habit of taking my top off at work Jackson." I said stopping to look directly at him.

"I didn't mean right here, right now!" He held his hands up in defence. "I just meant at some point."

"Well, you might not like it."

"I think I will."

"Well, I'll show you the top bit now, but you'll have to wait for the rest." I turned my back to him and swept my hair up and off my neck. I knew that wearing my hair loose covered the top of my tattoo, where it emerged over my right shoulder, up the back of my neck to my hairline. I also knew that it would give him an idea of the size of it, which might put him off. The small trail of stars was delicate at the top, on my neck, but they trailed down from there over my shoulder and across my back, swirling around a beautiful dragon and finishing at my waist. It had taken ages, but as large as it was, I still loved it. I held my breath as I heard him stand up behind me. I suddenly felt self-conscious and wondered what he'd think but suddenly warm fingers touched my skin, gently tracing the design up my neck.

"It's pretty." He said, and I dropped my hair, turning back to face him. "Does it go all the way down your back?"

"It does. I'll let you see the rest at some point, but not here." I replied, smiling up at him. There was something about him that just made my stomach tie up in knots and a stupid grin appear on my face. His presence literally reduced me to mush, it was worse than being a teenager again! He smiled back which resulted in my tummy flipping over again. It was actually ridiculous the effect he had on me. In fact, it was probably easier back when I thought I annoyed him. At least then we didn't have any reason to interact, and things weren't so full on. Now, he seemed to always be near and much as I wanted to believe his intentions were genuine, I really had no idea whether they were or not. This could be a huge game to him, and I was the only one in the firing line to get hurt. I just wasn't prepared to let that happen.

"How come you haven't got a girlfriend?" I asked later as we slid into a booth tucked away at the back of the restaurant Jackson had brought me to for dinner.

"How come you haven't got a boyfriend?" He replied.

"Touché." I said with a nod, then smiling added, "But it's still a valid question and I asked first."

"Fair point." He took a breath, "I guess, it's hard to see if a girl is genuine or not. A lot of them, they don't really want me, they want to date an actor. Or they want my money, or my status, or my character."

"Your character?" I asked him puzzled.

"Yeah, it's like, they see me on TV and think that is me, that that's who they're getting. It's like they're after the action, they think I'm this badass cop, and you know, that's all a story for TV. It's just my job."

"That must be hard."

"Yes, it is. Funny story," He said and then stopped, "No actually, it's not appropriate. Forget I said anything."

"You can't say that and then stop." I said scowling at him.

"I wasn't thinking, you really don't want to know."

"Well that's making it worse. You're just making it sound even more interesting."

"Okay." He rubbed his hand over his face, and sighed, "One of the last girls I was 'serious' with, well, I knew she liked the show, but I really thought she liked me too. She seemed to, but then one night, we were in bed, and well we were..." He stopped, unsure of how to word it eloquently.

"Yes I get the picture. Go on."

"Well anyway, she called out my character's name, rather than mine. That kind of killed the moment." He took a sip of his drink, "And the relationship."

"Oh no! That's unbelievable. How could someone treat you like that? How can they just forget that you aren't your character?"

"Yeah, but you get it. That's one of the things I like about you. You see me." He smiled. "Oh, and the fact you're beautiful."

"Oh stop it." I said shyly. "You could have your pick of women."

"I know, that's why I'm here with you tonight."

"Jackson, I'm really not the sort of girl you want to get involved with." He looked at me and probably saw that I was no longer smiling.

"Why not?"

"It's complicated." I let out a breath, unsure of what to say.

"Complicated?" He raised his brow, "You're going to have to do better than that Imogen."

"I have a lot of messy history." I told him. I wasn't prepared to elaborate on that. Not now certainly, maybe not ever.

"I'm not interested in your history Imogen; I want to get to know you now." I looked at him, again, wondering if I was seeing the truth of his feelings. "I just hope that you might want to get to know me better too?"

"Nah." I said letting my smile return, "It's only your money I'm after. Have you got a lot of it?"

"I hope you're joking?" He shook his head at me. "See, you're funny, you're beautiful, and you're talking to me like I am just a normal guy. It's really nice Imogen."

"It is really nice. I do like spending time with you Jackson, and you're not so bad to look at either." He burst out laughing.

"Yeah, that right there is one of the reasons I like you."

Later that night as he walked me to my door, Jackson's hand found mine and our fingers laced together.

"Thank you for tonight." I said softly, looking up at him.

"You're welcome. Thank you for coming out with me." He paused, "Can we do this again?"

"I'd like that." I nodded, coming to meet his gaze as we stopped walking and came to face each other at the bottom of the front steps. There was something so reassuring about him. He was so tall, and so strong, and yet there was a gentleness about him that comforted me, I felt safe with him, which was a really nice feeling. Feeling brave, I took the initiative stepping in and resting my palm gently against his chest. It felt solid beneath my hand. Lifting up on my toes I reached up to press my lips to his. He bent his head to meet me in a slow, gentle kiss and I relaxed as his arm wound around my waist, pulling me closer to him while his other hand found its way into my hair.

"I need your number." He said as we eased apart a few minutes later. He pulled out his phone from his pocket and unlocking it, passed it to me to input my number. "I'll text you now so you have mine," he said as he took it from me and quickly tapped out a message. My phone alert went off almost immediately. "So 8am?"

"Only if it's no trouble?" I replied. I couldn't help but feel like I was putting him out.

"None at all." He leaned down gently kissing me one last time, and for a moment I wondered if I should go back on my promise. Suddenly I didn't want to say goodnight, and instead wanted to invite him in. He stepped back from me and smiled. "Goodnight Imogen."

"Goodnight." I replied watching him go.

Later, my phone lit up with a simple message that made my heart flutter, "Goodnight sweetheart x."

CHAPTER 4

In the morning Nicole was up and out before I was even out of bed. It made me wonder if she had come home at all, despite our long-standing plan to let each other know we were okay if we weren't planning on coming home. I knew how things could go, and if Nicole was in the middle of something, it was likely that I was the last thing on her mind.

I dressed quickly after my shower and checked out the window as I applied my makeup to see if he had arrived yet. It was surprising how excited I was to see him, considering it had only been a few hours since he kissed me goodnight, and I felt the butterflies in my tummy flutter a little again.

"Hey." I smiled across the pavement at him as I pulled the door shut behind me. The sun was shining again and it looked like it would be another beautiful day. Jackson was out of the car and leaning back on the bonnet, two cups in his hands. "You know, a girl could get used to this." I said as I reached him, stopping just in front of him.

"Morning beautiful." He stood and stepped towards me, putting one of the cups in my hand before sliding his free arm around me, pulling me to him and pressing his lips against mine.

"What a pain we have to go to work." I said as I pulled back.

"I know. I'd say we could skip it, but I think they'd notice we were missing, and then people might guess we were together and then you'd have to admit it, even though you are ashamed to be seen with me."

"I am not ashamed!" I said laying my hand on his arm, "I'm just not sure what people would say. I don't want anyone to get the wrong impression."

"Well that's fine, and it's okay, for now." He leaned down and kissed me once more, "But eventually, if we're together, I'm going to want people to know we are. I don't want anyone hitting on you either."

"Oh, the jealous type are you?"

"Maybe a little, but more protective really, I just want everyone to know that you're with me."

"But Jackson, it's only been a few days, we aren't really 'together' are we?"

"Maybe not quite yet, but I hope that's the way we're going." He looked down at me, "Isn't that what you want too? It feels like you do but tell me if I'm reading things wrong."

"No, I do. I just don't want to rush it. It's new, and it's good and I don't want to spoil it. I've never been with anyone famous before, and it's all a bit scary."

"Scary huh? Well at least I don't seem to intimidate you anymore." He smiled, "Come on, we'd better get going."

For a while we drove in silence and I wondered if I'd been too honest about the way I felt. I really liked him, but the thought that this was a game to him still played on my mind.

"I meant to say, I'm not going to be around much of next week. I don't know if you knew or not." Jackson said as they pulled up to some traffic lights.

"No I didn't, I hadn't looked at the schedule yet." I replied looking over at him, "What are you up to?"

"There are a lot of filler scenes that I'm not needed for so we've scheduled them all in together so I have a few days off. I told my Mum and Dad that I'll fly up and see them. It's my brother's birthday, so he and my sister are coming too so we'll just have a few days together."

"That sounds nice." I said, wondering how I was going to cope for a week without seeing him. "Where do they live?"

"Texas, not too far outside of Austin." He replied, "We're close, and Mum and Dad still live in the house that I grew up in, so it's kinda cool to go back every now and again and see them all."

"That sounds lovely. I don't have anyone like that, it's just me and well Nicole. I think that's why we're so close, because for a long time we're all we had."

"Then you are lucky to have each other, I guess you're pretty close to being sisters then?"

"That's how we think of it." I smiled, "I know it's early days Jackson, but I'll miss you."

"It's only a few days, but I'll miss you too." He leaned over and rested his hand on my thigh, gently giving it a squeeze, "And I promise I'll come back."

"Good. You'd better." I replied, and softly placed my hand over his, linking our fingers together.

* * *

The days passed slowly without Jackson around. I was surprised at how quickly I'd grown accustomed to his company, and every time I heard the door to my makeup trailer open, I found myself hoping it would be him. We'd text each other a few times which was lovely, although I was conscious that I didn't want to seem needy either by bothering him too much. He'd also sent me some photos of the horses on the ranch his parents lived on. I was shocked when I saw them, I'd been expecting a house, not a farm, and it was a lovely looking one at that. Part way through the week he'd phoned me. He said he wanted to hear my voice and we ended up talking into the early hours, about everything and nothing. The more I got to know about him the more I came to trust him, to see that he was being genuine, at least, I hoped he was. He was kind and selfless and had even offered me the use of his car while he was away because mine still wasn't fixed. It was so lovely of him, but I thought it was a step too far and eventually told Nicole that mine was in the garage so I could car share with her. As the week went on, my car was returned with a hefty bill of course, but actually running and reliable which was always a bonus.

Home alone in the evenings, I noticed how much time Nicole was spending out with her 'someone'. I was dying to ask, but didn't want to put my friend on the spot, so kept my nosiness to myself, I was confident that Nicole would tell me what was happening when she was ready to.

When Thursday arrived I was so excited to finally see Jackson, and knowing his flight would have returned him in time to come to work, I was on edge all day. Despite repeatedly checking my phone I hadn't heard from him, and doubt began to creep in. It seemed like my first thoughts were right, and he'd just needed space to realise he didn't want to be involved with me. I kicked myself for letting my guard down, for letting myself get so close to him and I wondered what it was about him that had made me let myself fall for his charms. Even Nicole commented on my grumpiness, it was just so frustrating not to have heard anything at all from him.

On Friday I still hadn't heard anything so despondently, I drove to work. I was caught between feeling grateful for having my car and independence back and sad that I had seemingly lost what I thought was beginning to grow between me and Jackson. I made it through security and pulled into the car park nearest to our studio. I had no idea what the plan would be for the day and I found that unsettling. I wasn't confident that I'd manage to last the day given the way I felt. Taking a deep breath I swung the door open and stepped out into the car park to see Jackson's car already parked there.

It was so strange having him back, and his attitude did nothing to help me work out what was going on. It seemed that Jackson was there in body but not in mind. He made no effort to talk to me, and even seemed to be keeping a distance from me. On set he looked like he was just fine, laughing and joking between the scenes with the other members of the cast, but it wasn't my imagination, he was definitely keeping me at arm's length. Although he spoke to me when he needed to it wasn't like it had been before and to be honest, it hurt a little. We didn't have a moment alone to speak all day, even during make-up others were floating around, all trying to catch up with him and so by the end of the day I was just as confused as I had been at the start. I gave up in the end, and knowing he at least had my number, I hoped he'd call sometime in the evening. As I left my trailer I pulled my sunglasses down as a defence for myself, hoping no one would catch me on my way to the car. There was no sign of him anywhere and I'd almost made it when I heard someone call my name.

"Imogen!" I heard again, the unexpected shout had made me jump and I stopped in the middle of the car park to see where the voice had come from. I saw Mason leaning out of the window of his truck beckoning to me.

"Hey Mason, what's up?" I answered as I walked over to the car. As I reached the window, I realised Jackson was sitting in the passenger seat. Oddly, he smiled and waved at me.

"A few of us are going down to this bar we know for a few drinks. Do you want to come?"

"Oh." I suddenly felt lost for words.

"Come on Imogen." Another voice called and I peered in to see Nicole sitting in the back of the car. "Some others are meeting us there, it'll be fun!"

"I'm the designated driver, so I'm dropping these guys home later, but there's room for one more if you want to jump in?" Mason said smiling.

"Are you sure?" I asked and when Mason assured me he was, I opened the back door and climbed in next to Nicole. It was nice to be invited, but I couldn't help but feel a little bit of an afterthought as the invitation hadn't come earlier in the day, or from Jackson. I wondered if maybe they wouldn't have even bothered if they hadn't just driven right by me. It made me wonder again if I'd done something wrong or perhaps he just didn't want to spend any more time with me. Maybe I was crowding him. Maybe he was just bored of me. It would be about right, even though it made me feel incredibly sad.

"Imogen!" Nicole's voice broke through my thoughts, and I looked at her quickly.

"What?"

"Jackson was talking to you."

"You were? Sorry." I said looking towards him in surprise.

"It's okay, are you all right?" Jackson said, looking straight back at me.

"Yeah, just thinking. What did you say?" I asked him, well aware that a car full of people were able to listen.

"I just said it's good that you could come tonight. I looked for you earlier, but I couldn't find you." He said holding my gaze. "We try to get the team together fairly often, it's good to kick back a little together, when we work so hard. It keeps the team close." I nodded feeling even more confused by him.

"It's cool. Thanks for inviting me."

I looked out of the window for the rest of the journey. I could barely focus on the conversation and in the end gave up, letting the sounds of the voices just wash over me. Eventually they turned into a car park and Mason found a space, turning the engine off.

"You're being weird babe." Nicole said linking her arm through mine as we got out of the car.

"I'm not."

"You are. What's up?" The two men had walked ahead and slowly we followed them towards the bar.

"Nothing is up." I said again.

"Wait." Nicole stopped me and stared hard at me. "Do you like him?"

"Like who?" I asked, panicked. The last thing I wanted was someone knowing about me and Jackson.

"Mason?" Nicole said hands on both hips. "You've been weird since he called out to you."

"No!" I answered with relief, "Well, as a friend of course, but nothing more."

"Are you sure?" She still looked extremely suspicious which in turn made me feel suspicious, while also making me wonder why Nicole hadn't asked me about my feelings towards Jackson too. She only seemed to care about Mason and so I wondered if that might be who Nicole was spending all her extra time with.

"I'm sure. What's with the 20 questions?"

"Nothing. Forget it." Nicole said walking away and following the others into the bar.

It was far busier than I had expected in the bar, and the moment the cast and crew of 'LA Rescue' walked in, everything just got busier. There seemed to be people everywhere and fans were crowding around. Music was pumping and our group pushed through the crowd to a long table near the back. A few drinks in, and I was beginning to feel a little more relaxed, even though I still felt that Jackson was giving me a wide berth. It was awkward, because I wasn't sure how relaxed and chatty I could be without seeming too flirty in front of the others. Not that I could really even try to chat with him, he'd barely made eye contact with me after speaking to me in the car, and we weren't sitting anywhere near each other at the table the majority of the team were sitting at. I really wanted to enjoy myself and accepted another refill of wine when it was offered, but found my attention and eyes wandered considerably, and instead of chatting with those near me, I found myself watching Jackson as he chatted to those approaching him for autographs or photos. I tried to catch his eye when he got up to go to the bar again, but he didn't seem to see me, and carried on walking. In fairness it was really busy. Pushing my chair back and grabbing my bag I followed, determined to have a few moments with him. I hoped that if I knew how he was feeling then at least I would be able to gauge how I should act around him. As I passed the dance floor, I saw Nicole and Mason dancing together and smiled, they seemed to be having a lot of fun and appeared far too close for just people who worked together, unless of course they'd both had a few too many to drink, although Mason had said he was driving? I scanned the crowd again for Jackson, and stopped when I saw him standing with another woman near the bar. They weren't touching, but they might as well have been, considering how close they were. He leaned down tilting his head to hear the woman better, and she reached up putting her hand on his shoulder. It made sense, I thought to myself, that he was meeting someone else and that was why he hadn't found me to invite me here himself. I was just surprised as to how much it hurt and kicked myself for ignoring my first instincts to trust him. What a fool I'd been! Before I had even thought about what I was doing, I was walking out of the door and into the street. Outside it was dark and I stopped, wondering what to do. I had no car, but I wasn't going to walk back into the bar to feel a fool, so I started walking hoping I'd see a taxi before long. Upset as I was, I would be damned if I'd let anyone see me cry.

* * *

"Yes, she's here." Nicole's voice was loud and so was the light that had been flicked on over my head. I closed my eyes again, trying to shut out the light, groaning as I rolled over and tried to look at my clock.

"Nicole, it's after 2am, why are you in here shouting?" I said as I sat up.

"Yes, tell him and I'll call you back in a moment." Nicole said into her phone before ending the call and plopping down onto the bed next to me. "Is your phone broken?"

"What's going on?" I asked, still struggling to work out why Nicole was in my room in the middle of the night.

"You disappeared from the bar. No one knew where you'd gone and," She picked up my phone, and after looking at it held it up to my face. "You have about a million messages from everyone because we were all trying to make sure you were okay." Through my sleep added mind it dawned on me that Nicole was actually angry with me, and I took the phone from her, seeing messages and missed calls from not only Nicole, but Jackson as well.

"Sorry Nic." I reached out and squeezed her hand. "I just wasn't feeling it last night, and I didn't want to stop you. You looked like you were having so much fun-"

"I was!" Nicole interjected.

"I didn't think you would notice. I'm sorry."

"Well," Her tone dropped a little, "It wasn't me actually, it was Jackson who noticed you'd gone. He asked me where you were and I didn't know so he and Mason have been out looking for you, especially because you didn't answer your phone." I groaned feeling like an idiot.

"Shit, sorry."

"I've told them both now, so they're going home." Nicole said shoving me hard in the arm. "I am so angry with you. I was having a really good night."

"I said sorry."

"I know. It's just urgh! You know? Things were good, and then I had to go looking for you, and you were just here, ignoring us all."

"Thank you for checking on me. It means a lot."

"You're welcome, but don't do it again. I'm going to go and call Mason back and explain. Night." She leaned in for a hug and then left the room, leaving me to my thoughts.

CHAPTER 5

I woke up early the next morning after another restless night.
Needing to clear my head I decided to go for a run and after
pulling on my running kit I crept to the door hoping not to disturb
Nicole. After the previous night, the last thing I wanted was to
face her wrath again. I was just grateful it was Saturday and that I
didn't have to face work at least.

I don't really like running. The thought of it stresses me out and I
don't look forward to it, but I've also found it's the best thing for
clearing my mind. As I fell into a rhythm, my feet pounding the
pavement I began to feel the tightness in my mind loosening.
An hour later, and with a much clearer mind I arrived back home.
As I walked up the stairs I popped my earphones out, stretching
out my arms as I did. I still wasn't used to the LA heat and
running early in the morning was the only way I managed to get
out for a run now. If I left it too late, I found it impossible. I
unlocked the door, pushing it open and walking into our little
hallway as I kicked off my trainers. Our apartment had an unusual
layout, with the front door opening into a long hall leading to the
bedrooms and the bathroom. Off the hall through a large arch

was an open plan living area consisting of a lounge and kitchen with a dining area tucked to one side. It worked for us, giving us a nice balance open plan living while also ensuring a degree of space and privacy.

"Morning!" Nicole shouted through to me from the bathroom, sticking her head around the door. "Nice run?" She asked and I stopped flashing her a smile, relieved that she was no longer angry with me.

"Yeah, good thanks. You're up early."

"The door woke me up. You have a visitor." She nodded to the living area. "And will you please take your phone with you the next time you go out? I'm not your answering service." She smiled as she said it, but there was a tone to her voice that told me she meant it.

"Oh really?"

"Yeah, and later, I want details, but not now - I'm going out in a minute." She raised her eyebrows.

"Anyone interesting?" I asked.

"Yes, and later I will tell you, in return for some secrets of yours."

"Sounds like a plan."

"Now go and say hello."

"Yes Mum." I said with a grin walking towards the lounge. Sometimes it seemed like Nicole was more my older sister than my friend. I know she only acted like it because she cared about me, but occasionally it got a little bit much. I rounded the corner and stopped when I saw Jackson sitting on the sofa scrolling through his phone. He looked like he had made himself at home.

"Jackson? What are you doing here?"

"Hey, good morning." He stood up, slipping his phone into his pocket and looking me up and down, "I didn't know you ran?"

"Yeah, not as often as I like, but it clears my mind." I replied with a nod. "Why are you here?"

"I just wanted to talk, if you have a few minutes?"

"I was just going to grab some water and jump in the shower. I probably stink." I replied, trying to brush him off. I was still feeling hurt over the way he'd been ignoring me, and I couldn't imagine what he wanted to talk to me about, other than to finish things between us. In honesty, I'd rather take the easy way out and just leave it, letting it fade away, rather than have an awkward conversation.

"I can wait. I'm not in any rush." He said jamming his hands into the pockets of his jeans, his blue-green eyes not leaving mine.

"I'm just going to interrupt to say bye!" Nicole called, popping up next to me. "Now, do you need me to show you how to use your phone before I go?"

"Ha bloody ha." I frowned at Nicole. "Have a good time."

"Oh, I will." She grinned, "Oh, there's coffee in the pot if you want it. See you later, bye Jackson." He raised his hand in a wave and then turned his attention back to me as the door closed.

"See, I have my phone, and your TV, and coffee, go and have your shower, I'll be fine here." He sank back into the sofa and picked up the remote.

"Okay." I nodded, backing out of the room, feeling even more puzzled than I had the night before.

"Don't rush!" His words followed me to the bathroom.

I knew he'd told me not to rush but I couldn't help it. I didn't want to keep him, and I also wanted to know why he had come round. Hopping out of the shower I dried off, loosely towel drying my hair before putting a little mascara on. Despite not wanting to waste time putting on any more makeup I couldn't face him without anything. From my wardrobe I pulled out a yellow sundress I liked and deciding I was done, barefoot I walked back out to the lounge.

Nicole and I only have one sofa, so I had no choice but to sink down next to Jackson leaving a little space between us. Nervously I pulled my leg up beneath me, almost as a bit of a defence.

"Hey." He watched me as I arranged myself, "You look beautiful."

"Thank you." I blinked and looked down feeling suddenly shy. I felt his finger before I saw him move, gently under my chin, tilting my face back up to look at him.

"Have I done something? What's changed?" His eyes searched mine and I saw that he looked genuinely worried. When I didn't reply straightaway, he dropped his hand, covering mine with his own and continued, "I was worried about you last night, and when you didn't answer your phone…" He trailed off, still looking at me.

"Yeah, I'm sorry about that, I put it on silent when I went to sleep and didn't think about it until Nicole came into my room shouting at me." I shrugged. "I didn't think anyone would notice I was gone."

"I noticed."

"But you didn't even invite me Jackson. I felt like I was tagging along, and then you didn't even talk to me." I admitted, again unable to meet his eye.

"I wanted to, but you said you didn't want anyone knowing about us and I was trying to respect that." He replied frowning.

"What, by chatting with other women?" I asked, for the first time looking up at him voluntarily.

"Are you jealous?" He asked, "Because they were just fans. Going out in public can be hard work. Mason and I tend to attract a bit of attention, and if we just ignore fans it can affect how we're perceived but it means nights like that aren't always easy. I try to give them a bit, but of course I wanted to spend time with you. When I went to look for you, you were gone."

"The woman at the bar, was she just a fan?" I asked doubtfully. To be fair, I probably sounded suspicious, I certainly felt it.

"I didn't speak to anyone who wasn't, except for the crew. Imogen, I'm not interested in anyone else. I meant it when I said it before, I really like you. A lot."

"Really?"

"Yes." He sighed. "You've got so many walls up, I'm trying to be understanding, but you're going to have to trust me a little bit too."

"Okay, so why didn't you call me? I was expecting you back on Thursday and I didn't hear from you and then yesterday you were just at work like nothing had happened. It felt like you were avoiding me."

"Not at all." He shook his head, "My flight was delayed. I was going to call you, but I managed to lose my phone."

"You have it now." I said unsure of whether he was telling the truth, it made no sense, I knew I'd seen it in his hand.

"Yeah, I do. My battery was low, so I was charging it in the departure lounge. When they finally called my flight, I was so keen to get back that I was rushing, and I must have left it there." He smiled, catching my doubtful look, "I know it sounds ridiculous, but it's true. I didn't even notice until I was already on the plane and then I could hardly go back."

"Well how did you get it then?"

"One of the staff there noticed it, and they managed to get it couriered to me, I guess it wasn't too far behind me. It was a real pain in the ass though, I forget how much I rely on it."

"If that's true, why didn't you talk to me yesterday?"

"I thought you wanted to keep 'us' quiet?" He asked.

"Well yeah I do, but I didn't expect to be back to being ignored."

"I'm sorry if that's what you think I did. It certainly wasn't intentional. I was just trying to give you space. I hoped I could talk to you on your own, but every time I saw you, you were with someone else. I thought I'd get the chance last night, but then you disappeared." I looked at him, so unsure, trying to work out from his face whether he was really telling the truth. "You're going to have to start believing me. There is no one else."

"I'm trying." I admitted. "It's just hard."

"Tell me what I can do to make you believe me." He said, and at that moment, I could see it was genuine.

"I think I'm slowly getting it; I'm just scared." I moved onto my knees, scooting closer to him, so the full length of my thigh pressed against his, gently placing my hand on his jaw, "I'm sorry," I whispered stretching up and planting a kiss on his lips.

"What are you so scared of Imogen?" He asked holding back a little.

"That you'll hurt me I guess. That I won't see it coming." I admitted. Softly he stroked my cheek.

"I can promise you that I will never intentionally hurt you Imogen." He tilted my face up so he could hold my gaze. "If we're together, I'm all in. I won't look at another woman, I certainly won't cheat on you. I've told you, I'm not playing here, and while I can't promise things will work out for us, I promise you I will talk to you if I have a problem."

"Okay." I nodded, completely taken aback by his honesty. He kissed me then, and I softened into him, my skin tingling as he moved one hand up my back, resting the other on the bare skin of my thigh. "I am sorry." I repeated, breathing the words into the side of his face.

"It's okay, but don't ever leave somewhere like that in the middle of the night again. Not on your own. I was so worried about you." He said breaking away for a moment. "Anything could have happened to you."

"I won't." I said meeting his gaze. Slowly I moved closer, climbing up so I was sitting astride his lap, lacing my arms around his neck as his hands moved around my waist. I felt him exhale as I moved in closer to him, before he dropped his mouth to my neck.

Much later we lay in bed together on our sides, looking at each other. Between us our hands lay intertwined.

"Well, I wasn't expecting that to happen when I came over this morning." Jackson murmured raising my hand momentarily to his lips.

"I can't say I was either. So much for taking things slowly. I've clearly got no willpower when it comes to you." I smiled back at him. "It was pretty amazing though."

"I'll agree with that." I closed my eyes, feeling completely content at that moment. There was silence for a few minutes before Jackson said, "Imogen?"

"Hmmm?" I opened my eyes again to find him watching me.

"I know you don't want to rush things, but I kinda think we're past that now."

"What do you mean?"

"Only that, well if you're sharing a bed with me, I want to know it's just me, that there's no one else. I don't want to share you."

"There's no one else Jackson." I squeezed his hand hoping he didn't think I was the sort of woman to be sleeping with other men behind his back.

"I mean, I want to make it exclusive. Us, I mean officially. If that's okay with you?" He stopped and looked at me. Suddenly this was moving way faster than I ever would have imagined, but at the same time, nothing had ever felt so right. "I told you I'm serious, and I want you to be able to trust me, to know that I'm committed to you too. I want to tell people, well at least our friends, that we exist."

"That's so sweet of you." I smiled, leaned forward and kissed him again, "Exclusive? So you mean…"

"Yes, I want you to be my girlfriend." He said softly to which I shyly replied,

"Jackson I'd love to be your girlfriend."

It was lunchtime before we actually managed to leave the bed, and as I dressed, I wondered if Nicole would be home soon. I couldn't remember if she said where she was going or how long she might be. I stepped into my underwear, stopping to watch Jackson as he stood to pull on his jeans - he looked amazing without a shirt on. He caught me looking and grinned at me. "Like what you see?"

"Oh, I think you know I do." I walked over to him, stopping in front of him to slip my arms around his waist, laying my head against his bare chest. He returned the embrace, wrapping his arms around me too, resting his chin on top of my head.

"You know the feeling is mutual, and I like this too." He said running his fingers down over my shoulder following the cascade of stars that ran down my back to my hip. His fingers made my skin tingle.

"I'm glad, I wasn't sure you would." I admitted.

"Of course I do, it's big, but it's delicate. Can I ask why the dragon though?" I could feel him tracing the dragon that was nestled between the stars in the centre of my back.

"Do you really want to know?" I asked uncomfortably.

"Yes, even more so when you say it like there's something more to it." He said leaning back to meet my gaze and looking at me carefully.

"Well, it's not really anything that important. There used to be a name there, and then that part of my life was over, and I didn't want it to say that anymore. I decided dragons are fierce and that's what I wanted to be. I had the name covered with the dragon."

"I prefer the dragon." He smiled, "It's a good coverup. You can't even see there was a name there."

"That was the plan." I relaxed into him and closed my eyes.

"I could get used to this." He softly murmured into my hair.

"Me too, but Nicole might be home anytime, and I don't know that I want to tell her everything just yet."

"Do you want to come over to my house? I'll even cook for you, and if you want, you can spend the night with me?"

"Yes that sounds lovely." I said stepping back, "I'd better finish getting dressed."

I quickly finished dressing and threw a change of clothes into a bag with my hairbrush and some makeup. "Do I need anything?" I asked as left the bedroom and I dropped the bag on the sofa, before going to find my shoes.

"You could throw your swimsuit in?" He replied looking over at me.

"You have a pool?" I asked and he nodded, "Of course you do. What was I thinking?" I smiled; it was so easy to forget what a different world he lived in compared to me. "I'll get it."

***

The differences between Jackson and myself were huge, and they seemed to be getting more noticeable, not less. On the one hand, when I spoke to him, I forgot he was any different to me. He acted in the same way, he wasn't pretentious, talking to him felt natural, but seeing him being fawned over by women like the night before, and knowing he had his own pool when I could barely keep my car on the road just highlighted the differences. It felt a little like I was walking through a dream, and I still couldn't quite get my head around the fact that he was interested in me. I pushed my doubts as far to one side as I could and tried to accept things as they seemed to be, the last thing I wanted to do was to push him away with my worries.

Jackson's hand rest on my thigh as he drove, and I relaxed, looking out of the window. Something had certainly changed between us, and at least for me, there didn't seem to be any awkward silences. It seemed somehow natural for us to be together. I'd left a note for Nicole, I didn't want to aggravate her again, and although I told her I was going out and staying out, I didn't say who with. In hindsight I realised it was probably obvious, as Nicole had seen us together earlier in the day, but I wasn't ready to spell it out for her. It was only as we drove that I realised I didn't even know where Jackson lived.

"You're quiet. Are you okay?" Jackson asked after a few minutes.

"I'm fine," I replied quickly, covering his hand with my own, "I was just thinking, there's so much we don't know about each other. I don't even know where you live."

"Santa Monica." He replied, "Do you know it?"

"I think Nicole and I ate at a restaurant down by the beach one night, but I don't know it well. Is it far?"

"Not really, it's about twenty minutes from the studio, so it's convenient. Mason lives there too actually, but he is right on the beach, and my house is a bit further back. It's a little quieter there."

"That must be nice having a friend close by, but not on your doorstep?"

"It is, we don't see each other all the time, but we do eat together occasionally, or have people over to one of our places. It's nice."

"You two are really close aren't you?"

"Yes we are. He's like another brother really. It's weird to think I didn't know him growing up, we hadn't even met before we got our parts on the show, but something clicked, and we just got on instantly."

"That's great. I can't imagine working so closely with someone you didn't get on well with. It must be hard."

"It's really important for our show to be tight knit though, we're more of a family than anything else. It's just a bonus that we work together too."

"I have to admit, it's a great team to work with. I don't think there is anyone I don't get on with."

"Only me at the beginning?" Jackson laughed.

"Yeah well, you scared me. You were all silent and brooding and it made me nervous."

"I was trying to work out the best plan to get you into my bed."

"Well it worked."

"So, intimidation turns you on?" He asked raising one eyebrow, "Should I keep it up?"

"Don't be daft. We're past that now."

"Ah okay. I'll remember that." He smiled at me. "We're nearly there. This," he said making a turn, "Is my street." I looked out of the window at the wide street in front of me, and suddenly the nerves returned. Each house was set far back from the road, most nestled in trees.

"They're huge." I said without thinking. The last thing I wanted was to seem like I was in awe of him or his home, but this was way more than I had ever been expecting. He nodded but didn't reply, there was little he could say really.

"This one is mine." He continued as he swung across the road into a gated driveway. Hitting a button he dropped the driver's window and leaned out to tap a code into the keypad, pausing as the gates swung open.

"Oh wow." I whispered as they moved up the wide treelined driveway and a house emerged at the end. "I wasn't expecting this, you should have prepared me."

"What did you expect?" He pulled up in front of a double garage to one side of the house. "A trailer?" He grinned. "I just decided to invest my money in property, to have something tangible to show for my work."

"I get it Jackson, I just forget who you are when it's just you and me, if you know what I mean? I forget you're rich and famous and I just see you."

"And that sweetheart is why I like spending my time with you." He leaned over and kissed me, before unbuckling both of our seat belts. "I bought this place because who knows how long my career will go on for? I might make more shows, but realistically 'LA Rescue' could get axed tomorrow. I didn't want to look back in hindsight and wish I'd done something. Come on, I'll show you around."

* * *

The house was far bigger than anything I had expected, split over four floors with an open plan living area as well as a snug, office, separate dining room and cinema room. Of course, that was just the downstairs, upstairs there were five or six bedrooms, all with ensuite bathrooms. In the basement was a gym, I remembered Jackson telling me that he liked to work out in the mornings, but I'd just assumed he went to the gym, it never crossed my mind that he would have one of his own in his home. In the end, I felt like I'd been shown so many rooms that I lost count. Outside he showed me a beautiful patio area, a lawned area extending down to the trees and an infinity pool that took in the view of the world below us. Jackson had shown me around his home, not letting go of my hand once as we walked.

"It's beautiful." I told him when we arrived back in the entrance hall and I meant it.

"Thank you. Do you know what my favourite part is?" He asked and I shook my head. "Listen." I did and heard nothing. "Exactly," He continued, "It's so quiet. There are so few places I can just relax and be myself, it means a lot to me to have this. I could walk around here naked and no one except you would see, and of course, seeing as you have seen me naked before, I think that's fine." He smiled down at me. "Can I get you a drink?"

"Yes please."

"Wine?" He asked again and I nodded, "Go and grab a seat by the pool, I'll be right there."

Wandering outside by myself I was once again overwhelmed by the beauty and simplicity of the place. It was amazing and yet it wasn't flashy either. It really felt like a home, albeit it, an expensive one. I took a seat at one of the loungers, stretching my legs out along the length of it, enjoying the feeling of the warm sun on my face.

"Here you go." Jackson appeared in front of me a few minutes later holding out a glass for me to take.

"Thank you." I replied, as I took the glass from him.

"You're very welcome." He smiled, running one hand through his short hair, gently ruffling it as he settled down onto the lounger next to mine, "Thank you."

"What for?" I asked taking a sip of wine as I watched him. It tasted good.

"For taking a chance on me." He said and I saw a hint of vulnerability in him. "It means a lot Imogen." I put the glass down and swung around to face him.

"Don't thank me. I'm not doing you any favours." I smiled, and reached up, laying my hand on the side of his face. "I was nervous, but you're showing me that I can trust you, and that is pretty special."

"I know we are taking things faster than you wanted, but it just feels right, you know?" He said earnestly.

"I know exactly what you mean. It's been a long time since I've felt this comfortable with anyone. In fact, I don't think I've ever felt this comfortable with anyone. It's lovely." I stopped and bit my lip; I knew the time had come to tell him about my past. It wasn't fair to keep him in the dark any longer. He must have seen the look on my face, because he asked,

"What's wrong?"

"Nothing's wrong Jackson. But, there is something I should probably tell you before we go much further."

"What is it?" He sounded concerned, and looking up I saw his brow was furrowed.

"It's nothing really, well, I uh, I just don't want you to find out from someone else and it change how you feel about me. I probably should have told you before we slept together."

"Are you married?" I shook my head, "Seeing someone else?"

"No!"

"Have you got kids?"

"No Jackson." I laid my hand on his knee, it was strange to see him so nervous, springing from one idea to the next. "Stop jumping to conclusions and let me explain?"

"Okay." He looked a little sheepish.

"So, do you remember me saying I lived with someone in London?"

"Yeah, your ex?"

"Adam Carter." I nodded.

"Is his the name you had covered up?"

"Yeah. When I left I just wanted to forget all about him. It's never that easy though is it?" I let out a breath.

"It must have been pretty serious if you had his name tattooed on your back."

"Well yeah, it was. I'm going to start at the beginning if that's okay?" I said and he nodded, "Back then, you know at the start, things were great. He was kind, he treated me like a princess to be honest and we moved pretty quickly."

"Did he hurt you?" Jackson almost growled the words.

"No, no, nothing like that. I'm just trying to give you the full picture."

"Okay." He nodded, softening slightly.

"I've known Adam for a really long time, but the speed he and I moved once we were in a relationship is one of the reasons I wanted to be sure before jumping into something with you. He never hurt me, but he was pretty controlling. Over the time we were together he convinced me I needed him and he was always there, so it was hard to remember who I was on my own if that makes sense?" I could see him nodding as I spoke. "He wanted me to move in with him pretty quickly and so I did, and it was all good. His family welcomed me in and I felt part of something, but once I was all in, I couldn't get back out."

"Go on." A deep frown played across his forehead as he leaned forward, one hand under his chin, and both elbows on his knees.

"In the beginning I knew his family were involved in business, but it was mostly private. I'd known them for years, and I'd never had a reason to question what they did. I didn't know that they were tied up in organised crime. More than that, I didn't realise that they actually controlled a lot of the business in London, both the legal stuff and the illegal stuff. To be honest most of it was illegal, everything else was a front." I stopped to clear my throat. I found talking about my past difficult. "When I did find out I turned a blind eye to start with. I knew, but it didn't affect me, and I wasn't doing anything wrong, so everything seemed okay. Adam kept most of the details from me, so it wasn't too bad, but the longer we were together, the more came home with him. He took more control of the business, and his guys used to come into our home after a job. When it was protection or drugs, it was one thing, not that it was okay, but I could sort of put it out of my mind. I felt like everyone that was involved had chosen to be, but then something went wrong and one of Adam's guys got shot." Although I had chosen to look away, mostly from embarrassment, I could feel Jackson's eyes on me and knew he was listening to every word. "Adam went out looking for trouble and found it. Everything escalated from there. He just changed, he got so distant and there was violence, drama and men with guns everywhere I looked. I just didn't feel safe anymore, and it was like what we had between us died."

"So, what happened?" Jackson asked, and I looked up to see his face had softened and he looked more concerned now than worried.

"Adam wasn't the man I knew anymore, he was vacant, and I felt like I was just an object to him. I tried to talk to him, but I knew he couldn't leave the family business, and I didn't want to ask him to. In the end I left him. His mum didn't want me to go, she thought I knew too much to be allowed to walk away. I'm not sure what she would have done if she'd had the chance, but his dad trusted me, he didn't think I'd go to the police, and you know, I wouldn't, because as much as I disagreed with what was happening, Adam and I had history. Charlie gave me the money for my flight and took me to the airport. He was the closest thing I ever had to a father."

"I don't understand why you were so worried about telling me. Is there something I'm missing?" Jackson asked reaching his hand out and taking mine.

"I just wonder if it makes me weak, or a bad person, or that you might think less of me, knowing that I knew what was going on. Even now, I know enough that I could bring the family down. But I'm not sure that I should. It wouldn't stop anything, there would always be someone else ready to try to take over, so I'm not sure that it would do any good."

"Listen Imogen," He held my hand between both of his and it felt safe to talk to him. "Thank you for telling me, but it doesn't change anything. You might have known, but it doesn't sound like you did anything?" I shook my head.

"No, never."

"Then you really don't have to worry about it do you? Of course I don't think any less of you, how could I when it sounds like you did what you had to do to survive?" He shook his head. "I didn't realise that guns were so freely available in the UK?"

"Well they're not supposed to be, but the family controlled everything, they practically owned the police, so they could get pretty much what they wanted."

"Christ. That's crazy."

"Yeah. So they don't know where I am exactly, but I do keep in contact with Adam. He was upset when I left. Angry. Not with me exactly, but with the fact that I just disappeared. I just didn't think he would let me go, especially with his mum wanting to keep me there."

"You still talk to him?" Jackson seemed surprised.

"Not all the time, but yes, he likes to know I'm okay. He knows vaguely what I do for work, he knows I'm in this country, but not exactly where I am."

"Imogen, you know that could change if we're out and the paparazzi see us together. A photo could show up anywhere and he could see it. Even something from the set. How would you feel about that?"

"I guess that's why I'm telling you Jackson. It's not just me that it affects anymore. I don't want the mob turning up here without you at least knowing it could happen." With my free hand I reached down to pick up my glass from the floor beside me, taking a large mouthful. Jackson followed suit, reaching over for his beer. "The thing is, with the contacts Adam has, he could well already know where I am, and just not have told me. I honestly don't think he'd be a problem. I just don't want to have secrets from you and I understand if it changes things. I mean, I get it if it's too much to be involved with me. That's what I meant when I said I should have told you sooner. I just didn't know how." He shook his head.

"It's a lot you know? It's just taking me a minute to process it, but I don't regret getting involved with you. Of all the things I was expecting you to hit me with, it wasn't that you were involved in a gang." He laughed, "'My girlfriend was in the mafia?' It sounds like a movie." He said with a smile.

"I wasn't in the mafia though. Maybe it should be 'Almost Married to the Mob'?"

"Almost married? You didn't tell me that part?"

"We hadn't set a date or anything, but I did tell you we lived together." I suddenly felt embarrassed at my omission, "I think it was more that he felt when I was wearing his ring, other guys would keep their distance. But then, I also always had one of his minders with me whenever I went out, I wasn't allowed out on my own, so I was always pretty safe and controlled." I looked up at him, "And it was a long time ago, like two years."

"Okay." He nodded.

"There's one more thing." I said, knowing this might well be the hardest thing I ever had to tell him.

"What is it? It's okay sweetheart, you can tell me anything." He said softly.

"I know, it's just hard bringing it all up. I didn't think I'd ever want to tell anyone all this." I took a deep breath, I needed it for strength. "Adam was all about family. We were committed to each other, and he wanted us to start a family of our own. It was before things got bad between us." I stopped and looked down, unable to meet Jackson's gaze. "I had a miscarriage. It was devastating. We didn't try again, and sometimes I wonder if that was one of the reasons we fell apart. It hit us both really hard."

"Oh Imogen, I am so sorry honey. That must have been awful for you." Almost instantly he pulled me up across, settling me into his lap, "I don't even know what to say." He lowered his head to my neck, nestling there. It was a small action but very comforting.

"There's nothing you can say. It happened, it's a part of my story. It's just not a part I tell many people."

"Does Nicole know?"

"Not about the baby, no. It's something we kept between us."

"I won't tell anyone. I understand it's private, but thank you for telling me."

"I wanted to. It's difficult, but I don't want to have secrets from you." I told him, "Sometimes I find it a little hard when people close to me have babies, but to be honest, not many people close to me do. I'm not jealous so to speak, it just reminds me what I lost."

"I understand that."

"Thank you. Does it bother you?"

"No, it's okay." He answered, "Well, you know, of course I'd prefer you to have no history with anyone else, but it's unlikely either of us would get through life without any baggage."

"I guess." I said quietly, "How old are you Jackson? There's an awful lot I don't know about you."

"Twenty-six. What about you? I'd guess twenty-three?"

"Lucky guess!"

"Am I right?"

"Yes."

"That's funny, but it doesn't matter how old you are, or your history, because I think you're amazing." He said softly, and having had enough of talking, I pressed my lips to his.

"Do you think we could stop talking for a bit now Jackson?"

"If you insist sweetheart." He replied, pulling me even closer to him.

* * *

The rest of the weekend was spent in a blur. We spent most of our time together in the bedroom or eating, but I have to confess it was wonderful. On Sunday evening, Jackson drove me home. He had told me that he was more than happy for me to stay over again and that he'd take me to work the following day, but I insisted that we shouldn't run away with themselves. I didn't want to rush any more than we were already doing and spoil things, and I felt we needed some time apart in order to appreciate each other fully.

"Do you want to come in for a coffee before you go?" I asked as Jackson parked outside my building.

"Yeah, that would be good." He nodded and climbing from the car, he followed me in.

I'd just finished making out coffee when I heard keys in the door, followed by the sound of Nicole's voice chattering away. I wasn't sure if she was talking to someone or was on the phone, and I panicked, wondering what I should say about Jackson being with me. I couldn't panic for long because the door swung open and Nicole walked into the apartment followed by Mason. Jackson was sitting on the sofa and out of their eye line, so I plastered a smile across my face and shouted out to greet them.
"Hello." Nicole's face dropped when she saw me.
"Imogen, I didn't think you were home!" She said in surprise as she pushed the door closed.
"We only just got back a few minutes ago." I replied.
"Where have you been all weekend? I got your note."
"With me." Jackson must have heard them coming too, because suddenly he was next to me, his hand resting on my waist.
"Oh?" Nicole said with a look of shock, just as Mason jumped in, "Congratulations man!" He clapped Jackson on the shoulder, "I knew you two would end up together, I could just see it." I smiled, happy and yet surprised at the reaction.
"What have you been up to?" I asked Nicole.
"We've just been out to dinner. It seems you're not the only one with secrets." Nicole replied coyly.
"I knew you were seeing someone!" I was certain she had been she was just being unusually cagey about it too. "I just hadn't worked out who it was yet." I looked at them both, "You suit each other. How weird, that this has worked out like this. What an amazing coincidence." If we'd tried to set each other up with our

partners friends it would never have worked and yet here we were, unplanned but together.

Without a word Nicole grabbed my hand and dragged me to my room.

"Girl talk!" She called out as she pushed the door shut behind us, before turning to me, "So, are you really with Jackson?" She asked leaning back on the door, as if to hold it closed, and raising one eyebrow at me.

"Yes." I couldn't work out if she was happy or not, or why she'd felt the need to drag us both away from the men. "Why?"

"Ooh! I am so happy for you!" Nicole squealed throwing her arms around me, and I saw that she was excited, but unsure.

"Thank you!" I replied as we held each other, "It's still fairly early days, but it's good. How about you and Mason?"

"He's amazing. He's such a good man. I feel so lucky!" Nicole gushed. "Does Jackson know about Adam?"

"Yeah, I told him everything. I didn't want any secrets."

"Was he okay with it?"

"Better than I could have hoped for." I said sinking down onto Nicole's bed. "He just listened and didn't judge."

"Imogen, that's good. You deserve to be happy." Nicole replied settling down on the bed next to me.

"It is. It's nice too, I think because he's close with Mason, he gets how close we are. I don't think he'd become jealous of our friendship like Adam was."

"That wasn't normal Imogen, his behaviour wasn't normal." Nicole looked at me and squeezed my hand.

"I know, but you always saw the very worst in him. I thought it was okay because he cared." I shrugged. "I wouldn't let someone change me to suit them anymore. At least I don't think I would."

"This is so cool. We can leave them out there on their own, and we don't have to worry if they have anything to say to each other or not. We just know they're okay." She squealed again, "Oh and also we won't get dragged to meet any of their best friends weird girlfriends because it's just us." She smiled again, "It's so good!"

CHAPTER 6

I felt more at home with Jackson than I had ever done before.
Even with the man I was supposed to marry. He just seemed to
accept me for who I was with no complaint and no question. I
didn't feel I had to try to be anything I more than the person I was
with him, and that alone made me feel very special. More often
than not, lazy mornings followed more energetic nights in bed
and as I lay there, I snuggled closer into Jackson's side, one hand
absentmindedly stroking his chest. He held me tightly too him,
and I felt like I could have stayed there forever. He had other
plans however.

"Much as I hate to say it…" Jackson murmured into my hair.

"Oh don't!" I pressed my lips to his in an attempt to silence him.

"We have to be at Mason's soon. It's nearly lunchtime." He said
removing his arm from around my shoulders and reaching for his
phone from beside the bed to check the time. He groaned, "I'd
rather stay here with you, but we said we'd go, and they will be
expecting us."

"Okay, but I need a shower first, would you be interested in
joining me?" I asked with a grin.

"You are a very bad influence on me. My timekeeping has slipped and..." I leaned in, cutting him off before he could finish with another kiss.

The first time I saw Jackson's house I had been awestruck, but the first time I saw Mason's I was just lost for words. It was even bigger than Jackson's and the gardens and pool area opened up on to the beach below the house. It was stunning. Now I was more used to seeing it and being there, having visited a few times it wasn't such a shock, and although I noticed it's grandness still, it wasn't such a shock and didn't hit me with the same force as it had done before.

The driveway was reminiscent of a car showroom as we pulled in and Jackson parked his truck between several other large, shiny SUVs. Under normal circumstances, I would have hated events like this, but there was something about both Jackson and Mason that made them seem completely down to earth. Due to their attitude, most of their friends were of a similar mindset, which made being around the others less difficult. Although many of their friends were famous, wealthy or both, there didn't seem to be competition between them, and that alone made me feel comfortable around them.

Not long after we arrived Jackson got caught up in a conversation and I excused myself to find Nicole. Although she didn't live with Mason, she'd made herself quite at home. She knew her way around well and offered everyone drinks, acting very much the part of a hostess. It was busy though and after a while Nicole suggested we walk down to the beach. We didn't get much time to chat now, we were both spending a lot of time with Jackson and Mason respectively and it was nice to have a few minutes to catch up. Leaving our drinks behind we headed outside.

I knew Jackson was watching me as Nicole and I walked across the deck, down the path and through the garden to the steps to the beach. I could feel his eyes on me, and I stopped for a moment, turning round to look back up to the house. Jackson was leaning against the railing, cradling a bottle of beer and chatting with Mason. They were both looking down and raised their hands in return when I waved. I turned back to see Nicole had gone ahead without me and kicking off my shoes, I followed her barefoot on to the sand. The warm sand felt delicious between my toes. I felt reassured by Jackson's behaviour, it was so lovely to know he was okay with me being with my friend. Adam wouldn't have liked it at all. In fact, I'd never been able to leave his side at a party or event. Sometimes it made me feel like I was his property rather than his partner. He said it was for my protection, and while I don't doubt there was an element of that, enjoying the freedom I had now to be able to be with my friends or on my own actually made me want to be with Jackson all the more. I made a mental note to tell him that later on.

Up at the house Mason didn't take his eyes off the girls, watching as they both revealed their bikinis as they shimmied out of their dresses, leaving them on the sand before walking into the shallows. "Our women are different to the other girls I've known." He said in passing to Jackson.

"What, because they get their hair wet and have fun rather than walking round being fake and plastic?" He had a grin on his face as he spoke, but like Mason, he hadn't looked away from where Imogen and Nicole were now splashing about in the sea.

"Yeah, they're pretty special. It's refreshing how real they are. No games, you know what I mean?" He sipped his beer.

"Exactly. I hope if I keep telling Imogen that, one day she'll believe me."

"You two seem happy." Mason said questioning whether he was seeing the reality of his friend's relationship.

"We are. Well I am definitely."

"Imogen seems happy too, dude."

"I hope she is. She just doubts herself sometimes and then me." He took a mouthful of his beer. "I'm working on it."

"I didn't know she had a tattoo like that. It's interesting." Imogen's back was almost completely bare in her halter neck bikini, giving anyone looking a view of the full extent of the tattoo running down her back. "It must have taken ages."

"I don't know, I've never asked her that. She'd tell you it's from her old life, but you know, even though I've never really been into tattoos, I like hers." Jackson told Mason.

"You mentioning her old life, Nicole told me a little bit about Imogen's ex. He sounded pretty extreme." Mason said and Jackson turned to him with a frown.

"I'm not sure that Imogen would feel happy about Nicole telling people about that."

"Hey, it's not everyone, just me, and there were no details. Nic just said he was a control freak. She said he stopped Imogen from seeing her, and didn't let her go anywhere on her own. I just thought it must be hard for Imogen to get over that."

"Yeah, I think it has been." Jackson said, relieved to find out that more details hadn't been shared. "Imogen told me he was into some heavy stuff and liked to protect her, but I think in the end it just smothered her. I don't want her to ever feel like that with me."

"I'm sure she won't. You give her freedom, that's all most people want. Well, that and to know they are loved."

"I agree." He looked down to beach again, "Shall we take them some towels?"

"Hey guys!" Nicole shouted from her place waist deep in the water, watching as Mason and Jackson approached us.

"Are you coming in?" I called to Jackson. "The water is lovely." Jackson looked at me doubtfully before glancing towards Mason. "Ah what the hell! It's a good job I wore shorts!" He laughed, and pulling out his phone and wallet from his pocket, he handed them to Mason before pulling his t-shirt up and over his head and throwing it onto the sand. I squealed as he ran towards me, splashing water everywhere before scooping me up into his arms, planting a kiss on my lips.

"Ew! Get a room!" Nicole complained, walking up the beach to where Mason was waiting, letting him wrap her in a towel.

"We'll just leave them to it, shall we?" He joked, slipping his arm around her as they slowly began their walk back to the house.

"Peace at last." Jackson said setting me back on my feet next to him. "Shall we swim for a bit?"

CHAPTER 7

The sun had risen and was shining through the open window and it felt warm on my face. I liked sleeping with the windows and blinds open, although Jackson's house had more than efficient air-conditioning, it just felt more natural. The sounds of birds from the trees outside along with the sunshine woke me gently and I was always in a better mood when I woke naturally than when I was pulled from my sleep by an alarm clock. As time passed, I spent more and more time with Jackson at his house, and was beginning to feel quite at home with him, especially in his bed. Slowly I stretched, pressing my back into the hardness of Jackson's chest. I closed my eyes again relishing the feeling of safety and care that I felt being held in his arms, even when he was still sleeping. It was a feeling I felt I would never tire of. Sometimes I still felt like it was a dream, that I'd wake up and none of the time I'd spent with Jackson would have been real. I felt so lucky to have been given this chance with him.

Feeling me move, Jackson twitched, sliding his arm away. I didn't feel ready to get up yet so gently caught his hand, holding it in place, as I rolled onto my back so I could see him properly.

Leaving my hand on his I felt him relax and his fingers stretch out on my bare stomach, enjoying the freedom of being close to him. He looked incredibly peaceful while he was sleeping.

After a while, I decided to go and make breakfast for us both. Carefully sliding out from under his arm I swung my legs out of the bed and sat up.

"Where are you going sweetheart?" He mumbled sleepily.

"Going to make you breakfast. Go back to sleep for a bit." I replied quietly, turning to lay a kiss on his lips.

"You are too good to me." He slipped his arms gently around me, pulling me back to him, and soon the thought of breakfast was forgotten.

Eating breakfast with Jackson was another one of my favourite things. I loved the peace and quiet of his home and I loved spending time with him, without the presence of others. The sun was high in the sky now, shining through the open French doors and into the kitchen where we sat together at the breakfast bar. He caught me watching him and smiled over his coffee at me.

"This is a good breakfast." He was busy tucking into a full English, something I had introduced him to a few weeks before.

"I'm glad you like it."

"You know, if you moved in with me, you could cook for me every morning." He said, his eyes twinkling with amusement. He often joked about me moving in, but I didn't for a moment think he was serious, it all seemed a bit too good to be true. Even more unbelievable than him wanting to be with me in the first place.

"What an offer!" I replied. "And would you expect me to clean too?" I said batting his arm.

"Of course not! Mrs Jones does my cleaning, and she likes working for me, I don't want to put her out of a job." I laughed, but before I could reply, my phone started to ring on the counter, and I got up to retrieve it.

"Oh." I was surprised when I saw who it was flashing up on the screen, and looking at Jackson I told him, "It's Adam."

"Really?" He turned to me, "I've not got a problem with you answering it Imogen." I nodded apprehensively; it was unlike Adam to call me out of the blue. Sliding back into the seat I had vacated; I swiped the screen up to answer the call.

"Hello?" I felt self-conscious sitting so close to Jackson while answering the phone to my ex. Especially when I had no idea what he wanted.

"Imogen, have you seen the news?" The voice on the other end of the line said, all in one breath, without so much of a hello.

"Hi Adam, no, I haven't. Why?" I replied raising an eyebrow at Jackson.

"Turn it on. Sky News, although I think any of them will be covering it."

"Hang on." I realised Jackson must have overheard as he had already reached for the remote to turn the TV in the corner on and was flicking through the channels to reach the news section. I smiled gratefully, mouthing the word 'thank you' to him. He settled on a channel and I focused on the main headlines moving across the screen. "Oh my God." I murmured, my hand flying to my mouth. The news reporter was announcing the death of Charlie Carter, Adam's father. "Adam, I am so sorry."

"It wasn't an accident Imogen; it was a hit. They haven't announced it publicly yet, but we know."

"Right." I let out a breath, "This is a lot to take in."

"Where are you Imogen? Are you with the actor?" Adam asked and a chill went down my spine.

"How do you know who I am with?" I looked worriedly at Jackson. "Adam, hold on, I'm putting you on speaker phone." I swiped up, selecting speaker and laying the phone down on the surface between them, "Okay, we can hear you."

"Who am I talking to?" Adam asked, and I remembered how he never sounded worried, only ever perfectly in command of the situation. It was one of the things that had drawn me to him, but now, it just unnerved me.

"I'm here with Imogen, my name is Jackson." Jackson said looking at me as he spoke, as if for reassurance.

"Ah, the actor." Adam said knowingly.

"Yeah, I guess that would be me." He replied with a frown, looking with interest at me. I didn't know how Adam knew about him and unsure of what to say I shrugged in response. I had no idea what Adam knew about us, and to be honest, it freaked me out.

"I'm so sorry about your Dad, Adam." I said quietly. It was hard to process, I had been so close to Charlie. For a long time, he had been like a father to me, and for far longer than just the time Adam and I had been together. Now probably wasn't the time to explain all that to Jackson though. To think he was gone was terrible. Jackson reached over, gently covering my hand with his and giving it a reassuring squeeze. I could see he remembered what little I had told him about Charlie.

"Thank you Imogen." Adam cleared his throat. "We are closing in on those who were responsible, but I am concerned that you need to be careful in the meantime. They might target you in an attempt to get to me."

"Me? Why me? Surely they wouldn't after all this time? Why would they?" I stopped, feeling completely in shock, and at a loss to know what to say.

"It's what they do, you were close to me, it could make you a target." Adam said, his voice quiet, before asking, "Jackson, I know we don't know each other, but can I presume you care about our mutual friend?"

"I'm not sure what business it is of yours?" Jackson said slowly, his voice so low it was almost a growl.

"I'm not trying to compete with you, I know she's moved on, but I need to know you can protect her."

"Of course I can." He looked at me, "You can move in here, it's safer than your place. I'd sleep better knowing you were close." I smiled at him, touched that he would offer, but thinking there would be little sleep if we were sharing a bed every night.

"It's a gated property isn't it?" Adam asked, and I scowled at Jackson. Adam clearly knew more than I thought about my life now.

"Are you keeping surveillance on us?" I asked him crossly.

"Mostly you Imogen, I just needed to know you were safe."

"By spying on me?" I realised that my voice was getting louder, and Jackson motioned for me to relax.

"Imogen, please." Adam said softly. "It's only because I care about you. I didn't want you ending up in a bad situation."

"With all due respect, it isn't any of your business what situation I am in now." I sighed, softening my voice a little, "But, Jackson is a good man, and he cares about me. So you don't need to worry okay?" I suddenly felt embarrassed that I was talking openly about my relationship and hoped I hadn't overstepped the mark.

"That's good. I was thinking I could send one of my men for security. Would that help?"

"I appreciate the offer Adam, but I don't think it's necessary." I sat back, crossing my right leg over my left and gently rubbing my toes against Jackson's leg.

"If you change your mind, just let me know and I'll send someone." Adam replied, "I have to go. Call me if you need anything." I had barely managed to say goodbye before the call was ended.

"Well," Jackson said thoughtfully, "He's straight to the point, isn't he?" I nodded, still processing everything that had been said. I couldn't quite believe that the news was true, but there it was in front of me, still part of the loop of news being shown on the TV. It wasn't everyday such a prominent businessman was gunned down, even if they were portraying it as an 'accident'. The tears came then, and I couldn't stop them rolling down my face, silently at first, before it really hit me. It was more than that though, I suddenly felt scared, if Adam knew where I was then it was possible anyone could find me, without too much trouble. Jackson stood up and helping me to my feet he pulled me into him, kissing the side of my face as he held me. "I am so sorry Imogen. I know he meant a lot to you." He said eventually pulling back enough to look into my eyes. He gently wiped the tears from beneath them with his thumb.

"It's just such a shock. I thought I'd escaped all that drama." I whispered, more to his chest than anything else.

"Yeah, I bet. Nothing can prepare you for news like that." They stood together for several minutes while I tried to compose myself. I felt so safe in his arms. "Will you move in with me?" He said after a while. I pulled back from his arms so I could look up at him. It was a lot to take in, and I was so nervous of making a mistake. "Before you say anything, just think about it. I love having you here with me, it's weird when you go back to your place. I know I've joked a few times about you moving in, but I'm serious Imogen. You can still have your independence; I don't expect you to be tied to me or anything. It just seems like a natural progression for our relationship, and I'd know you were safe if you were here with me." He stopped.

"You don't think it's too soon?" I said still feeling unsure.

"No. I think it would be perfect." He dropped his lips to my face, kissing my cheek, and as he pulled away he whispered, "I know it hasn't been that long, but sometimes you just know, don't you? I know what I want, and well, I love you Imogen." I looked at him in shock, I hadn't been expecting to hear that just yet, despite feeling the same way myself.

"You do?"

"Yes Imogen, I do." He smiled down at me, making the butterflies return.

"I wasn't expecting that." I reached up, sliding my hand up his arm, feeling the muscle tighten beneath the skin, over his shoulder and to the back of his neck. I tugged him back down to meet me as I whispered, "But it's good because I love you too."

* * *

Later that evening we drove back to my apartment. Jackson told me he was keen to get me moved in as soon as possible, before we were caught up at work again, especially given that there was a potential threat to my safety. Everything was moving so fast that it was hard to keep up, but I felt happy in the knowledge that

Jackson wanted to look after me. Protect me even. I wasn't used to liking that, but it was a nice feeling.

Explaining to Nicole that I was moving out was hard, especially given that it was a complete surprise, but she took it well, especially when we explained why. Packing didn't take long and was fairly easy, although I was a little embarrassed when Jackson seemed surprised at how little I actually owned. I'd told him, but I suppose seeing it in person is different. When someone is helping you pack up your life, there's nothing to hide. Other than my clothes and personal items, very little in the house was mine, and while I told him that I it was mainly because I hadn't accumulated much after my time travelling, he admitted I travelled far more lightly than he ever had imagined. He told me he found it endearing that I wasn't really into possessions, and refreshing that I was able to live without the numerous material things that so many of the girls he had known had needed. I meanwhile hid my embarrassment by folding up some items in the wardrobe for as long as I could. When I eventually came out, and as I put the clothes into my bag, I explained that so much of my time with Adam had been based on money and possessions that it was wonderful to shake it all off, shunning the things that reminded me of him.

"I don't like the idea of you driving back by yourself tonight." Jackson said carrying a box down the stairs as we finished loading my belongings into his truck. Nicole padded down the steps behind us looking a little lost. "Just in case anyone is watching, or following…" He trailed off. I understood where he was coming from, I didn't want to take any unnecessary risks, but I also didn't want to let fear rule me. Or him. It was a difficult line to tread.

"You could leave your car tonight, and drive back with Jackson. Mason and I can bring it over one day for you." Nicole added, "You don't need it for a few days do you?"

"No, I guess I don't." I nodded, "Okay, if you don't mind."

"It's no problem."

"Nicole?" I waited until she was looking at me, unsure quite how to broach the subject. "I think you should go and stay with Mason. What if someone is watching but gets us mixed up? I don't want anything to happen to you."

"To be honest, I was thinking the same thing. Plus, it gives me an excuse to stay there more often." She had a twinkle in her eye as she spoke.

"Do you want us to wait while you grab your things?" Jackson asked her.

"Thanks, but no. You two go, I'll call Mason and he can come and get me."

It was the end of an era to know I was moving out of the home I'd shared with my best friend, but at the same time it was exciting knowing Jackson and I were moving with our relationship. Even if it was fast. It was more than I had ever imagined, and I still couldn't quite believe I was lucky enough to have found what I had with Jackson.

"Look after her." Nicole said firmly, putting her arms up to hug Jackson. He hugged her back, replying,

"Of course I will. You know she means the world to me."

"I know." Nicole let him go and stepped towards me, embracing me as she did. "I am so happy for you, but I am going to miss you so much!"

"I'm not going to be far away, and you spend so much time with Mason that it won't make a huge difference anyway."

"I know. It's just comforting knowing I had you to come home to."

"You are welcome at our place anytime Nicole." Jackson added and she smiled up gratefully, wiping a tear from her eye.

"Why am I even crying?" She said laughing at herself.

"Don't! You'll start me off." I giggled, letting go of Nicole and looking at her. "I'll see you at work anyway!"

"Yes, you will." She smiled. "Well, you'd better get going then."

CHAPTER 8

As much as I was beginning to trust that my new life was real, I still couldn't be surprised at how much things had changed for me since I had met Jackson. He welcomed me into his home, and made me feel like it was mine too, encouraging me to add or change anything I wanted. His generosity and kindness made me realise just how lucky I was to have found him. It just seemed like it was meant to be, and I honestly never felt as home with anyone in the way I did with him.

"I've got something for you." Jackson said sliding a small box past his cup of coffee and across the table to me one morning. I looked at it warily and he grinned, adding, "Open it, it won't bite." I contemplated it, it was too big to be a ring box, not that I was expecting it to be, but it still had a special look about it. Carefully, I picked it up and turning it towards me, I popped it open. Inside were a set of three keys.

"Keys?" I asked as I took them from the box.

"I know you have the spare key, but I had them cut for you, I thought you should have your own. They're for the front and back door, and you know the gate code, so you can come and go as you want." He said softly. "I want you to feel that this place is yours - ours."

"That's really kind. Thank you, Jackson." I got up and walked over to him, gently touching my lips against his. "But what's the third one for?"

"A surprise for you." He stood up too and placing his hands on my waist, gently steered me from the kitchen to the front door. "It's outside. Come on." As he opened the front door, he gently put his hand across my eyes, telling me, "Close your eyes." I did as I was told, wondering what on earth he could have done. There were few gifts he would have hidden outside and I wondered if the surprise could be what I thought it might be. I doubted it, even Jackson wouldn't make such a grand gesture surely? Feeling him grasp my elbow I allowed him to guide me through the doorway and down the front steps. Eventually we stopped and his hand slip from my face, coming to rest on my waist. My breath caught as his hand moved around, across my stomach, gently pulling me back against him. I loved touching him, feeling the firmness of his body against the softness of my own, and there was something intense about having my eyes closed and being able to trust him completely. "Okay, open them." Opening my eyes I looked across the driveway to see a shiny red Audi parked next to his SUV.

"What?" I exclaimed in surprise turning to look at him. The things he did were unbelievable.

"Yes, it's yours." He smiled, suddenly looking nervous, pressing the key into my hand.

"Why?"

"Well sweetheart, because I want to know you are safe, and your car is so old and unreliable." He looked hopeful, "Do you like it?"

"I do, but Jackson, it's too much. You shouldn't have done this."
My emotions bubbled to the surface and I tried to push them
back down, resting my hand and forehead against his chest so he
couldn't see the tears welling in my eyes.

"Hey." He leaned back looking down at me. "Are you crying? Oh
man, this is not how it was supposed to go, you were supposed
to be pleased and then take me for a spin." He slipped both arms
around me, holding me tightly to him. He sounded devastated.

"I'm sorry, pay no attention, I'm just shocked." I sniffed, "It's so
kind of you. I just, well wow, no-one has ever bought me a car
before."

"So, you're happy?" He sounded so confused it made me feel
terrible.

"Yes, you wonderful man, I am very happy. But you still shouldn't
have!" I rest my hand against his chest again, feeling the rhythm
of his breath and letting it soothe me.

"I just want you to be happy, that's all that matters to me."

"I don't know how I got so lucky." I murmured.

"What do you mean? Lucky that I got you a new car? Because in
all honesty, your old one was a bit of an embarrassment parked
outside." I looked up to see him grinning down at me.

"No, you fool." I scowled at him, "I meant you. I'm lucky to have
you."

Having the new car meant I had more freedom, and instead of car
sharing each day, I was able to slowly begin to fall into my own
routine, travelling to and from the studio independently rather
than having to fit around each other. Of course, the fact I had my
own car didn't stop him worrying about me and while I didn't
want to admit it to him, I actually liked the feeling of being looked

after and cared for. It was different to the time I'd spent with Adam. He had been possessive, and Jackson wasn't like that. He didn't smother me or treat me like an object. I knew that Adam had loved me in his own way, but it had been overpowering. Sometimes I felt like I was drowning and that was without the complications of his family.

"Are you sure you don't want me to hang around?" Jackson stood in front of me, looking down, hands in his pockets and a thoughtful look on his face. I'd driven myself in to work knowing he wasn't filming in the afternoon and hoping to stop him having to wait for me. I knew it was only because he worried, but he needed a lot of encouragement to leave me alone.

"No, it's silly you just waiting around for me." I bit my lip as I looked up at him. "I've got to start doing things on my own again at some point."

"All right." He sounded doubtful, but moved closer, leaning down to kiss me softly. "I'll see you later then? At home." The way he said the words 'home' made my heart flutter, and I tried to stop myself from grinning.

"Yeah, you will."

"Bye." He waved as he walked to the door, "See you Mason." He called, I had almost forgotten Mason was there too, waiting in the chair for his makeup to be done before he could film his scenes.

"Later man!" He called as Jackson left.

"Right." I picked up my notes and checked through them. "No special effects, just normal character this afternoon?" I looked at Mason for confirmation.

"Yep, just normal old Tyler." He said referring to his character.

"Okay." I opened the drawer on my case and began to extract the items I would need.

"So, Imogen..." Mason started, looking at me with a smile, "Things are pretty serious between you and Jackson?"

"Yeah, it's good I think."

"You think?" He said sounding surprised. I pulled over a stool and settled in next to him, getting comfortable so I could work quickly.

"Well, sometimes it still just seems a little too good to be true you know? Sometimes I still can't believe he is really interested in me. It feels a bit like a dream."

"Oh, I see." He nodded, "I thought it took him a long time to convince you to start seeing him. It was longer than it took for Nic to start dating me."

"Nicole knows what she wants, and she hasn't had her fingers burned like I have. I just don't want to get hurt, or look a fool. It's scary admitting you have feelings for someone, especially someone so different to me." I told him, adding, "I'm not that good at letting people in. It takes a while." He nodded.

"I get that, but you know that Jackson isn't playing games don't you? He loves you Imogen, and the two of you really aren't that different."

"Well, yeah maybe, but things change. I might not be enough for him. He could get bored of me. He might think this is a huge mistake, and then where would I be?" I said doubtfully.

"No." He shook his head. "He won't. I know how he feels about you, I can see it. I've known him for a long time Imogen, he's my best friend. No, he's more like my brother. He isn't leading you on, or anything like that. He really cares about you. He wouldn't have asked you to move in with him if it wasn't serious." He finished, but it didn't matter, Mason didn't know the details, he didn't know about Adam and Charlie and the family business that Jackson was trying to protect me from.

"It's more complicated than that though Mason." I told him, not making eye contact, and moving my position to gain access to the other side of his face.

"Are you talking about that stuff with your ex?" He asked and I looked at him in confusion wondering what he knew. "Nic told me he was a bit of a dark character and Jackson told me you were involved in some, er, difficult situations." He looked unsure of how to word it. "Don't be upset with him, he didn't go into details, but surely it was obvious he would tell me? He wants to know you are safe when he's not around. He just wanted to make sure I was aware in case you needed anything."

"Oh. I see." I hadn't expected that.

"But listen. That stuff, it doesn't affect anything about the two of you. He loves you and I think from what I can see, that you love him too. He told me that he had wanted you to move in for a while, but I think all of this," He circled his arms around, "It just made it easier for him to have a reason to move things along more quickly. It stopped you having too many excuses."

"You think so?" I asked pursing my lips.

"I know so." He replied and I smiled. It was reassuring to hear it from someone else. It meant a lot and I decided she would try harder to let my doubts go.

"Thanks Mason. That's good to hear."

It was early evening by the time we'd wrapped for the day. After cleaning up I left to go to my car, saying goodbye to the few remaining crew as I passed. I had to admit, it was a huge relief to know in all good faith that my car would start. My mind wandered back to the conversations of the day, and I thought about what I could do to show Jackson how much I appreciated him. A sudden noise behind me made me jump, pulling me from my thoughts and I wondered if someone was behind me. I was still in the habit of trying to hide my car away even though the new one didn't warrant hiding, and now I kicked myself for it. I picked up my pace, too nervous to look around and check behind me and I fumbled in my bag as I walked for my car keys, clicking the unlock button as I found them. The lights flashed and the familiar sound of the central locking releasing was reassuring. I knew that in a couple more steps I'd be able to lock myself in, and then I would be able to laugh at myself for being so jumpy.

"Stop right there." A gravelly voice spoke just as I put my hand out for the door handle and I felt something hard dig into my back. "Do as you are told, and you will be fine. Cause me any trouble and I will shoot you. Do you understand?" I opened my mouth, but my voice cracked, and no sound came out. I nodded quickly but the voice said more harshly, "Do you understand?" I felt another sharp dig in my back.

"Yes."

"Good girl. Do not look at me." A hand grabbed my arm, forcing me against the side of the car with a thud. "Drop your bag and your keys." I did as I was told, dropping them to the floor without thinking. "Where's your phone?" He said again.

"In my pocket."

"Slowly take it out, and pass it back to me." I did as he asked, I wasn't sure what else I could do, there seemed to be anything I could do to help myself. There was no one passing, no sound or movement from any of the few remaining cars nearby either. As soon as I held my phone out it was snatched from my hand.

"We can't have you trying to call anyone, now can we?" He laughed as he dropped it to the floor. It made an awful noise as it smashed and for good measure, he ground his foot down on top of it, making a terrible crunching noise. "Right, is there anything else you have that I need to know about?"

"No." I whispered, the man stank of sweat and cigarettes and having him so close made my stomach churn. This was it; I was going to die. I wouldn't even be able to say goodbye to Jackson, I couldn't tell him how grateful I was to him or how much I loved him. That was the last thought I had, and I tried to blink back tears as the man shoved me back against the car again. There was an intense pain in the back of my head, and everything went black.

My head throbbed. I tried to move but I couldn't. It seemed like my hands were stuck, but for the life of me I didn't know why. I blinked trying to focus on what I could see, but that was very little. My mouth tasted disgusting and as I moved I realised there was something in my mouth pulling tight across my face and preventing me from speaking. I tried to clear my mind clear my throat as best I could, and gradually my eyes became more accustomed to the dim light. It was dark, but not night. I struggled to get a perspective, across from me, to one side of the room I saw there were some curtains. From behind them a glimmer of daylight shone through. If there was daylight outside, did that mean I'd been here since last night?

"Oh, you're awake are you?" A voice said from the darkness breaking my thoughts. "If you're going to be quiet, and sit there nicely, I'll untie your hands. But if you mess me about, I'll shut you up again. All right?" He asked and I nodded. I'd forgotten about how much my head hurt and as I moved it the pain increased, making me wince. "Okay." The man approached, still staying in the shadows and tugged the rope from my hands as well as from my mouth. Grabbing my elbow, he roughly pulled me up to sitting. "Water?" He asked picking up a glass from behind him and offering it to me. I was so thirsty I didn't actually care if it was clean water or not. I gulped it down quickly. It tasted strange, but then my mouth was so dry I wasn't sure that my senses were even reliable.

"Thank you."

"You're just here to send someone a message, okay? As soon as he does as he is told I'll get the message to let you go. I don't have a problem with you, all right?" He said gruffly, taking the glass from me and moving back into the shadows again.

"And if he doesn't do what you want him to?"

"You don't want to think about that." I was so tired, despite just waking up, and though I tried to fight it, it wasn't long before my eyes drifted shut again.

***

"Where the fuck is she?" Jackson roared down the phone. His patience had run out, not that there had been a lot of it in the first place. Ever since he'd realised Imogen was missing he had been on edge; he wasn't used to having problems he couldn't solve. Mason and Nicole were in the kitchen too, watching on helplessly as Jackson paced the length of the room.

"We're working on it." Adam's voice was much calmer than Jackson's. There was a cold almost disconnected element to it that unnerved Jackson even more. "We'll get her back."

"You don't know that! What do they want from her?"

"Only a few weeks ago I told you this was a real possibility, it's what I was worried about. What I warned you both about." His voice was patronising, "She is nothing more than an insurance policy to them, all they want is to make sure I talk to them."

"It's been too long. I'm calling the police." His frustration at his lack of control was beginning to show through.

"Not yet!" Adam answered sharply, the first time he'd raised his voice slightly. "Give me a little more time. You could get her killed."

"Give me the phone Jackson." Nicole asked holding her hand out to him, gently placing the other hand on his arm for reassurance. He passed the phone over, shaking his head and sinking down onto one of the stools at the counter. "Adam, it's Nicole." She spoke softly into the phone. "What can we do? Jackson is going out of his mind here."

Jackson watched Nicole speak on his phone, shifting her weight from one foot to the other she listened to the voice at the other end. This was an impossible situation to be in. It was like living his worst nightmare, he had failed to protect Imogen and now she was just gone. Two days before he had worried because she was home late. He'd tried not to worry, to give her space, but as time went on, he couldn't help himself. Her phone going straight to voicemail had done nothing to reassure him, so he'd phoned the studio and asked them to check the trailer. The call back had informed him that her car was still in the car park, the door left open, her bag and smashed phone on the ground beside it. Nothing had been taken, so it was clearly not a robbery. Remembering hearing that there was no sign of her made him feel sick and he resumed pacing. Watching the CCTV footage back with the security guard was the worst part, seeing as she dropped her phone before crumpling like a rag doll as the guy behind her hit her over the head with the butt of his gun.

"Jackson?" Nicole came to stand before him, he hadn't even noticed she had ended the call. She reached out and laid her hand on his forearm. "He said to give him a few hours, he's working on something. If we haven't heard anything by 4pm, he said we should call the police."

"Okay. What do you think? I don't know the guy? I don't know whether to listen to him or not?" She nodded.

"If he's asking for time, I'm inclined to think he has a plan. I honestly don't know Jackson, but we've left it this long, let's just give him the benefit of the doubt. It's only a little bit of time." She reached out and laced her arms around his waist, "It'll be okay, I'm sure of it." She said giving him a squeeze before she released him.

"I hope so." His voice was barely a whisper, "I don't know what I'd do without her."

"Let's hope you don't have to find out." Nicole looked to Mason, "Why don't I stay here in case there's any news, and you two go out for a drive?"

"We could go back to the studio, see if there's anything we missed?" Mason said thoughtfully. He could see Nicole was just trying to give Jackson a distraction, to make him feel like he was doing something productive.

"Okay." Jackson stood, checking his phone once more. "You'll call me if you hear anything?"

"Of course I will." She replied as Mason leaned in for a kiss goodbye. "Now, go and see if you can see anything that might help us."

There was no sign of Imogen anywhere, no obvious clues, no hidden meanings. If it hadn't been for her car and her bag, she would have just vanished without a trace. It was hard enough to figure anything out with the fragments of information that they could piece together. With heavy hearts eventually Jackson and Mason turned back to return to the house. There was still a little bit of hope that Nicole would have heard something, although in all likelihood they both knew that she would have phoned them the moment she had any news, good or bad. Jackson felt like he was in a living nightmare, he knew Mason was talking to him, but nothing was going in, he just watched out the window, hoping for a sign that would help him find Imogen. His phone ringing startled him, bringing him back to reality.

"Hello?" He didn't even check the screen before answering.

"I have her." Adam's voice came down the line. "Meet me at the hospital."

"You've got her? Is she...?"

"She's alive, but she's unconscious, I think she's been drugged. Meet me there as soon as you can, I'll be there shortly." The line went dead. Jackson relayed the little information he had to Mason, who without missing a beat swung the car around, accelerating away.

***

I felt like I was underwater. Everything felt heavy, even my eyelids. I tried to open my eyes, but everything was so bright I could barely keep them open. Blinking a couple of times, everything became clearer, and I saw several people around the bed. It was such an effort to look that I closed them again, softening into the bed. Why was it so bright? With my eyes closed I began to tune in on the voices, gradually deciphering them in my muddled mind.

"Except for the head wound, there doesn't seem to be any signs of trauma." A voice said.

"What about her wrists?" That was Jackson, I was sure of it.

"Well yes, she does have a few minor cuts and grazes, and her ankles and wrists look like they were bound, but other than that, our examinations show her injuries look minor. Of course, we'll know more for certain when she wakes up." There was a pause, "I know it's a horrible situation, but in cases like this, we see an awful lot worse, Mr Stone."

"I'm sure you have, but I haven't." It was Jackson again, "This is the woman I love. No one could see the person they care about being hurt as a good thing."

"No, but you've got her back. The signs are good." The voice said again. I didn't recognise the voice, and found myself trying to find the source of it.

"Hey Jackson, look! She's opened her eyes!" Well, that sounded like Nicole. Now they were all close to me, looking down at me, and it looked like Nicole was crying. Jackson's eyes were red too.

"Imogen sweetheart!" He grasped my hand, pressing his lips to my forehead.

"Where…" I wanted to ask where I was and what had happened but after a croak, coughing stopped me.

"No, don't talk. Just relax. Don't worry about anything." Jackson said softly. "You're safe, at the hospital. Nicole and Mason are here too, and the doctor." Nicole had hold of my other hand.

"You scared us Imogen." She said gently.

"Okay everyone, let's clear back a little and give Imogen some space. I just need to do a few checks if that's okay?" The doctor said and I panicked, my eyes finding Jackson's. The last thing I wanted was to do was be on my own now and I tightened my grip on his hand.

"Can Jackson stay?" I croaked. My throat was so sore.

"I'm not going anywhere unless you want me to sweetheart." He said quietly, and as he squeezed my hand, I attempted a small smile.

"We'll reassess in the morning, but I think you'll be able to go home tomorrow." The doctor said when she had completed the examination. "You're recovering well, and it seems your injuries are minor. You're dehydrated, so we need to address that, as well as make sure that the sedative you were given is completely out of your system, and that there are no side effects, so we'll just keep that IV drip in for a little while longer."

"What about her head?" Jackson asked.

"Well, we're monitoring for any after effects, but given the time since the injury I think she'll be fine, sore, but fine. You've been very lucky." She gave us both a warm smile. "The only thing I would suggest Imogen," she perched on the edge of the bed, "Is that you talk to someone. Now, there's no rush, but you've been through a traumatic experience and I for one don't want to see the people that took you take anything else from you." Squeezing my hand, she stood up. "I'm assuming you will be staying here tonight Mr Stone?"

"Yes, if that is okay?"

"It's absolutely fine." The doctor replied nodding, "If you need anything at all, just press the call button and one of the nurses will be right with you."

"Thank you." He said, for the first time looking a little more relaxed. "I'm so glad there isn't anything serious, but, how are you really feeling?"

"I don't know." I hadn't let go of his hand since I had woken up and he swapped his hands over, stretching his fingers before settling into the chair next to me, pulling it as close to the bed as possible. "I don't remember... what happened?" I asked confused.

"Are you sure you want know?" He asked softly. "We don't have to talk about it now if it's too much?" I nodded and taking my nod as an assent to continue, he did. "Well, that night I left you at work, it looks like some guys were waiting for you. I guess they'd been watching and waiting until you were alone. I'm not sure what happened, but when you didn't come home, I tried to find out where you were and instead of you, I found your car, your bag and your phone, all abandoned. We checked back the security footage and saw someone following you before they knocked you out and then put you into the back of a car. It was horrible to watch, but that was all we knew." I nodded and gently he raised his hand to my face, "I hate that they did this to you." He said running his fingertips gently down the side of my face. From the way it felt I had a fairly bruised cheekbone, but I hadn't looked in a mirror yet.

"It's blurry, but I remember some bits."

"The doctor said that they think the people who took you gave you something to make you sleep and it would probably make you a bit disorientated."

"Hmmm, that makes sense."

"I felt so helpless Imogen. I had no idea of how to find you, or if you were okay, we were at a dead end with the security footage and no one had seen you." He looked quite emotional, but I wasn't sure what to say to make it any better for him. I squeezed his hand once more hoping to reassure him, and gently he lifted my hand brushing his lips across my knuckles. Lowering my hand he continued, "I decided to call Adam, and we tried to work out where you might be, but it was impossible. I think he knew more than he let on, because he was adamant I shouldn't phone the police. I didn't, but it was terrifying to think that I was just sitting around waiting."

"How did you get hold of him?"

"I trawled your social media until I found him, then sent him a DM with my number asking him to call me." He sighed. "To be fair he got straight back to me and without him I might not have got you back."

"Without him, I might not have been taken in the first place." I said quietly.

"Well yeah." He agreed. "I didn't even know he was in the country, and suddenly he was on the phone to tell me he'd got you. I arrived here at the same time as him. He was carrying you in from his car, but you looked in such a bad way, I can't believe just a few hours later you're sitting here talking to me." He smiled.

"I was so scared; I didn't know if I'd ever see you again." I said quietly, tears forming in my eyes.

"I felt exactly the same sweetheart." He gently catching a stray tear with his thumb as it streaked down my cheek. A knock at the door interrupted made me jump.

"Come in." Jackson called out, though I noticed he didn't move from my side. The door swung open slowly and a bouquet of flowers made its way into the room.

"Hello Princess." Adam's smooth English voice echoed through the room and I looked up in surprise to see him approaching me. I hadn't really taken it in when Jackson had told me that Adam was here, that he was the one who found me and brought me to the hospital. He approached the bed, laying the bouquet down on the surface by the window as he passed, leaning down and laying a kiss on my forehead. "How are you feeling?"

"Hey. I'm okay thanks." I stopped, "Well, my head is sore, but I'm okay."

"That's good." He smiled, and I looked back at him, noticing for the first time that he was almost the complete opposite of Jackson in many ways. He was looking sharp, wearing a suit, which was his signature look, while Jackson was far more relaxed in a polo shirt and jeans. The only thing that was remotely similar was their eye colour, but even that was different. While they were both shades of blue, Jackson's were warm with a tinge of green while Adam's were colder, more calculating. He always seemed to be assessing the situation he was in. "I have a plane to catch, but I just wanted to pop in and see you were okay." He paused, "I also wanted to tell you both that the men responsible won't bother you again." He caught my eye and holding my gaze he continued, "You're safe now Imogen, do you understand?" I saw Jackson frown, and I wondered nervously where this conversation was heading.

"What did you do?" I asked Adam quietly.

"You don't need to worry yourself about it." He smiled, "I just want you to know that it's over now. No one will bother you again."

"Thank you." I replied. I didn't know what else to say to him.

"It's no problem." He leaned down, and once again kissed my forehead. "Goodbye Imogen."

"Bye Adam, take care of yourself."

"I'll walk you out." Jackson stood, gently releasing my hand, "I'll be back in a moment sweetheart."

"Okay." I told him, and watched as Jackson followed Adam to the door pulling it closed behind him.

Jackson pulled the door closed and crossed his arms across his chest, looking directly at Adam. Adam didn't back down, instead meeting his gaze without wavering.

"What's the problem Jackson?" Adam asked cutting straight to the point.

"She left you." Jackson stated.

"She left my family."

"Well, I think you and your family are pretty closely linked."

"I would have given it all up in a heartbeat for her."

"I doubt that." He shook his head.

"Wouldn't you?" Adam looked Jackson straight in the eye, giving him pause. "If she said she didn't want you to be on the TV any more or to film with other women, would you choose her or your career?" He asked.

"Her of course, without a doubt." Jackson answered truthfully.

"Well, it would have been the same for me, if she'd given me a chance to make the choice. We could have been happy." For a second, Jackson thought he could see a chink in Adam's armour, but he shrugged it off quickly.

"Do you still love her?" He asked, even though he dreaded the answer.

"Of course I do. I wouldn't be here otherwise." He was so matter of fact about it that it surprised Jackson. "I'm glad she's happy though. I want you to know I won't pursue her, but I will stay in touch with her. She's still part of my family, whether you like it or not."

"I appreciate your honesty." Jackson nodded, "And thank you for your help, I'm more grateful than you know."

"Of course." Adam held out his hand and Jackson shook it, noticing his knuckles were raw, as if he'd been fighting. It was at odds with his smart appearance. "Take care of her for me." Without waiting for a reply, he turned and walked away down the corridor.

***

"It's so good to be home." I told Jackson. As soon as he'd brought me home he'd scooped me up in his arms and carried me to bed. If I hadn't been so tired and fragile it would have been a lot more romantic, but even still, he made me feel light as a feather. Being in his arms was a feeling I would never tire of. He'd laid me down on our bed and told me I needed to rest but I didn't want to go. Reluctantly he laid down next to me and I snuggled in against his chest, relaxing as he carefully put his arm around me, holding him tightly too him. I ran my hand over his chest, feeling his heart beat beneath my palm.

"It's pretty damn good to have you back." He told me, his breath warm against my face. A few moments passed before he asked, "Do you think you'll be okay going back to work? I don't mean now, just like when you're better?"

"I don't know, I guess so." I stopped. "I haven't really thought about it, but I suppose it helps knowing that those men aren't out there anymore."

"I still don't get how Adam could be so open about that."

"I told you what he was like. Violence is normal for him, it's just a part of his life. It's what the family did, if someone didn't agree with them, they got rid of them. I guess he thought he was putting our minds at rest." I took a breath. I didn't agree with Adam's motives or actions, but I did sort of understand them. I knew deep down he was only trying to protect me, but it made me wonder if living with him had de-sensitised me. I'm not sure how normal it was for me to be so accepting of his behaviour.

"Jackson, you know, I don't want to talk about Adam right now."

"Okay, good." He kissed me softly. "I was thinking…"

"What?" I asked intrigued. His tone had changed, and I wondered what he was going to say.

"Well, I've spoken to the team, and they aren't expecting us back in work for at least a week. Maybe two. There is no rush, so I was wondering if we could get away?"

"Really? That sounds lovely."

"Good. Well, I thought it might be nice to have a change of scene, and I wondered if you'd come with me to meet my parents?" He finished. I wasn't expecting that and moved quickly, propping myself up on one elbow to look at him.

"Are you serious?" I asked in surprise.

"I am. Why?"

"It just seems a lot. Isn't it a bit soon?"

"Really? Is that your excuse?" He replied looking back at me with an amused expression. "We live together now; I think it's a good time for you to meet my family. If they lived closer, I probably would have asked you sooner. Maybe we would have just seen them for dinner, but having to organise flights and all, well, it's just harder."

"It makes sense, I just wasn't expecting it, that's all." I said feeling overwhelmed.

"It's okay, it was just an idea. We don't have to do it now, but I do want you to meet them one day." He stroked the side of my face, gently tucking a loose bit of hair behind my ear.

"What if they don't like me?"

"They will." He smiled. "And, to be honest Imogen, if they don't it won't make a difference to the way I feel about you and that's the only thing that matters to me."

"Okay then." I conceded, "If you're sure you want me to."

"Yeah?" He said with a huge grin, "Sweetheart, that's amazing!" He leaned up and kissed me. "I really want my family to meet you. I don't think you have a clue about how much I care about you."

"I think I'm working it out, it's just taking me a moment to believe it's true." I closed the gap between us and returned his kiss. "I just don't want to wake up one day and find it's all been some sort of a dream."

"I am not going anywhere sweetheart. Us, this thing we have, I'm not letting it go."

The flight itself was uneventful. I couldn't shake the nerves I had at meeting his parents, but I did the best I could. We took only carry on luggage, and wearing a baseball cap and sunglasses Jackson managed to make it through the airport unrecognised, leading the way and not once letting go of my hand. It was sweet, and yet it made me wonder if he thought I was likely to run away. I'd slept for a lot of the flight, even though I pulled my book out of my bag, it was more out of habit than something to do. Once we disembarked we made our way to the vehicle rental area where our car was waiting, and everything suddenly seemed very real. Jackson drove, much as I didn't mind driving, I never really drove if we were out together, and as he knew where he was going it would have been silly to. I did wonder as we pulled into the long driveway, that if I had offered to drive, I would have had something to take my mind off my worries and stop the nerves bubbling in my tummy. Surrounding the drive was farmland where horses roamed freely. It was beautiful, and yet overwhelming. Jackson looked over to me, momentarily taking his eyes from the road to catch my eye.

"Don't be nervous." He said gently squeezing my hand.

"Wouldn't you be?" I replied, returning the smile.

"Yeah, I guess. But you don't need to be." He pointed ahead to the end of the drive, "We're here."

"Oh God." I groaned, the house was an imposing build, an older build with more recent extension, but well-kept and in keeping with its surroundings.

"Just try to relax." He smiled, "Oh look, the welcoming committee is coming out to meet us." The front door swung open as the car reached the end of the driveway and two people, presumably Jackson's mum and dad were now waiting at the top of the steps for us. I pushed my sunglasses up on top of my head, watching the couple as they stood gently holding onto each other. I loved to see older couples looking so happy and always found it impressive when a couple managed to survive after so many years. Jackson put the car into park and jumped out, moving round the car to open my door for me, "Come on sweetheart, come and say hello."

The introductions couldn't have gone better, Jackson's mum and dad seemed genuinely pleased to meet me, hugging me and telling me how grateful they were to have me come and stay with them. They rightly assumed that it would all be a little much at once for me and after a little while they left Jackson to show me around the house, and freshen up before dinner.

"So, you met at work?" Anne, Jackson's mum asked me later. Jackson and I were sitting together opposite his mum and dad at the dining table in the open plan kitchen. There was another separate dining area in another room, that I suspected was kept for special occasions.

"Yes Mom, Imogen is our lead make-up artist on set." Jackson replied. "Her special effects are amazing. She makes me look like I need to be in the hospital half the time."

"That's nice that you have something in common." She nodded, with a smile, then looking at me, "Have you been doing the work for a long time?"

"A few years now actually, although this is the biggest set I've worked on. It was intimidating to start with." I smiled at Jackson. "She means that I intimidated her. Apparently I made her nervous." Jackson added. "I just didn't want to tell her I liked her on her first day, so I tried to give her space." He smiled back at me.

"It seems like you've got over that hurdle now." Robert said with a laugh.

"I have to say, you two make a lovely couple. It's good to see you looking so happy Jackson." Anne added.

"I am." He looked at me again, "We are." Robert leaned over to refill their glasses from the bottle of wine on the table.

"He doesn't bring many girls home." Anne said conspiratorially to me after a moment, "So we know you must be special." I smiled, feeling embarrassed, but pleased.

"Thanks Mom, nothing like letting all my secrets out." Jackson said with a laugh. It was easy to see how comfortable he was with his mum and dad though, there didn't seem to be any tension in their relationship and being in their presence put me at ease.

"I didn't like to ask earlier Imogen, but how did you hurt your face?" I looked nervously at Jackson for reassurance at what to say. It was an awkward subject, and we hadn't discussed what we might say. I didn't want to worry them, and as if he sensed how uncomfortable I was, Jackson answered for me.

"Well, it's a long story, Mom, and there isn't really an easy way to say it but recently Imogen was abducted." He laid his knife and fork down and folded his arms on the table.

"Oh, that's funny. What really happened?" She said with a smile.

"No, I'm not joking. I know it sounds crazy, but unfortunately it happened. I would have told you, but it was chaos, and then it seemed too much to explain over the phone."

"Oh, my goodness!" Anne exclaimed, her hand flying to her mouth. "I am so sorry!" Robert reached out to reassure her, gently rubbing her back.

"It's okay, Mom, she's okay." Jackson replied, then looking back at me added, "Now at least."

"So, have they caught whoever was responsible?" Robert asked, looking concerned.

"Imogen, is it okay if I explain?" Jackson asked quietly.

"It's okay, I will." I answered reaching my hand out to lay it on his leg for reassurance. He laid his hand down on top of mine, gently stroking it. I cleared my throat and then looked up at Anne and Robert who were looking at me expectantly. "I er, I used to live with a man who was really heavily involved in organised crime back home. I left him because I didn't want to be a part of it, of that life anymore." I took a breath, "Just recently his father was assassinated, and the people behind it took me. I believe they did it in an attempt to get to Adam."

"That's terrible! How did you get away? Have they been arrested now?" Anne asked, her words coming in a rush.

"I, I don't think they were arrested, but I don't think they'll be a problem anymore." I said, unsure of how to voice it, unsure of how much I should really say to them. Even when telling the truth, I could keep it toned down for them.

"What do you mean?" Robert asked, looking from me to Jackson and then back again.

"She means Adam took care of them. They're most probably dead." Jackson said softly. "He was trying to protect her, and I guess it was the only way he could be sure they wouldn't come back again. I'm not condoning his actions, but these people are beyond the law. It's the reason Imogen broke away from them."

"I can't believe it." Robert said, while Anne looked speechless next to him.

"I know, I couldn't either. It's a bit much to take in isn't it?" Jackson agreed.

"Are you okay though? They didn't hurt you?" Anne asked eventually, looking at me with concern in her eyes and I felt relieved that she wasn't completely horrified.

"It was probably the worst experience of my life. It was so scary." I paused, "But I'm okay. Except for these." I gestured to the fading marks on my face.

"I'm glad to hear it wasn't anything more serious."

"If we take the positives from this, it means we have time off work to come and visit you both." I said with a smile.

"I love your positivity." Jackson laughed and leaning over, laid a kiss on the side of my face. "You definitely find the silver lining, don't you?"

"I try." There was quiet for a few minutes, with only the sound of eating and cutlery being moved. I really hoped that the truth wasn't too much for them. The last thing I wanted was for them to think I wasn't good enough for Jackson. I bit my lip as I thought and pushed my food around my plate, suddenly feeling too uncomfortable to eat.

"Jackson, I don't think we told you, but Justin and Ashleigh are coming up tomorrow. They want to meet you too Imogen." Robert told us both, talking about Jackson's brother and sister. "As Anne said, it isn't often that Jackson brings someone home, so they're excited."

"Run Imogen, let's go home." Jackson joked, I ignored him, instead asking his parents,

"I feel like although I know their names, I don't know anything about them. Will you tell me about them?" I let out a silent sigh of relief. It seemed I had thankfully been over-worrying about their reaction after all.

Over the rest of the meal Jackson and his parents relayed information about Justin and Ashleigh, Jackson's older brother and younger sister. Both single they were coming together and bringing Ashleigh's young son Theo. Much to the disgust of the rest of the family it seemed that her partner had left her to bring up their child on her own, and despite the difficulties she was doing a good job. From the way Jackson spoke about her, I could see how much he doted on his younger sister and his baby nephew. It opened up a whole other side to him.

"Let's go for a walk. I'll show you the horses." Jackson took my hand after dinner, leading me out of the back door and down the steps.

"Can you ride?"

"Yeah, since I was really small. But this is Texas, most people can." He grinned.

"Hmm" I said thoughtfully. "It's a different way of life to back home."

"Tell me about it. You never tell me anything about it. It's almost like you're trying to erase that part of your life."

"I don't want to bore you."

"Imogen, you don't bore me. I want to know everything about you. Maybe one day we could go? You could show me around? I've never been to London. Actually, I've never been to the UK."

"Maybe." I nodded feeling unsure. "It just feels a little like my old life. I don't know that I want to introduce you to my past."

"You mean Adam?"

"Well no, but yeah, I suppose there is that too. He'd know if we were there. If not straightaway, then soon, and I don't really want to run into his mum. She's scary."

"He kills people, but you're scared of his mother?" He asked and I looked up at him, meeting his gaze.

"Who do you think he learned from?" I replied. "Trust me, she is one lady you don't want to be on the wrong side of, and without Charlie in my corner…"

"I see." He paused. "Maybe not London then."

"Maybe one day, just not right now." I said pushing up on my tiptoes to kiss him. "It's so beautiful here. Thank you for bringing me."

"It is, isn't it? I think I take it for granted because I grew up here. I'm trying to see it through your eyes."

"It's amazing. I wish I'd brought my camera."

"Did you leave it at home?" Jackson asked. He knew how keen I was on photography.

"No, it's in my bag. It's just with the sky like that…" I gestured to the setting sun and stopped walking.

"If you think that's beautiful, then you need to see the sunrise. Hey one morning we'll do that. There's a place I used to love as a kid. It would be great to take you."

"Yeah, that would be lovely." I loved it when he relaxed and I could see genuine enthusiasm and excitement in his face. It was infectious.

CHAPTER 9

"Here she is." Robert said as I walked into the kitchen. "Would you like some coffee?" He asked me gesturing to the pot.

"She likes tea Dad. Do we have any?" Jackson interrupted, walking over to kiss me on the cheek and lead me back to the table, pulling out a chair and pushing me gently into it.

"Hmmm. Only herbal I think."

"Coffee is fine, thank you Robert."

"Of course Imogen. Coming right up."

"Stop being so polite, and actually say what you want." Jackson murmured into my ear. "They want to get to know you, don't be scared of letting them."

"Okay. Sorry." I smiled sheepishly at him, before taking the mug Robert was offering to me. "Thank you."

"No problem. We thought we'd do a late brunch. Justin and Ashleigh will be here soon to join us. They're driving over together."

"That will be lovely. " I replied and I realised Jackson looked a little nervous. "What?" I asked him.

"Justin is laid back, he's going to be no problem, but Ashleigh, well, she's…" He trailed off with a frown.

"What Jackson is probably trying to say is that our youngest child is possibly a little bit overwhelming at times." Anne said with a smile. "I'm not saying she's spoiled, but she had a lot of attention growing up, and well, she's excitable." There was a tenderness in the way Anne spoke about her daughter, and I wondered what sort of a nightmare I was about to meet.

Luckily I didn't have too long to wait, as less than twenty minutes later there was the sudden sound of voices in the hall, and an older Jackson walked in carrying a baby seat, followed by a petite blonde woman.

"Oh my God! It is so good to finally meet you! I'm Ashleigh." The woman worked her way around the table to me, wrapping her arms around me as if we'd known each other for years. "I was beginning to wonder if you were even real." She said with a smile, before moving on, "Your poor face, Mom told us what happened." There was no space for me to get a word in edgewise, and I realised what Jackson had meant when he described his sister, she was a real whirlwind. I looked over at him for a moment, and saw him trying to contain a smile as he watched the scene unfold. Justin however was much more like Jackson. Older yes, but he had many of the same mannerisms, it was like looking at a future Jackson. Setting the baby seat in the corner of the room, he'd greeted me by name, pulling me into a hug, and I felt immediately at ease with him. Easy conversation followed as they ate their brunch, and I realised again how lucky I was, not only to have met this man, but for his family to accept me so readily.

I had almost finished eating when the baby began to stir, quietly at first and then more loudly and more demanding.

"I need to feed him. He's a hungry little thing." Ashleigh said, rising from the table and going to the bag she'd left on the side. "Jackson, can you?" She asked as she pulled out a bottle and began to make a feed up.

"Of course I can." Jackson replied, although I noted, he was already on his way to the maker of the sound, crouching on the floor and pushing the hood of the seat down before unclipping the straps and releasing the baby. He held him like an expert, cradling him against his chest and my heart fluttered a little. Since my miscarriage I'd tried to push the thought of babies to the back of my mind. The thought of having children rarely crossed my mind, I didn't want to hope for something that might not be possible, but seeing this side of Jackson almost made me feel strangely broody.

"Okay, I'm ready, I'm going to get comfortable on the sofa, Imogen, come and keep me company?" It was a direction rather than a request, but I didn't mind. It was refreshing to meet someone that actually said what was on their mind rather than beating around the bush.

"Of course." I took a sip of coffee before setting the mug down on the table. It was getting cold.

"Go on through, I'll bring you another one in a few minutes." Jackson told me.

"Thank you." I replied as I left the room.

"It's so good to finally meet you. I've been wanting to since Jackson first mentioned you, but I don't really want to fly with this little one just yet and well, it's hard enough juggling him and work,

119

without adding anything else into the mix." Ashleigh said once she had settled the baby.

"I bet." I replied. "You certainly have your hands full, but you look like you have everything under control." Theo now looked settled and happy in the arms of his mother, getting his fill of milk. "How old is he?"

"Six months."

"Wow, you look amazing!" I wasn't just being kind, I really meant it.

"I suppose that's the benefit of being a working single Mom. I don't get much time to sit around!" She laughed. "It's hard, but I really wouldn't change it. He's my life now."

"That's lovely." I reached out and touched his little foot. "I forget how small they are."

"He didn't feel that small when I was giving birth to him!" Ashleigh replied with a laugh that made me giggle.

"No, I can imagine. Were you on your own?"

"No, Mom came in with me, and stayed. I thought who better than a woman who has had three kids, if I can't have my partner with me?"

"So, is he not in the picture at all?" I asked carefully.

"No, and you know, now I think good riddance to him. He's missed out on all of this, which I don't mind, I'm fine on my own, but he'd better not come swanning back in and want to get to know Theo when he's older." She had a smile on her face, but I was sure I could hear a lot of bitterness underneath it too.

"It must be hard."

"Yeah it was. I just couldn't process it to start with. You know, I thought we had something special, and he just walks away. I thought we were going to get married and live happily ever after, but instead he decides he is too young to settle down and heads off to a new city, with a new job and probably new women too. When I told him I was pregnant, he was like, well good luck with that!" She shook her head, "For a long time I was so angry, but now, I'm just thankful for this little one."

"You should be. He's gorgeous."

"He is. I'm lucky." She nodded. She barely took a breath between sentences, let alone subjects. "Anyway, Jackson tells me that we're like the same age, which means we can be best friends! I've always wanted a sister, but I ended up with two brothers instead, and I've never been that keen on any of Jackson's past girls but you're perfect."

"Steady Ash, you're going to scare her away with your stalker tendencies and I'd really quite like to keep her." Jackson walked in to the room holding two mugs, setting one down beside each of us, leaning down and laying a kiss on the top of my head as he passed.

"You think talking about keeping her isn't going to scare her away? I think you're the creepy one!" Ashleigh giggled. I could see what the family had meant about her, she was like a ball of energy, but there was no harm in her at all. In fact, I really liked her, and felt almost instantly comfortable around her.

"So, tell me, now you're living together, when are you going to give Theo a playmate?" She asked, looking from me to Jackson and back again.

"Ash!" Jackson shook his head at her. "You don't have any boundaries, do you?"

"It's okay, it's just not something we've really talked about it is?" I replied a little uncomfortably. We hadn't really discussed the future at all, and I had no idea what he wanted long term. I hoped that it might be marriage and kids one day, but the speed we moved in together made me question that we might not both be on the same page. Seizing the moment I asked him, "Do you want kids?" Then I panicked, adding quickly, "Not now, but in the future?"

"Well yeah of course. I've always thought that I'd like to get married one day, and have a fairly big family, until now I hadn't met a girl I could see that future with." He stopped speaking and winked at me before coming around to sit down in the armchair across the room from us. He looked thoughtful, "I think, for me the most important thing is to be in a solid relationship first, sorry Ash, but you know what I mean."

"Yeah of course, this isn't how I would have planned things." She agreed.

"It's just you know, with Mom and Dad, they're such a big part of my life even now, I want to be able to give that to my kids. I know none of us can predict the future, but I want to do everything I can to make sure I give my family the best chance I can."

"I think that's lovely. It's great that you have them as role models. I wish I had a close family like you both have." I said truthfully.

"Hey, you're part of ours now honey. If Jackson loves you, so do we." Ashleigh said, giving my hand a squeeze.

"That's very kind of you." I was really touched by the way she'd welcomed me into their family.

"You know, you don't talk about your family Imogen, like, not ever." Jackson said in a low voice. I knew he was prompting me to talk to him, but also not pushing. It made me feel comfortable enough to tell him.

"Well, that's because I don't have any real family. It's not something I really think about now, it happened so long ago." I said wondering how much was appropriate to say. It seemed that there was never quite the right time to tell people certain things.

"You don't have to talk about it if you don't want to." Jackson said kindly, but I could see he wanted to know everything, and I didn't feel I really had any reason to keep it to myself any longer.

"It's okay." I said, before continuing, "Well you see, there was a car accident when I was really young, I walked away, but my parents and my brother didn't. I was about eight I think so I don't really remember it. It's more like a story I've been told than something that actually happened to me." I stopped and reached for my coffee.

"Oh my God!" Ashleigh exclaimed.

"I'm so sorry." Jackson said looking worried. The truth was obviously worse than the things he had imagined.

"No don't be. Like I said, it's a long time ago."

"So where did you grow up?" Ashleigh asked.

"I was actually taken in by a friend of my Dad, well someone my Dad worked with." I took a breath, "His name was Charlie." I stopped, looking at Jackson and waited for the news to sink in.

"Charlie?" Jackson frowned. "Adam's father?"

"Yeah." I nodded, "I told you he was the closest thing I had to a dad."

"So, you grew up with Adam?"

"Not really, he was away at college for a lot of the time."

"Right." Jackson said slowly. He looked pretty shocked, and I rushed to keep talking to ease the silence in the room.

"Adam's six years older than me so he was fourteen or so when I moved in. He barely even noticed I was there, I think I was more of a nuisance in the house, just a little girl getting in the way. Where possible they kept me busy, a driver took me everywhere and I was sent to a private school, which was where I met Nicole. Charlie was always kind to me and used to spend more time with me than anyone else did. He treated me like the daughter he never had, but I've often wondered if he knew more about how my mum and dad died than he said, and looked after me out of guilt. It just wasn't something I ever felt I could ask him." I looked down, I could feel both Jackson and Ashleigh looking at me and hoped neither was too shocked at the story I was explaining. I hadn't thought it mattered, and now, it just seemed bigger than ever. "I really didn't know what the family were up to, and just got on with things. It's not an excuse, but I didn't know any different." I paused before going on, "I guess I was about fifteen when Adam noticed me. That was when things started to change, and although Nicole and I travelled, whenever I went home he was there, and then once we were together, they drew me in, and I began to realise just what the family business was."

"Your girlfriend could use her life story to write scripts for soap operas!" Ashleigh said with a smile. It seemed to me that she was trying to make light of the situation.

"I'm sorry I didn't tell you everything. It's just, it happened a long time ago, and not that that's an excuse, but well, I…" I stopped. I suddenly felt ashamed of my past, ashamed that I had fallen for Adam's charms, ashamed that I hadn't walked away sooner. It was a lot to deal with.

"Hey." Jackson's voice was soft, and I looked up to see he was now crouching on the floor in front of me. "I'm not angry." He told me gently, "Shocked maybe, but not angry. I just wasn't expecting to hear that you and Adam had so much history, but then, it makes more sense as to why you stayed so long and why he still cares so much about you now."

"Thank you." I said with a small nod. When I looked up at him, I saw the gentleness in his eyes.

"You must have been with him longer than I realised then. Quite a long time?" He asked.

"Yeah, about six years." He let out a low whistle.

"Wow, no wonder he was pissed when you left him."

"It doesn't mean I should have stayed."

"No. It doesn't, I just… Well Imogen, I wasn't expecting that today." He said quietly.

"All I asked was whether you were planning on having kids anytime soon." Ashleigh said with a giggle. "Jackson told me, but Imogen, you didn't." She shuffled the now sleeping baby in her arms. "Here, would you like to hold him?" She said holding him out to me.

"Yes, if that's okay?" I asked, grateful again that Ashleigh had diffused the tension in the room.

Later that evening I excused myself and went up to bed earlier than the others. I was exhausted and let out a sigh of relief as I opened the door to the peace and quiet of Jackson's room. It had been redecorated since he had moved out, but it was still very much his room. It was simple and modern, but with a homely feel, decorated in shades of blue, with a soft pile carpet that felt delicious under bare feet. I pushed the door shut behind me and flicked on the lamp on the bedside table allowing myself to flop face down on the bed like a starfish. It had been one hell of a day emotionally. Not only had I had to tackle Jackson's parents but meet his brother, sister and nephew, and then of course explain all the stuff from the past that I'd really rather leave alone. I just hoped the truth wouldn't make Jackson feel differently about me or push him away, but I reasoned that I would have had to tell him at some point. There never seemed to be the right time to bring up old relationships, and to explain them.

I heard the door opening slowly and lifted my head as I felt the bed depress next to me. Looking up I saw Jackson holding a mug.

"I brought you this up. It's herbal, but it's tea." He said with a smile, "Are you feeling okay?" He asked, and once more I was touched by his kindness.

"Thank you." I said sitting up and taking the mug from him. "Yeah, I'm okay. It's just been a lot today."

"I know."

"I'm sorry Jackson." I looked down.

"What for?"

"I've never intentionally kept things from you. It's just hard to tell you things like that. It's like, they're in the past, so they shouldn't matter, but they do, and there's never a good time to say them, and then it just comes out, and it's a shock and I feel so bad about it."

"Imogen, it's okay. Yes, it was a shock, but none of it changes you, or the way I feel about you." He said gently stroking my face. "Although I admit, I do feel a little more threatened by Adam than I did before."

"You shouldn't feel like that. You have no competition." I smiled shyly as I looked up at him. I couldn't believe it when he said things like that, it made me feel like I was more important to him than I realised.

"That's good to hear." He nodded, then taking a breath he continued, "Imogen, I get what you mean about things being awkward, but is there anything else, I mean anything at all, that you haven't told me?"

"I don't think so." I replied.

"I wouldn't normally ask, but I was wondering if we could have five minutes where we can ask each other anything."

"Anything?" I asked raising my eyebrow.

"Yeah, and if there's anything you want to ask me, I'm up for it. No boundaries, no offence, no judgement, and after that, we leave the past where it is?"

"I don't know what I'd ask you, but yeah, go ahead." I answered with a smile, reaching behind me to set the mug on the nightstand and then stretching out on the bed again. "To be honest, it always seems easier to answer your questions than it is to just tell you things out of the blue. Ask away, I'm an open book, well to you at least."

"Okay, totally open book Imogen. Did you love Adam? No, I mean do you still love Adam? On any level?" He turned as he spoke, drawing his legs up on to the bed, stretching out next to me as he leaned back against the headboard.

"That's two questions. Yes, I did, and no I don't. But, even when I did, it was never like what we have though. This is stronger, and better, if that makes sense."

"Well that's good to hear."

"I was young Jackson, and yes he meant a lot to me, but I wonder really if it was more of a security thing? It was nice to be loved."

"Yeah, I guess that makes sense." He nodded before continuing. "Did your Dad work in the same business as Adam's family?"

"I'm not really sure. I think so. I also think the accident that killed my family might not have been an accident. From what I do know, my Dad did work with Charlie, and closely, but I can't be sure if it was on the legal side or not. I assume not."

"Other than the contact you have with Adam now; do you have any ties to that part of your life?"

"No. I cut them all when I left. I just wanted to move on. The only person I keep in contact with is Adam, and of course Nicole, but she was never involved anyway." I bit my lip, looking up at him, "Do I get to ask you any questions?"

"Of course, sorry. Go ahead."

"How many serious relationships have you been in? I mean like, how many times have you been in love?"

"Hmmm. Not counting the teenage infatuations with the gym teacher and stuff like that, I'd say twice. Two serious relationships, and in love both times. One of course is with you."

"Oh really?"

"Yes really and you're the only woman I've lived with." He leaned over kissing me softly. It was reassuring.

"How many women have you slept with?" The moment I asked I regretted it.

"Too many." He stopped and looked at me. "You don't really want to know do you?"

"Probably not." I laughed, "No, I don't really want to think of you being with anyone else."

"What about you?"

"I haven't slept with any women." I said deadpan, causing him to laugh out loud.

"You know what I mean Imogen." He said when he'd recovered, "I meant men, but thank you, that's good to know too."

"Only you and Adam."

"Really?"

"Yes, I'm not some cheap slut you know." I said in mock offence.

"I never said you were."

"Hmmm." I huffed at him. "Any more questions?"

"Loads of them, but you look tired, and I have plans for you tomorrow."

"Oh do you?" I asked.

"Yes, but it's a surprise, I'm taking you out so you can have a few hours away from my family. I think you need a break, and I want to have you to myself for a bit, so you'd better think about getting some sleep, because it's an early start tomorrow."

CHAPTER 10

It was dark and too early to be up, but Jackson had woken me up seeming full of enthusiasm following on from his cryptic clues the night before. I wanted to make him happy so sleepily I'd pulled myself out of bed, thrown on my jeans and a hoody and climbed into the car with him. I had no idea of what he was planning, and I wasn't sure where we were going, but I relaxed into the seat, just happy to be with him. The drive wasn't too long, and it was still dark when we pulled up in a small parking area.

"We have to walk from here." Jackson said swinging his door open and coming round to help me out.

"Walk!" I said jokingly, "You didn't tell me there would be effort required!"

"Trust me, it'll be worth it." He said kissing me softly before moving to the back of the car where he pulled out a backpack and swung it up onto his shoulders. I was surprised he was so organised, I hadn't seen him pack the bag. All I had to carry was my camera, which I carefully put over my shoulder, before taking Jackson's outstretched hand and falling into step next to him. The path was stoney and uneven. It was hard to pick our way through in the dark, and while Jackson seemed sure of himself, leading the way with his torch, I felt a little more nervous. I clung to his hand, letting him guide me along the path, between the bushes and trees. Once or twice I stumbled, but he was always there to stop me from falling. After we'd walked for about half an hour, light began to break through in the dark sky. We'd climbed a fair distance, not a mountain, but certainly a trail up a steep hill. It was disorientating in the dark though, and I didn't think there would be any way I'd be able to retrace my steps on a different day. I doubted I'd even find my way back to the car without Jackson.

"I think we'll stop here." Jackson said thoughtfully, looking about himself. The sky was getting lighter by the minute now, and before I knew it, he'd shaken a blanket out onto the ground, "Here, sit down." He said gesturing to the middle of the blanket.

"Okay, thank you." I sat down crossing my legs in front of me and waited as Jackson lowered himself down behind me, stretching his long legs out, one either side of me and pulling me back against his chest, his arms gently wrapping around me. It was wonderful spending time with him alone, especially after the exhaustion I had felt the night before after the day spent with his family.

"Are you warm enough?" He asked, his breath tickling my ear.

"I am now." I replied, curling my fingers around his forearm. There was something so safe and reassuring about him, and I loved the feeling of his arms around me. It felt good to be close to him, and it reassured me that he was okay with everything I had told him.

"Good." He replied, "Not long now."

He was right. We hadn't been sat for long on our blanket when the sun began to break through. The sky reddened and if you didn't know, it could have been mistaken for an out-of-control fire. Reds and oranges filled the sky, beginning to overpower the blackness of night, and breath taken I reached for my camera, aligning it carefully to snap several landscape shots. Neither of us spoke a word, it was mesmerising. As the sky began to become more blue, the landscape came into view too.

"Wow." I murmured, leaning back into him once more.

"You like?" He asked.

"I love it. It's amazing."

"I'm glad. I hoped you would." I could hear the smile in his voice as he spoke. "Sorry it was so early."

"Don't be, it was worth it." I turned my face, tilting my head back so I could kiss him. I felt so content and happy in the moment. "I did wonder where you were bringing me." I smiled as we separated. "Who knew the sunrise would be so beautiful."

"It's awesome. We used to camp up here when we were kids. Then Justin and I did as we got older and we got to know the places that were a little bit more unknown."

"I have no idea how you found this place in the dark."

"I just know it well; I've had years of practice! But you're the first girl I've shared it with." He reached for the rucksack and rummaging in it, he pulled out a camp stove. "Breakfast?" He grinned.

"Were you a boy scout?" I asked in surprise.

"No." He shrugged. "I just spent a lot of time outdoors when I was younger."

"This is a whole new side to you I'm seeing!"

He shrugged it off, but it was so sweet to see Jackson looking so proud of what he had achieved. I could see he was pleased with himself for the way the morning had turned out, and so far, everything seemed perfect. Sometimes he looked so young, and almost vulnerable that I completely forgot he was famous and well known. Every time he opened up a little and showed me that softer side, I fell a little bit more in love with him. After we had eaten Jackson packed up the stove and stood up, holding his hand out to pull me up to my feet.

"First things first." He said pulling his phone out of his pocket and switching the camera view. "A selfie of us." He held the camera up and stepped in behind me, making sure to capture the hills in the distance behind us.

"You are so sweet." I said to him, smiling as he took another batch of photos.

"I know. I'm adorable." He pressed his lips to the side of my face. "Come on. There's more I want you to see." Leading the way again Jackson walked ahead, the path seemed wider now it was light and except for a couple of places we were able to walk next to each other.

"Where are we going?"

"You'll see." He grinned and didn't tell me anymore. "It's just somewhere I loved as a kid." Eventually after another long walk the path began to open up. It took me a minute to work out that the sound I could hear was rushing water. I looked up at him questioningly, but he ignored me, instead continuing to lead me along the path. "Here we are." He said eventually gesturing in front of us. Below the path I could see a large river with a waterfall tumbling into pool at the bottom. It was quiet and looked beautifully calm and peaceful.

"Oh wow!" I said softly.

"Another reason I wanted to bring you so early is that this area is much quieter earlier in the morning. Late afternoons are often jam packed. It's a destination for hikers, a reward for their effort, I guess. Well, that and the fact the water is always warmer after a day in the sun."

"I bet it's freezing." I said eyeing it nervously.

"Refreshing." He corrected me with a grin and a twinkle in his eye. I began to wonder what he was planning, and watched as he shook the blanket out onto a patch of short grass, laying it out and dropping the backpack down on top of it. Without a word, he pulled off his sweater and dropped it down onto the blanket.

"You're not thinking about going in, are you?"

"I am indeed." He pulled his t-shirt up and over his head too, revealing his toned abdomen and bare chest. Even though we'd been together for a while, I didn't think I'd ever have enough of looking at him.

"But…" I didn't even know what to say.

"I have towels in my bag, and your bikini, so you can't even complain that anyone might see you naked." He smiled, and crouching down, dug around in the bag to pull out those items.

"You really have thought of everything." I returned the smile, touched at how thoughtful he was being, and took my swimsuit from him.

After quickly changing, he led me down to the water. While the waterfall itself was fierce, creating a strong current, to one side the large pool that had formed was almost still. It was peaceful, and not nearly as cold as I had imagined it might be, although as I stepped in, it was still a little bit of a shock. I pulled my hair up into a bun, fixing it out of my way with the tie I kept around my wrist.

Slowly we waded out, and eased ourselves into the water. It was far deeper than I had expected, but the wildness of it made me feel alive, to be out in the outdoors like this, enjoying the elements with the man I loved was amazing.

After swimming for some time, we left the water, finding a rock that had been warmed by the sun and stretching out next to each other. Jackson laid back, propping himself up on one elbow, while I stayed sitting, still captivated by the beauty of the view around me.

"It's very rare you let me see the whole of your tattoo." He said quietly, touching the stars on my neck.

"It's not intentional, I just forget it's there." I smiled at him, turning to face him. "Thank you for sharing this with me. It means a lot."

"I want to share everything with you Imogen. I've never met someone that fits into my life with me the way you do. I don't ever want to be without you. I hope you know that you mean the world to me."

"You know, I wasn't looking for a relationship when I met you Jackson, but I wonder if that's why I found you? I wasn't pushing or hoping something would work out, and instead it just did. I can't imagine being without you either. I feel very lucky."

"I consider myself the lucky one." He said sitting up. "Stay there. I'll be back in a moment." He said as he pushed himself to his feet, and walked over towards where we had left our belongings. I watched him walk away openly appreciating the way he looked without his shirt on. He caught me watching and called over, "I hope you want me for more than just my body?"

"Nope. It's only about your body." I replied, "Well that and the sex of course." I laid back on the rock and closed my eyes.

"You Miss Cole are awful. I can't believe you'd objectify me in that way! I feel so cheap!" He was suddenly next to me again, laying a kiss on my lips.

"Oh, you know I love you for your mind too." I replied as he moved back.

"I do." He knelt back so he was leaning over me, "There's something else I wanted to show you."

"What's that?" I rolled onto my side, and looked at him.

"Come over here." He stood and pulled me to my feet, before leading me down to the water's edge. "So. You know I love you?" I nodded, "And I'm serious about wanting to spend the rest of my life with you." I held my breath, nodding again but wondering what was coming next. Slowly he dropped down onto one knee in front of me, producing a black velvet box from his pocket and I gasped. "So, what I wanted to ask Imogen, is if you would marry me?" I looked down and saw the smile on his face, the hope there in his expression and knew it was real. There was no doubt in my mind that I wanted the same thing he did, but hearing him say the words meant so much to me. I could see how genuine he was, and all of my doubts were blown away, replaced by the certainty I could see in his eyes.

"Yes." I replied. I'd never been more sure about anything in my life.

"Yes?" He questioned, seemingly in disbelief. His eyes didn't leave mine.

"Yes!" I replied once more, throwing my arms around his neck as he stood up. He lifted me gently in his arms, pressing me against him, leaving a long, lingering kiss on my mouth. "You don't think others might think it's too soon?" I asked after a moment.

"Others?" He asked with a smile. "You mean my family?"

"Yeah, I guess."

"Screw what anyone else thinks. I know what I want, and I hope you do too. I want you to be my wife. That's it. It's got nothing to do with anyone else. But I'm sure they'll be happy for us." He set me back on my feet and popped open the box, revealing a beautiful diamond solitaire.

"Oh wow. That's huge."

"Is it too big?" He asked gently sliding it on to my finger.

"No. It's beautiful. I couldn't have chosen a better one myself. I love it. Thank you."

"I just wanted to give you something that would remind you how special you are to me." He said softly.

"It's lovely. Thank you."

"And I was thinking, we don't have to rush anything. Like, we don't have to get married this year, or even next year, although I don't want to put it off too long either. I just want you to know that I am serious."

"I know you are, and I appreciate you caring, but stop worrying." I reached out and stroked the side of his face, gently tilting my face to his for a kiss. I was so grateful that we were on our own in this beautiful secluded spot.

We returned back to house later that afternoon. I felt like I was in a daze, albeit a happy one and occasionally I looked down to check my new ring was there, sparkling in the sunshine and reminding me it was all real. The house seemed quiet as Jackson swung the door open, holding it back for me to walk in front of him. I hadn't taken more than a step inside before Ashleigh ran down the hall, closely followed by the rest of the family.

"What did she say?" She screeched, looking at us in excitement.

"They knew?" I asked looking at Jackson in surprise. That meant he'd been planning this for longer than I realised.

"Yeah, I really hoped you say yes, and I wanted them to share in this. I wasn't expecting Ash to pounce on us before we'd even got through the door. Little sisters are a pain in the ass." He frowned at her.

"What did you say?" Ashleigh asked me, completely ignoring her brother's remark.

"I said yes." I replied holding my hand up so the family could see my beautiful new ring. There was a chorus of congratulations from the family.

"This calls for champagne! We need to celebrate." Robert exclaimed, returning to the kitchen.

CHAPTER 11

"I'll see you later sweetheart." Jackson said laying a kiss on my cheek.

"Have fun!" I replied.

"Hey, Ashleigh, have you seen the photos Imogen has taken?" Jackson asked as he was about to leave the room, and she shook her head, looking up expectantly. "Show her." He said probably knowing I would be unlikely to show anyone my work without encouragement, and then he was gone out onto the ranch with Robert and Justin for the day. Anne was busy in the kitchen but was expected through soon, until then Ashleigh and I were on their own.

"Yes, show me." Ashleigh said encouragingly after a moment.

"Um, well, I have some of the sunset the other morning." I said fumbling for my camera. I skipped through the photos until I found one I liked and passed it to Ashleigh. In return, Theo was passed back to me. Not long ago I'd have been nervous, worried about the feelings holding Theo might bring up but now I was relaxing I was enjoying the feeling of holding a small person in my arms, even though it made my heart ache for what I had lost. On the positive side it was endearing to see how good Jackson was with him too.

"Wow Imogen, these are great." I looked up to see that Ashleigh was flicking through the whole set of photos on the camera. Some of them dated a long way back, I wasn't so good at deleting old photos.

"Ah, some of those are probably really old." I mentioned a little nervously.

"You are really talented Imogen, don't be modest." She said looking up from the camera and catching me with a serious look.

"Thanks Ashleigh."

"I'm serious." She paused, "Hey, just a thought, I've wanted some professional photos of Theo done for months. Would you take some of him?"

"Yes, of course, if you want me to?"

"That would be brilliant. We can ask Mom, and clear a little of the furniture away to have a clear space. It's exciting!" She grinned. "Let's do it now!"

"Okay!" Her enthusiasm was infectious.

We spent the next few hours watching Theo wriggle around while I took photos of him and Ashleigh. Afterwards flicked through the photos together, sitting side by side with our backs against the sofa as Theo laid happily on the floor beside us.

"I'm sorry I don't have my laptop so we can look at them on a bigger screen." I told Ashleigh; I hadn't thought I would have any need for it so had left it at home.

"It's no problem, they're great Imogen."

"I'll email you them all when I get home." I told her as I turned the camera off.

"That would be great, thank you." Ashleigh put her arm around me, giving me a hug, "Oh, but hey, would you mind not posting them anywhere? Online I mean?"

"Yeah, no worries, I wouldn't anyway, that's not my place, but can I ask why?"

"Well, since Theo was born, I've just been a lot more private. I think, because Caleb left me, I don't want him to know anything about this little one's life. He was the one who chose to walk away, and he is the one who hasn't made contact. I don't want him to share in it, at least, not without him contacting me first. Maybe it sounds petty or selfish, but it's just the way I want it."

"I don't think that sounds selfish Ashleigh. You're a lioness, protecting her cub. I totally understand that. It makes a lot of sense, and I think if I were in the same situation, I'd feel the same. If you let me have your email, I'll send them to you so no one else has them. Then it's up to you who you share them with." I did understand, it was the way I probably would have been with my own baby if I had ever had the chance.

"Thanks Imogen. You are like a breath of fresh air." She smiled. "I always wanted a sister, and now it's like I've got one."

"That's sweet."

"I don't know what you've done to Jackson, I've never seen him act the way he does with you, I mean, with other girls. It's cute."

"Haven't you?" I asked in surprise.

"No. He's usually a lot more guarded. He's wary of letting anyone too close, too quickly, and with you, it's like he knew you were meant to be. It's lovely. He deserves someone to make him happy, and I'm so glad you found each other."

I was touched by the authenticity in Ashleigh's words. I had never felt so accepted, well and truly part of the family, and more

141

importantly, I didn't feel I had to change any part of myself to be here and wanted. It was like they had opened their arms and just drawn me in. Days spent with them were relaxed and calm, a far cry from anytime I had spent with the Carter family. I just hadn't realised at the time what a lot of drama surrounded them. This was a wonderful and welcome relief to that.

CHAPTER 12

"So, how are you really?" Nicole asked looking questioningly across the table at me. It was like she was trying to read my mind, the intensity of her stare almost hurt. We'd booked a table at a restaurant, wanting to share our news with our best friends, but so far all I'd done was try to hide my hand while remaining inconspicuous and answer Nicole's barrage of questions.

"I'm okay honestly." I replied. "We had a lovely time with Jackson's family. It was really good to get away."

"I bet. What about Adam, is he out of the picture now?" Nicole was relentless.

"Yes. Well I hope so at least. I don't need any more drama."

"No, because now you've got me. Mr Reliable." Jackson smiled at me.

"Being reliable is good. That's why I love what Mason and I have. I know exactly where I stand." Nicole said in answer.

"We have some news." Jackson said gently reaching for my hand and giving it a squeeze.

"Oh my God!" Nicole squealed, "Are you pregnant?" Mason hushed her as he looked cautiously around to see if anyone was listening.

"No!" I replied quickly, shaking my head. "Trust you to jump to conclusions."

"Yeah, not pregnant, not yet anyway." Jackson said with a twinkle in his eye. He looked quite amused.

"So, are you going to tell us?" Mason asked.

"Yes I am." Jackson told them, "This wonderful, beautiful, amazing woman, came into my life when I wasn't looking for anything special and yet somehow, we have built the most solid relationship I've ever had. I love her more than anything, and I'm not letting her go, so while we were away, I asked her to marry me, and she said yes." He turned to me, gently kissing my lips, ever so softly, without lingering long enough to make anyone else uncomfortable. Mason had a huge smile on his face and as I turned, I noticed Nicole did too.

"Congratulations! Oh, I am so happy for you!" Mason said. He looked genuinely happy, and I relaxed a little, I hadn't realised how nervous I had been about sharing our news. For someone without a real family, it felt like mine was growing and growing.

"Oh Imogen." Nicole reached across the table, squeezing my hand. "Congratulations babe." She had tears in her eyes. "Can I see it?" She asked and I knew she was asking about my engagement ring.

"Of course." I smiled, for the first time lifting my hand from my lap and holding it out to Nicole.

"Bloody hell! It's like a small iceberg!" She said, eyebrows raising.

"She's worth it. I'd give her the world if I could." Jackson told her.

"You have him wrapped around your little finger don't you?" Nicole joked with a smile.

"No. He's just a big softie under his hard exterior." I replied, nuzzling my head against his shoulder.

"The best of us are." Mason agreed making me smile.

It was good to be back at work finally. I still felt self-conscious about my ring and I tried to hide it where I could, and draw as little attention to it as possible, but it made me feel like I was being a little bit sneaky. Filming had been going on for a couple of hours and we were just about to break up for lunch when there was a shout.

"Hey everyone!" Jackson's voice could be heard from across the set and the crew stopped to look towards him. I looked over in surprise, it was unlike Jackson to create a scene and I wondered what was going on. I noticed he was standing on a crate, giving him additional height and making him more noticeable to those in front of him. "If I could have a few minutes of your time everyone?" A few more people moved in from the periphery and talking stopped as they looked at Jackson. "Thanks everyone." He said looking at the crowd before him. "Well, you know we're a family here, right?" There was a murmur of assent from the cast. "Hell yeah!" Mason bellowed from the side where he stood with his arm around Nicole. He made me laugh, he could always be counted on to share his enthusiasm.

"Thanks Mason." Jackson grinned, and continued, "So, I just want to share with you some good news." It suddenly dawned on me what was coming, and I just wanted the ground to open up and swallow me. I didn't like being the centre of attention, it made me feel uncomfortable. The only reason I had ever been able to handle large scale events with Jackson or Adam was because they took the majority of the attention. I felt his eyes on me and looked up at him, I felt like he was trying to gauge my reaction, but I was so nervous all I could do was bite my bottom lip as I looked back at him. "Most of you will know that our fabulous make-up artist Imogen is my woman, but I wanted to share with you all that last week I asked her to marry me," he paused for dramatic effect, "And she said yes!" There was applause from the crowd, people shouting out congratulations and suddenly I felt all eyes were on me. I would have tried to escape, I could only imagine what shade of beetroot my face had gone, but then he was with me. He slid his arm around me, holding me to his side calling out, "So I guess we'll be throwing an engagement party soon, and you'll all be invited!"

After that things snowballed, pictures of Jackson and I appeared on magazine covers and online, speculating that we were engaged and trying to show close ups of my ring. It was unnerving. I wasn't used to being in the public eye so much and it was hard to know how to cope with it all. I cringed when my phone pinged with a text message from Adam. It read just one word, "Congratulations." Of course Adam knew and I kicked myself that I hadn't had the common sense or decency to tell him myself. I hadn't appreciated that my personal life would become so public, it was a huge learning curve. The last thing I wanted to do was hurt him, he'd been a big part of my life for a long time, but now I was with Jackson I didn't want to encourage him, or even have as much contact with him as I'd done before. It was a balance because I also didn't want him to feel that I'd just cut him off. It was tricky and made me feel bad.

Living with Jackson soon became a normality. Days became weeks which became months, and after a while it seemed like it had always been that way. I settled into his home and began to think of it as mine too, rather than feeling like I lived in his home as I had done initially. That wasn't something I expected to happen so easily. Slowly I added touches to make it feel more shared space, and relaxed into my new life although in honesty I still occasionally pinched myself, I just couldn't believe how lucky I was.

CHAPTER 13

"Thanks for today." I told Nicole as we drove home from shopping. Nicole took her eyes off the road to smile over at me. "It's great. We should do this more often. It's easy to get out of the habit. Did you get everything you needed?" Nicole was referring to the birthday shopping I had wanted to do for Jackson. Time had passed and with Jackson's birthday looming I had been saving every penny I could for his present. It was the first birthday we'd be spending together as a couple and I wanted something special to show him how much he meant to me. I knew early on that he had a love of watches and so eventually I decided to get him a Rolex, but with the addition of an engraving of our initials together on the back. I was so pleased with it, and yet worried too that he wouldn't like it as much as I hoped he would. I'd gone backwards and forwards for weeks about it, but it was a lot of money and I didn't want to waste it. It wasn't even about the money really, I just wanted to get him something special that'd he would know had come from my heart.

I was so lucky, because not long after I bought it and having hidden it in the boot, out of Jackson's way, my car was broken into and my camera stolen. It must have been an opportunist because I'd only left the car for a few minutes, I just hadn't thought to hide the camera away and coming back to the car, I found the window smashed and my camera bag gone. They clearly hadn't looked any further because if they did, they would have found the watch too. It was annoying but I was relieved that the camera itself was insured. With my photos backed up onto my laptop, it was annoying, but I knew it was all replaceable. It all happened at such a busy time, when Jackson was working on directing a couple of episodes of the show, that I didn't even bother to tell him. I didn't want him worrying that anyone was following me again.

"Yes I think I did." I replied. Although the watch was expensive, I wanted to spoil him in the way he often spoiled me, and I also wanted to find some other small bits and pieces for him to open. We pulled up at the gate to the drive and rolling the window down Nicole input the code as I relayed it to her. Swinging the car around Nicole leant over and hugged me friend goodbye before I got out, both of us waving goodbye.

I rarely put my car in the garage and as I walked up toward the house, I noticed there was an unfamiliar car parked next to mine. I didn't recognise it and carried on pushing the front door open, my heels clicking on the tile floor in the hall as I entered the house.

"Hey, I'm back!" I called, unsure of where Jackson was. He appeared almost immediately in the doorway of his study. A frown played across his face, and when I looked closer, I realised he looked angry.

"Imogen, can you come in here?" He said stepping back into the office.

"Yes of course, let me just put these bags away." I said desperate to hide the gifts I had bought for him.

"No, just leave them and come in here please." He said gruffly.

"Okay." I said suddenly feeling anxious. He'd not said hello to me, let alone kissed me like he would normally have done. "Is everything all right?" I asked walking in and putting my bags down in the corner. It was a stupid question, it was clear that things were not all right, I just didn't know what was wrong. A man I didn't know was sitting behind Jackson's desk and Jackson retreated back there too, standing to the side of the other man, leaning up against the wall, crossing his arms across his chest. I felt like I had walked into an interview.

"Imogen, this is my lawyer, Lewis Harrington." Jackson said. He sounded like he was trying to keep his voice level.

"Hello." I said uncertainly, looking from one man to the other.

"Miss Cole, take a seat please." Mr Harrington said. I was wrong, it felt less like an interview and more like an interrogation was about to take place. "Mr Stone has a few concerns we would like to address with you."

"Concerns?" I blinked realising that I was right about Jackson being angry for some reason. I just hadn't appreciated that it was with me. "What is going on?" I couldn't understand why I was being addressed so formally and it was alarming.

"I have some photos here." The lawyer said, opening a folder and taking some photos out before laying them across the desk. "We believe that you took these, can you confirm that for us?" I looked at the selection of prints, all photos I had taken of Ashleigh and baby Theo that I had taken when we were staying with Jackson's parents.

"I did, yes. Why?"

"I don't believe it Imogen, I thought you were different. I thought I could trust you!" Jackson burst out. "Was it always about the money with me?" He barely stopped for a breath, "I bet you made a nice bit of cash selling those - they've been used everywhere. I can't believe you would violate our privacy like that, not just mine but Ashleigh's too!"

"What?" I asked, almost speechless, looking at him was like looking at a stranger. He was so angry.

"It was the one thing she asked you not to do and now her baby's face is everywhere. Anyone could see it. I can't believe you'd do that." He stopped for a second, his eyes locking with mine, "I let you into my life, and my family's lives. You know how private they are. I might have chosen this career, but they didn't, and they don't deserve this."

"But Jackson, I don't…" He cut me off before I could explain.

"Imogen I can't do this." He walked to the door. "It's over."

"Wait!" I said sharply, standing up to look at him, "What's over?"

"You and me Imogen." He said as if I was stupid. "We're over. There's some paperwork you need to go over with my lawyer. I need some air." Before I could say another word, he was gone, the door slamming behind him.

I sank back down into my chair in a stunned silence. I had no idea what had just happened. How could everything change so quickly? It took me a minute to realise the lawyer was talking to me.

"What?" I said in bewilderment, looking up, "I'm sorry, can you repeat that?"

"Yes." He said matter of factly, "I was just explaining that Mr Stone has expressed his need for you to sign this." He pushed a piece of paper across the table towards me.

"What is it?" I pulled it towards me and picked it up. I wasn't taking in anything at this point, it just looked like a jumble of words to me.

"An NDA." I looked at him blankly, "It's a Non-Disclosure Agreement." He explained taking a pen and passing it to me.

"I don't understand." I said trying to absorb what was happening.

"Miss Cole, it's a formal agreement, once you've signed it, it means that you agree not to speak about your past relationship with Mr Stone to any degree. It means that if you do, legal proceedings can be taken against you."

"My past relationship? He really wants this?" I whispered, fighting back tears.

"I'm afraid so Miss Cole. His words to me were that the trust he had with you has been broken. He wants assurance that nothing else that is personal to him or his family will be aired to the public."

"I can't believe he thinks I'd do something like that." I mumbled. I looked up to see Mr Harrington offering me a tissue. I blinked as I took it and wiped my eyes, smiling gratefully as I did. "Thank you."

"I'm not sure I understand you." He said looking puzzled.

"I just can't believe he thinks I'd do that to him, to any of them. There's no way I'd sell photos I'd taken privately of his family. I wouldn't even give them away. I thought he'd know that."

"But you took them?" He clarified, and I nodded. "So what are you telling me? Can you explain please?"

"What's the point? He doesn't believe me." I shrugged, again blinking back more tears. "He said he loved me, and now because he thinks I've done something, he is just ready to throw me away?"

"Miss Cole, can you explain please?" His voice was gentle. I took a deep breath and wondered how to explain things.

"A few weeks ago my car was broken into. I only left it for a minute, but I left the camera on the seat and someone must have seen it. I came back to find the window smashed and my camera bag gone." I sighed. "I didn't even think about the memory card in it. All I thought was that the camera could be replaced, the photos were backed up on my laptop and the insurance covered the damage to the car."

"If that is the case, why is Mr Stone so surprised?"

"I didn't tell Jackson. I didn't want to worry him, he was so busy. I wish I had now." I dropped my head into my hands.

"Well, if that's true, you must have gone to the police?" I nodded. "Of course I did."

"So, you'd have an incident report?" He asked.

"I do yeah." I briefly looked up, meeting the gaze of the lawyer. "I needed it for the insurance company."

"Let me call Mr Stone back in, we can explain to him, I'm sure he would be relieved to hear an explanation to this. We can sort this misunderstanding out." He said standing, leaning forward on his desk as he did so, but I raised my hand quickly to stop him.

"No!" He looked puzzled by my reaction, but sat back down at one. Looking at him I continued, "Like he told you, the trust is gone. He didn't even have the decency to ask me, he just thought the worst of me and called you in." I ran my hand across my forehead, I had the beginnings of an awful headache, but anger was beginning to replace the shock and sadness I felt. "It's too late for explanations."

"Are you sure?" He asked taking his glasses of and pinching the bridge of his nose. "It seems to me…" I stopped him with a wave of my hand,

"With respect, I don't really care what you think." I said holding his gaze. "Okay, so what is it I need to sign?" The lawyer doubtfully pushed the NDA across the table to me again and passed me a pen.

"So, this details the limits to what you're able to discuss with others regarding your relationship. Read it thoroughly, but in all honesty, it would be safer not to discuss anything about the time you've shared."

"Right." I nodded, trying to take it in, before scrawling my name on the bottom of both copies, returning one to the lawyer. "What else?"

"Are you sure about this?" He asked.

"Yes, and I'd appreciate you not telling him what I told you." I said softly.

"If you're sure?" He asked hesitantly and I nodded, I seemed to have really thrown him, but if this was how Jackson wanted it, I didn't see any point in trying to change things. "Mr Stone has asked for the keys to the house, your credit card…" He consulted the paperwork in front of him, and listed a few other items. With a nod I stood up, going to where I'd left my bag. I pulled my purse out and dug through it, laying the credit card and another bank card on the desk.

"I need my car. I don't have any way of getting anywhere without it." I said as I removed the house keys from my keyring.

"That's fine. I think Mr Stone understands that, he hasn't said anything about the car other than it was a gift for you."

"Thank you." I nodded and laid my phone on the table next to the keys.

"He hasn't said anything about your phone." The lawyer looked at me questioningly.

"It isn't mine. I don't pay for it, so he should have it back." I looked down at my hand, taking one final glance at my beautiful engagement ring before pulling it off my finger and laying it down on top of my phone.

"Miss Cole, he hasn't asked for that."

"I hardly need it now do I?" I said with a wry smile. "He should have it back. I won't take anything that isn't mine." I stood. "Is that everything you need from me?"

"I believe so."

"Am I allowed to get my things?"

"Of course." He replied and moving quickly I grabbed my bags from the floor, leaving the room.

I didn't see Jackson as I moved through the house, and there was no sign of him upstairs as I made my way to our room either. I couldn't believe it had come to this. It was heartbreaking. In our bedroom I sat for a moment on the end of the bed and tried to collect my thoughts. I felt sick, and resting my elbows on my knees I took a few deep breathes before attempting to get up again. At the back of the wardrobe I found my trusty old rucksack. It was the one I had used when I travelled, and I had never been able to throw it away. It had more than enough space for the things I counted as my own. Tatty but strong, I smiled, it was a little like me. I flicked through my clothes quickly. I had no intention of hanging around any longer than necessary. I left anything that was expensive, or that Jackson had bought for me, except for one pair of jeans that I liked. I was determined not to give him any ammunition against me, and closed the doors on the rows of shoes I was leaving behind. I folded everything up, squeezing it tight into my bag. I had a drawer of jewellery that I opened, once again only taking the few things that had been mine before I met Jackson. From the back of the drawer where I had hidden it, I retrieved the Rolex I had bought for him. Moving to our bathroom I picked through my toiletries, again taking only the things I knew were really mine. Looking around the room, it was suddenly like looking at a luxurious hotel room, it no longer looked like I had lived here, and all I had done was remove a few small possessions. Opening my bedside drawer, I took out my personal pieces of paperwork and tucked them into the side of my bag. Swinging it up onto my shoulder I walked back downstairs and dropped it in the hallway.

A couple of pictures were mine and I intended to take them, but once I had picked them up and looked at them, it felt wrong, so I gently laid them back down again, leaving them where they were. My laptop was out on a table, so wrapping up the power lead I tucked it under my arm. The last place I visited was the bookshelf in the corner of the snug. Running my finger along the spines I picked out my own books, removing a handful and adding them to the pile by the door. I had very little to show for a relationship that had been so permanent.

Jackson was back in the study talking in a low voice with the lawyer. Seeing them I stopped in the doorway and knocked. They looked up in unison to look at me, and without waiting I approached the desk. "I've got my things. Well, the things that are mine. I've left everything else. I don't want to be accused of anything else." I couldn't meet Jackson's eyes. I didn't even try to. "I just thought I'd leave you this." I laid the Rolex box on the desk. "I understand you probably won't want it, but I saved up for it for your birthday, and I can't take it back because I had it engraved for you." Jackson looked at it but didn't speak. After a moment of silence I asked, "Can I have my passport please, and my car documents?"

"Yeah, hang on." He replied gruffly, turning to a filing cabinet low on the ground and pulling it open, flicking through the documents to find the ones he needed. "Is there anything else?"

"No, I don't think so." I replied taking the items he was holding out to me. "Do you want to check my bag? I'd hate for you to think I stole anything." I knew I probably sounded sarcastic and unkind, but I was hurting, and it was his fault.

"I hope that's not necessary." He said in a low voice.

"Okay." I looked at the floor, once again fighting back tears, "Goodbye Jackson." I whispered, my voice cracking as I left the room, going back to the hall to pick up my things.

"Is that all you're taking?" Jackson said from behind me, making me jump. I hadn't heard him follow me out. I didn't turn around; I couldn't face looking at him. I knew I'd break down.

"It's all that's mine." I said quietly. Without a backward glance, I walked to the front door and pulling it open I left the house.

I had nowhere to go, and the full enormity of what had happened didn't hit me until I'd driven away. I had to pull over to let all the tears I had been holding back out, I didn't even to check to see if anyone could see me. I had no idea what I was supposed to do, and with an NDA in place, I didn't know if I could talk to anyone about it. I was terrified that saying the wrong thing would make everything a billion times worse. Without a phone I had no distractions either, but of course, no internet access, no ability to call Nicole. Thinking about Nicole reminded me that I probably wasn't even allowed to speak to my best friend. But then, I was pretty sure I knew which side Nicole and Mason would take in the argument. It wasn't even an argument though, what even was it? An accusation and then what, a dumping? Like I was nothing. Like I had never really mattered to him, like he was just done with me. I wondered how I could have been so stupid to let myself fall in love with him, to rely on him.

All I knew for certain was that I had been pulled over for so long that the light had begun to fade, which made me realise just how long I had been sat going over things in my head. For all the thinking, nothing felt any clearer, I just hurt more than I ever thought was possible.

Finding a budget motel was the first thing I felt I needed to do. I had a little money, but not enough to keep me going for long, especially without a job. At least, I assumed I didn't have a job. It was unlikely I could work with Jackson after the way he had ended things between us, and I didn't want to turn up to be thrown off the premises. I couldn't imagine for a moment that he'd want me there and I wasn't sure that I could face him. It was hard to know what to do. Selling the car was a priority too, it was sad but a necessity, as it would free up some money to tide me over until I had found work again. I didn't need a new car, something cheap and old would do the job, as long as it was more reliable than my last car.

Without the ability to search the internet for cheap motels I drove around looking for one. The neighbourhoods got less welcoming, but the price tags got lower and eventually I found somewhere I could afford with a vacant room. There was no delicate way of putting it, but the place was rough. There was little wonder that it wasn't fully booked, if I could have afforded anything better, I would have done, but for now needs must. The motel didn't feel particularly safe, and the lack of sleep I managed could have been caused by the noise of shouting outside as well as the events of the day. Unable to sleep, I pushed a small cabinet in front of the door to stop intruders, it made me feel like I was doing something to protect myself, but as I did it, I thought how easy it would be for someone to come through the window instead. As far as I could see, there was no choice, so I stayed in my room and wallowed in my own self pity. I didn't know what else I could do. Even after a couple of days had passed and I'd got more used to the noise, I didn't tend to leave the room after dark and only in the daylight once I had checked the coast was clear. On the third day I began to stop in at car sales places hoping someone would offer me a decent price for my car. By late afternoon I found a buyer, and although I wondered if holding out would have got me a better price, I felt at least driving my new dented and faded little runaround meant I had nothing to draw attention to myself.

Days passed in a blur after the breakup. I felt lost and alone and dazed, like I was moving through a fog, nothing seemed quite real, and I barely managed to function beyond getting up and having a shower. I think the shock hit me harder than I realised. Everything was hard, and the days seemed so long. Eating and sleeping were the two hardest things I found to do, although concentrating was particularly hard too.

I did a lot of thinking and realised I was always judging myself. I never felt like I was good enough. Especially for him. When he ended things, it was like he proved me right, everything I had ever expected to go wrong did and I was left with nothing. Actually, it was worse than nothing, before I met him, I didn't know what love like we'd had was. Once we'd split up, I knew that anything or anyone I ever had in the future I would compare to him and what we had. No one would ever match up; even given the way he broke my heart. Who knew that my loss would feel so physical, that it would actually hurt? If I'd know, maybe I would have done things differently, I might never have said yes to dinner that first night. Oh, the power of hindsight!

More than two weeks after we split up, I finally gathered the courage to go to the studio. I knew that realistically I had to apologise to the director Eric for my absence, and make sure he had found a replacement. I was convinced that there was already going to be someone in my place, instigated of course by Jackson, but I felt I owed the team, even though I couldn't really explain anything. At the same time, I wanted to pick up my things. The worst part was that given the way I'd had to leave, I doubted that I'd even be able to ask for a reference, and that certainly wouldn't help my job hunt.

Driving into the studios was strange, despite it being weeks since I'd been there, it felt like no time at all had passed. I pulled into a space having chosen a time when I hoped most of the team would be filming hoping I could be in and out without seeing anyone that I didn't need to. I felt on edge as I made my way to Eric's office and confused after I left. He seemed surprised to have seen me, but rather than being angry with me, he seemed more concerned about where I'd been. He seemed to be under the impression that I was ill or at least had been. When I explained that I was leaving and had just come to get my things he was even more surprised which was odd. I just told him that my circumstances had changed, and I hoped he would be able to replace me easily. He tried to change my mind and convince me to stay, but eventually listened and seemed to have no ill feeling towards me, so I began to wonder if Jackson had even told the team that we had split up. I was relieved that part of my mission was over, but I was still feeling puzzled as I left the office. Hoping to be able to make it all the way to the makeup trailer without being seen I moved cautiously looking ahead as I moved between the buildings. I was almost there when I heard a shout.

"Imogen!" Turning I saw Mason jogging towards me.

"Hi Mason." I smiled at him, but as he got closer his smile turned to a frown.

"Are you okay?" He asked pulling me into a hug.

"Yeah." I replied, I didn't want to get into this. Not now, and not with my ex's best friend.

"Are you sure?" He released me from the hug but kept hold of both my arms, gently assessing me. "You don't look so good. Have you lost weight?"

"I'm okay." I said brushing him off but touched that he seemed to care. "I just came to get my things."

"What do you mean?" He asked looking confused.

"I don't work here anymore." I said slowly, watching Mason's face and beginning to wonder if he knew. I had been surprised at his warm welcome, maybe Jackson hadn't told him everything. I was more confused than ever now. First Eric and now Mason, why on earth hadn't he told everyone?

"What's going on Imogen? Nicole has been so worried about you, she says you haven't been answering your phone."

"I, um, I lost it." I said without meeting his gaze. I wasn't expecting to have to deal with this.

"And you couldn't use Jackson's? Why haven't you been at work?" I wasn't sure what I could tell him and whether I was allowed to answer a direct question like that, but I was aware that if I didn't say anything, I would make things worse. There was little else I could do, so I decided to tell him the bare minimum.

"Mason, we split up." His mouth fell open.

"You what?"

"You heard. It was a few weeks ago now; didn't he tell you?" I asked and he shook his head. He looked stunned, "Look I need to get going. I just came to get my stuff."

"Well, where are you staying? You still haven't told me where you've been."

"Just laying low." I told him the name of the rundown motel where I'd been staying.

"You can't stay there! It's in an awful area." He said in horror.

"It's not so bad and I didn't really have much choice." I shrugged. "Look, I really have to go, I don't want to be here any longer than I have to. It was good to see you."

"Listen Imogen." He said quickly, "Come and stay with us."

"That's kind, but I don't think I can cope with you two being all romantic, and besides, I'd get in the way." I was touched by his kind offer, but couldn't imagine taking him up on it.

"I have guest accommodation in the grounds remember?"

"I'd forgotten that." I said and, in all honesty, I had completely forgotten about Mason's guest houses.

"They're empty, you can take either of them for as long as you want, you won't be in our way and we won't be in yours. All we'll share is the driveway, and dinner tonight. You don't look like you've eaten in days."

"I can't impose on you." I said carefully.

"You're not, but also, Nicole would kill me if she knew I'd let you go back to that place." He smiled. "I just don't know why you didn't come to us straightaway."

"You're his friend Mason. I didn't want to put you in the middle." I said, I was sure that by saying that I wasn't breaking any rules.

"I'm your friend too." He grinned, "Go and get your things from the motel and check out. You really are welcome to stay as long as you want to. I'll let Nicole know in a minute."

"Are you really sure?" I said still feeling doubtful.

"I am. I'll see you tonight."

"Thanks Mason."

"No problem." He said turning and beginning to walk away. "I'd better go and do some of the stuff they pay me for."

"Okay." The last thing I wanted was to run into Jackson, so I called after him, "Hey, do you know where he is?"

"On set last I knew." Mason replied as he jogged away. With that in mind I set off again, hoping to sneak in and out before Jackson knew I'd been there. All I wanted was my stuff, and then I'd have no reason to come back again. I passed no one else during the walk over, and opening the door found the trailer deserted which was a relief. Starting at one end of the room I began to check the cupboards, pulling out anything that I knew was mine and moving as quickly as I could. Emptying a box, I began to throw my belongings into it, a jumper I'd left behind months ago, my make up tools, a couple of pot plants and my mug. My make up case was there too, and that was all mine as far as I was concerned although to my surprise, I noticed it looked like it had been used. I wouldn't have left anything in such a mess. I was quite particular about how things were stored. The last thing I looked at was the photo wall I had created. I was surprised that hadn't been touched already, but even photos that I was in were still up. I slowly pulled them down, one by one until I had a small bundle in my hand. The last one was a photo of me and Jackson. We stood together, smiling at the camera, his arms wrapped tightly around me. It wasn't taken all that long ago and it was surprising for me to see it, to see how happy we looked. I wondered why Jackson hadn't taken it down. From the way he'd acted when he threw me out, I would have assumed he would have ripped down every last reminder of me. Distracted, I didn't notice the voices outside the trailer approaching until they were too close, and startled I realised there was no way out without being seen. The door opened and a woman I didn't know walked in.

"Can I help you?" She asked me briskly.

"No thanks." I replied, tucking the photos into the box and picking it up. "Just collecting my things."

"Imogen?" It was Jackson's voice, and he stepped into the trailer behind the woman. He looked like he'd been in a fight, with a black eye, bruised cheekbone and blood trickling from his eyebrow. I might have been worried except I recognised it as well applied stage makeup. "What are you doing here?"

"Sorry." I looked up at him, "I thought I'd be done before you came back. I'll get going now though, I think I have everything of mine."

"Why are you taking your things? Where have you been?" He asked and for a moment I thought he looked puzzled.

"I don't work here anymore." I felt myself frowning and tried to soften my face, I didn't want to embarrass myself. "If you'll excuse me, I'll let you get on." I said walking towards him, I didn't want to push past but there was no other way out of the trailer, and I almost held my breath as I passed him.

"Imogen?" His voice was quiet as I opened the door. I didn't look back, I couldn't, I was already on the edge of tears and I was terrified of letting myself down and looking a fool. The door banged shut behind me and I finally let myself take a deep breath, pulling my sunglasses down to hide my face as I hurried to the car. "Imogen!" His voice came again louder this time and I knew he'd left the trailer. I kept walking despite hearing footsteps approach behind me. I tensed but carried on walking, only stopping when I felt a hand on my arm. "Wait Imogen." He pulled me back to face him and I shook my arm free.

"What do you want?" I asked looking up at him.

"Why are you collecting your things? What do you mean you don't work here?" He asked and I snorted.

"Are you serious?" I raised my eyebrow in shock. "You kicked me out, made me sign an NDA to say I couldn't speak your name, because you thought I did something, and you expect me to roll into work with you the next day like normal?" For the first time I didn't bother to hide the anger in my voice.

"I didn't think it would affect work." He said looking dumbfounded.

"Yeah. You didn't think. If you had, you would have known I would never have done anything like the things you accused me of." Pushing my hair back behind my ear I shifted the weight of the box in my arms. "Am I even allowed to be talking to you or are you hoping to try to sue me? I haven't got a lot left to take." He looked taken aback by my words.

"You left a lot of your things behind." He said quietly after a moment.

"I didn't leave anything that belongs to me. If there's stuff there that you don't want, I suggest you chuck it out, or donate it." I took a step away. "I want to go now."

"Even your phone. I um… didn't know where you were."

"I don't see why you'd care."

"Imogen please?"

"Please what?"

"Please listen to me." He said quietly.

"Ha! What like you listened to me?" I stopped, and looked down at my feet, taking a deep breath. "Look, I don't want to argue, I'm just angry. I'm going to go now okay?"

"Wait! Are you free tonight?"

"Why?"

"You could come and get the rest of your things."

"I don't want them."

"Please Imogen. Don't be stubborn. They're yours." He watched me closely, and perhaps seeing the doubt in my mind he added, "Please? I'll be home by 7pm and I won't keep you." What an ironic use of words, I thought to myself, of course he won't keep me, he just tossed me aside when he was done with me. I just stared at him, feeling cornered, and once again he added, "Please?"

"Okay." I nodded. "I'll try."

"Thank you." He smiled at me, but instead of returning the smile, I turned and walked away.

Packing up the motel took little time, one of the good things about having such a streamlined amount of possessions meant I didn't have to spend time sorting through old items. I bundled it all into the back of the car and checked out, grateful that I wouldn't have to return to the motel again. Getting into the car I made the decision that I should go to the house and pick up my things. The last thing I really wanted to do was see Jackson again, but he had been so persistent that I didn't feel I had much choice.

It was strange making the drive back to what had been our home, but now was no longer mine. It never really had been I suppose. I'd always doubted things would work out, but I'd believed he had really loved me. How wrong I had been! I felt a mixture of sadness for what I'd lost and anger for the way Jackson had dealt with it, although underlying was annoyance at myself. I wished I'd told him when my camera had been taken, maybe we would have been able to overcome everything. I shook myself. There was no point in wondering about the what if's, this was my reality now. If this is how he was going to treat me over a misunderstanding, then much as it hurt, I would rather find out now than in the future when we could have been together even longer.

Pulling up at the gate, I fought the urge to enter the key code and instead pressed the buzzer.

"Hello?" Jackson's voice answered me.

"It's me." I replied determined to keep strong, to get in and out as quickly as possible. The gate swung open and I drove slowly up the driveway. Jackson was waiting at the top of the steps by the front door. I pulled up, suddenly conscious of what I was driving, but knowing there was little I could do about it. Taking a deep breath, I got out, leaving my bag and keys in the car so I could make a quick getaway.

"Hey." He said as I approached. His brown hair looked tousled as if he had just stepped out of the shower and he was barefoot, wearing jeans and a t-shirt.

"Hello."

"You didn't have to buzz in. I haven't changed the code."

"I wasn't just going to let myself in, it would be a bit rude considering I don't live here anymore." I said trying to keep my tone level.

"Yeah okay." He pushed his hands into his pockets, shifting his weight from one foot too the other. I wondered if he was as uncomfortable as I felt.

"So. How are we going to do this? Do you want me to wait here?" I asked quietly.

"No!" He looked surprised, but I didn't know the rules he was playing by. The last time I had been here, he was so angry, it was a weird situation and almost impossible to know how I was supposed to act. "Of course you can come in."

"Okay." I walked slowly up the steps and stepping to the side, he motioned for me to follow him in.

"Shall we start upstairs?" He asked and I nodded, pushing the front door shut behind me. "Where's your car Imogen?"

"Outside." I said without looking at him. I wasn't in the mood for polite conversation or any conversation to be honest.

"I meant the one I bought you."

"I had to sell it."

"Why?" He said glancing at me as they walked.

"Is it not obvious?" I asked.

"Not to me, that's why I asked."

168

"Well, when you threw me out, I didn't have anywhere to go, no money and no job. I spent the last of my savings on that stupid watch I bought you. The car was the only thing I had of any value. I had to sell it so I could pay for somewhere to stay. Is that a good enough reason for you?" He stopped walking and turned to me, running his hand through his hair and closing his eyes for a second.

"I'm sorry Imogen. I was so angry with you. I'm still angry, but I also admit that I didn't handle things very well."

"That's an understatement." I said continuing past him to what had been our bedroom. "I just wish you'd talked to me. It would have been nice to have a conversation rather than you jumping to the wrong conclusion." I shrugged. "Anyway... I forgot to bring a bag. Can I grab a couple of bin bags or something?"

"No. I'll get you a suitcase. You might need a couple; you have a lot of clothes." He left the room and I sat on the bed, not wanting to start packing until he came back. When he returned he unzipped a large blue suitcase and laid it on the bed. I stood up.

"Okay, what do you want to get rid of?" I asked.

"It's hardly like that, Imogen, they are your things, you should have them." He pulled open the door to the wardrobe and began to pull items out. "I can't believe you left all of this."

"Like I'm going to need dresses like these anymore!" I said shaking my head and raising an eyebrow. "Okay. Chuck it in, I'll decide what to do with it later." Moving in, I took some more down from the rail and roughly folded them into the bag too. We continued in silence for a few minutes, until the wardrobe was clear before I opened my drawer, pulling more clothing out and packing it away in the suitcase.

"I think you're about full. I'll get you another." Jackson said motioning to the suitcase.

"It's okay. I'm just about done." I said squeezing some more in and attempting to pull the zip shut.

"No, there's all your shoes too." He left the room, and came back a few moments later with another suitcase, unzipping it and laying it open on the bed. "You have your jewellery too." He said opening another drawer. "I was really surprised that you left your engagement ring." He said quietly.

"I had to really didn't I? I didn't want any more accusations that I'd only been after your money." I winced at the sound of bitterness in my voice as I tried to pull the closed suitcase off the bed, struggling with its weight.

"It's yours though. You should have it." He had picked out some of the boxes, and held them out to me, taking the full suitcase and lifting it down to the floor for me. I scooped up the rest of my belongings, including the shoes and threw them into the empty case. I'd forgotten I had so many.

"Those earrings are worth more than my car. I'd look ridiculous."

"Well take them and sell them then."

"Sentimental old thing aren't you?" I said with sarcasm adding, "All right, if you're sure you want me to?"

"I'd prefer you to have them."

"Okay. Is that everything?" I asked zipping the second case.

"No, I have your phone downstairs." He took the suitcase from me. "Hey, it's heavy, let me take it."

"Thank you."

I followed Jackson down the stairs, watching as he dropped both suitcases in the hallway for me.

"Your phone is in here, I put it on to charge for you." He said walking into the kitchen, "Are you hungry?"

"Hungry?" I asked in surprise as I followed him.

"Yeah, you know, for food." He said with a smile.

"I'm so confused by you." I said quietly, "Don't try to be my friend. I don't want that." I sank down onto one of the stools, watching as he checked on a dish in the oven, turning the heat down, but not off.

"Imogen, I was just offering because I cooked too much, and I haven't eaten yet. I thought you might want to have a bite before you go. It's fine if you don't want to." He looked down, "Here's your phone." He said passing it over to me.

"Can we sort out the billing for it?" I looked warily at him. "If you're paying for it, it isn't really mine is it?"

"Well yeah I guess." He looked taken aback by my question. "But there's no rush." I turned it on to find a sea of messages, mostly from Jackson's sister, horrible hurtful messages accusing me of stealing, of destroying my relationship with his family, but others from his Mum and Dad too. I scrolled through them and it felt like a knife had been twisted in my heart. All the people I thought were my family had turned on me too.

"You know, it might be better if I leave it with you. You can probably cancel the contract, can't you? I'll try to pick up a replacement at some point." I stopped scrolling and put the phone down. It was horrible to think everyone I had cared about believed the worst of me.

"What is it?" I looked up to see that Jackson had been watching me, a flicker of concern on his face.

"Some really lovely messages from your family." I said quietly. "I don't want it, but thanks."

"What did you expect Imogen?" He asked softly. Hearing those words just about tipped me over the edge and I stood up, shoving the stool backwards as I did. Suddenly I felt furious, it was like a dam had been broken and I could hear the venom in my own voice as I spoke.

"What did I expect?" I asked loudly, catching his eye, "I thought you would have the decency to ask me what happened, to believe me, not to throw me out without a care about where I would go or what would happen to me!" I shook my head. "But I suppose I should thank you. I always thought you'd hurt me, I just never thought it would be like this. I'm so glad we didn't end up getting married or having kids. What would you have done then, poisoned them against me too?" I was so angry I couldn't even think straight, and I could feel a pulsing in my temples. Raising my fingers to the sides of my face I gently made small circles with my fingertips. I knew I needed to calm down. "So much for trust!" I finished, stalking to the hallway and reaching for the bags.

"Wait, Imogen." He was suddenly behind me, catching my arm, spinning me back to face him.

"Why should I?"

"Imogen, I don't understand what you're saying. Can you tell me what you mean?"

"There's no point. You made up your mind about me and got your lawyer involved. You never once asked for an explanation then and it's a bit late now. It just shows how little I really meant to you." I dropped my head, the anger slipping away from me and leaving me feeling sad once again, "Please let me go." He did at once, looking at me with something that looked like concern. We stared at each other for a moment, quietly assessing each other.

"I'll help you to your car." Jackson said eventually, picking my suitcases up from the floor.

"Thank you." I murmured. We walked in silence out to the car, I couldn't even be bothered to be embarrassed about the car anymore, I was just grateful I had it.

"Have you got everything you own in there?" He asked as I opened the boot.

"Actually, I do." He looked at me questioningly and so I continued, "I've been staying at a really shitty motel, but earlier at work I saw Mason and he invited me to stay at their place for a bit. So, I'm going there later." I said, adding, "Don't worry I didn't speak about you, well I had to tell him we aren't together anymore, but that was it." I leaned in and dragged a box of papers out of the boot, making space. "It'll be the first night in weeks that I'll be able to sleep properly I hope."

"What's that?" Jackson asked as I took the box from the boot, shifting it in my arms before going to put it in the front.

"What?" I asked in confusion. He plucked a piece of paper from the box as I passed. "Hey, that's mine." I tried to grab it back, but he held it out of my reach as he looked at it.

"It's from the police." He said carefully. "A police report about a theft?" I gave up waiting and threw the box in the front of the car.

"That's right. It's when my camera was stolen from my car. It's from a few months back. I had to go to the police to be able to get the car window repaired on the insurance, well that and replace my camera." I stood, hands on hips looking at him as he digested the information. "I didn't tell you about it at the time because I honestly didn't think it mattered, you were busy with work and everything I lost could be replaced. I had the photos backed up, so it didn't even cross my mind that the memory card could be used. I thought whoever had stolen the camera just wanted that, and they'd throw the rest away. But you know, if you'd bothered to ask me, you'd know all of that." I stopped and went again for the suitcase, heaving it up the side of the car and tipping it into the boot. The good thing about having an old car was that I wasn't worried in the least about scratching the paintwork. "Although, with the way you've been lately, you probably just think it's a story." I looked back to see Jackson standing in a stunned silence just watching me.

"It wasn't you." He whispered, and I could see it slowly dawning on him the gravity of the mistake he had made. "Fuck."

"Hmmm. That's what I thought when you threw me out." I raised an eyebrow and pursed my lips. "Can I have that back please?" I asked reaching out to take the paper from him.

"Why didn't you tell me?"

"What was the point? You'd already decided what you thought of me, you didn't even ask me. And to be honest, if I really meant that little to you, then I'd prefer to find out now, than further down the line." I shrugged. "Shit happens, or at least it seems to happen to me. We have to move on."

"I am so..." I cut him off. I didn't want to hear his apologies now. "Whatever." I waved my hand at him, "I'm done. Goodbye Jackson. It was really good while it lasted." I turned my back and while I still had the strength to do it, I walked to the driver's door and got in, buckling up and starting the engine. As I pulled away, in the rearview mirror I saw Jackson standing in the driveway watching me go. He looked broken. I barely managed to hold in my tears until I got to the main road.

CHAPTER 14

It felt like my life had lost its meaning. I didn't know it was possible to feel worse than I already did, but I found it was. The only time I'd ever felt this lost before was in the days after my miscarriage, but then at least I had Adam. When I woke up in the night in tears, he would be there to hold me and make me feel safe. Despite our relationship difficulties, he'd never left me, but now I was utterly alone. I felt disorientated and distant from the world around me, and although I rarely drank in the evenings, I often awoke feeling like I had a hangover. There was nothing to get up in the mornings for, worse than that I just seemed to have lost my purpose. I did very little except check online jobs listings to see if there was anything available, which there wasn't. The majority of my day consisted of waking up, wandering down to the beach for a little swim, wandering back, maybe taking a shower, checking for jobs and wandering down to the beach again. The lack of purpose made me realise just how much I had lost. Nicole occasionally tried to drag me out, but she and Mason were so tied up with their own lives and jobs, that I didn't want to impose any more than I was already doing by living in their guest house.

The little guest house itself was beautiful, one of two on the property. One was a purpose built house while the one I had chosen was much smaller, more of a cabin than a house, but it was tucked into the gardens and almost hidden from view. I liked it because it reminded me of the beach huts we had back home in England, and while it was little more than a large room with the bed in the living space, it looked out to the beach which I found wonderful. If I left the door open, I could hear the sea from my bed. It was lovely having the beach so close, and I enjoyed the peace it gave me, often sitting down on the beach for long spaces of time just watching the waves. It was really the only time I ever felt properly relaxed.

A few weeks passed and Nicole and Mason invited me to join them in the evening, they told me they had already asked some other friends over for drinks. The invitations for me to join them came often and I realised what a thoughtful couple they were, always including me where possible, but I found it harder than ever to be around people, and avoided large groups whenever possible. Especially people that had known Jackson and I as a couple. I didn't want any more confrontations and I didn't know what to say about the way my life had fallen apart. It was just easier to avoid everything. In the afternoon before the guests began to arrive, I went out and pulled my car right up to the guesthouse, trying to hide it from view, or if not hide it, at least make it slightly less noticeable. I really didn't want to see or talk to anyone, it made things just too awkward, so I hoped by moving my car others wouldn't even think about whether I was there or not. Then, giving myself a few minutes, I quietly snuck down to the beach, knowing it was a bit of a cop out, but also just needing space, and I knew that wouldn't happen up at the house. The good thing about the property being so big was that it was easier to move about without being noticed. Trees and bushes lined the paths, and made for an interesting landscape with many nooks and alcoves where there was often a quiet place to be found amongst the greenery.

Once down onto the beach, I walked along a little way before finding a gap between some rocks. It was the perfect place to tuck myself out of direct sight, but with the view of the sea unobstructed. I had no intention of going back until things died down, or until it was dark enough to sneak back without being seen. The more I snuck about, the more I realised just how much I needed to find my own place, but until I found myself a new job, I was well and truly. stuck.

Up at the house the guests were arriving with Mason and Nicole greeting each one of them at the door.

"Hey Jackson." Nicole smiled letting him in through the front door.

"Hi Nicole." He returned the smile, bending to kiss her cheek. "Hi Mason." Things had been strained between the two of them recently, although Jackson didn't know why for sure. He assumed Imogen had told them and that Mason was on her side, but he was grateful he at least still managed to get an invitation. "I brought this." He said holding out a bottle of wine to Nicole who didn't seem to be as adverse to him being there as Mason was.

"Thanks Jackson." She motioned for him to come through into the kitchen area. "Can I get you a drink?" She opened the fridge and held out a beer to him.

"You know me well." He said as he took it from her. "Thank you."

"Imogen isn't here." Mason said catching Jackson's gaze wandering across the open plan living area.

"No?"

"No." Mason said firmly.

"Where is she?"

"Probably on the beach." Nicole added in, "That's where she normally is."

"Just leave her alone. I'm sure she remembers where you live if she wants to talk." Mason didn't look impressed at Jackson's interest.

"Can I go and say hi at least? I just want to make sure she's okay. I haven't seen her for ages." He replied hating that he had to explain things to his friends. It felt like he was asking a parent for permission.

"I'd prefer you didn't." Mason said, just as Nicole replied,

"I'm sure that's fine." Jackson frowned looking from one to the other of them.

"Thanks guys. I won't bother her for long." He went past the fridge, grabbing another bottle of beer on the way and popping it open. "I'll take her this!" He took a mouthful from his, carrying the other by the neck, and headed to the steps leading to the beach.

Imogen wasn't in sight anywhere, so Jackson kicked off his shoes, leaving them where they lay and walked along the beach, hoping to spot her. There wasn't any sign of her until he noticed a large rock. By the bottom of the rock two feet were half buried in the sand. He walked to the rock, making sure to keep his distance so he didn't startle her as he approached.

"Hey Imogen." I looked up from my book in surprise, before registering who it was that had disturbed me. Jackson was standing a little way away from me, a small smile playing on his lips. He looked really unsure of himself.

"Oh. Hi." I replied. "What are you doing down here?"

"I came down to find you. I hope you don't mind, I just wanted to see how you were." He replied and then holding out the bottle of beer said, "I brought you this."

"Thank you." I took it from him, laying my book down next to me.

"Can I sit down?" He asked and I suddenly felt wary.

"Uh yeah, I suppose so." I replied watching as he sat down next to me on the sand. He left a space between us, but he was still so close to me that it almost hurt.

"So, how are you?" He asked glancing toward me.

"Fabulous." I replied without a smile, "How about you?"

"Still feeling like a complete dick to be honest." He said taking a breath. "I am so very sorry Imogen. I was such an idiot. I wish I could take it back. I wish I could change what I did, but I can't. All I can do is say sorry."

"It's all right." I shrugged. "Well, it's not the highlight of my adult life, you know, but it's okay. Things could have been worse." Although I was trying to make light of the situation, I didn't try to pretend I was happy I was happy about it.

"Could they really?" He seemed doubtful. "I'm not sure how?"

"Actually, they could. For a while I actually thought I was pregnant." I sniffed. "Can you imagine how awful that would have been?" It had only been a worry for a moment, but it had been a worry all the same.

"Jesus. I'm sorry Imogen. You've been dealing with so much." He said looking shocked and running his hand across his forehead.

"Sometimes you just have no choice." I smiled a little, but didn't look up at him. "Anyway, despite the worry I wasn't. The doctor suggested it was stress. So, that was lucky."

"Why didn't you tell me?" He asked and I almost snorted with laughter.

"What because you've been so understanding lately?" I shook my head. "It's just easier to rely on myself. Then no one can let me down."

"What would you have done?" He asked gently after a moment had passed. "I mean, if you were pregnant?"

"God knows, Jackson. I'm glad I don't have to think about it to be honest." I took a sip of the beer he'd brought me. "Thank you for this."

"No worries." There was silence before Jackson said quietly. "I'm so sorry Imogen. I wish I hadn't jumped to the wrong conclusion and overreacted the way I did."

"It's okay. It's done. Stop apologising." I replied softly. "You can't change it so there's no point in beating yourself up about it." I was still looking out to sea, holding the bottle between my hands while my elbows rest on my drawn up knees. I couldn't have been wrapped up much tighter if I had tried. I felt like I needed to protect myself.

"How can you be so forgiving?"

"Because I don't want anger to eat me up. I've already lost enough." It seemed Jackson was processing what I said and neither of us spoke for a few minutes. All I could hear was the sound of the waves crashing, until he spoke again.

"I wanted you to know that I spoke with my lawyer. All the paperwork you signed; it's been destroyed. You can say whatever you like about me to whoever you like Imogen. Go to the papers and tell them what I did if you want. It's only what I deserve."

"Right, like I'd ever do anything like that." I didn't say that I didn't like the lack of proof, but he seemed to read my mind, pulling an envelope from his pocket and passing it to me. "What's this?"

"A letter from my lawyer to corroborate what I've just told you. I had a feeling you might not trust me."

"What's the saying? Once bitten, twice shy?" I folded the letter in half, not wanting to open it there, and tucked it into my book to keep it safe. "Thank you."

"I miss you Imogen." Jackson said after a while.

"Don't say things like that." I whispered. I could feel tears prickling my eyes and I tried to blink them back. He was sitting closer to me than I realised and out of the corner of my eye I assessed him.

"It's true." He offered. Hearing him speak like that hurt. It also confused me. I still didn't understand how the man I loved, who promised he loved me too, could treat me the way he had done. Slowly I dropped my head to one side, gently coming to rest on his shoulder. I heard him take a sharp intake of breath, perhaps in surprise but I ignored it, instead closing my eyes and just resting there. Jackson didn't move for a second, he seemed almost frozen, but then slowly and softly he slipped his arm around my shoulders holding me to him, and for the first time in weeks I felt safe and secure. It was heartbreaking. "I love you Imogen."

"I love you too Jackson." I admitted, before adding, "But, you're an arsehole, and you broke my heart."

"I know." His voice cracked, "If I could do anything to take back what I did, I would do it in a heartbeat. You mean more to me than anything. I was such a fool."

"Yes, you were." I smiled sadly, knowing he couldn't see it. "But you must know I can't trust you now, not after this. It took so long for me to believe you really cared about me and that I could trust you but at the first sign of trouble you just binned me off." I turned a little more to him slipping my arms around his waist, falling into him, and resting my face against his chest. He dropped his face to my hair, and I felt him kiss the top of my head softly.

"Is there nothing I can do?" He asked into my hair.

"No, I don't think there is Jackson." I breathed in the smell of him, so familiar and yet so sad. "It was nice at least getting the chance to say goodbye."

"Goodbye?" I felt him tense. "What do you mean?"

"I think, well, it's hard to know really, but I think I'm going to go home." I said finally.

"Home? You mean England?" He released me enough to be able to look me in the face.

"That's what I was thinking." I nodded.

"Why?" He asked, seeming completely stunned.

"Why not?" I shrugged.

"Is it Adam? Are you going back to him?"

"No." I replied with a laugh, "He doesn't even know that you and me are over. I didn't think it was a good idea to have him on your case."

"He didn't like me when we were together. You'd think he would be grateful that we're not close anymore."

"But you know he was protective. I'm not sure that he'd like the story of how I ended up in a trashy motel. It's just better to hope he doesn't find out." He nodded and there was a pause. Jackson seemed to be digesting what I had told him.

"I thought you were happy here Imogen?"

"I was. But that was when I had a cool job, an amazing partner, a future to look forward to. I don't even have a reason to get out of bed in the morning now, let alone to stay here. It's so depressing. I have no ties, and the only reason I am here is because I don't have enough money to fly home." I stopped and closed my eyes. "That sounded like I was asking for money, which I'm not."

"I didn't think that." He gently brushed a strand of hair behind my ear, "I thought you'd carry on working on the set. You were so good at your job and everyone liked having you around."

"Yeah, but that was before. Can you imagine us having to work so closely when we can barely say two words to each other?" I laughed, "I'm not supposed to even talk about you, so how would that work?"

"I told you that's all null and void now." He said slowly, "And you and me, we'd be fine. Come back, Imogen, at least while you decide what you're going to do. Eric isn't keen on the temp we have in for you, and well to be honest, you're the only make-up artist I've ever enjoyed working with. I won't get in your way or anything." He sounded hopeful.

"I don't know." I trailed off. This was the last thing I had been expecting.

"I won't push you Imogen, I'd give you space." He seemed so keen, and it was so out of the blue, I just wasn't sure what to say. "Well at least tell me you'll think about it?" He said when I didn't answer him.

"Okay, I will." I slowly began to untangle myself from him, shuffling across the sand to put a little bit of space between us.

"Oh, I have something else for you." He said and I watched as he put his hand into his pocket, fishing out a key.

"What's that?" I asked suspiciously.

"It's your car key. I managed to find your car and bought it back for you. I'm not having any arguments, this is non-negotiable. I bought it for you, and you should keep it. I don't know if I believe that thing you've been driving is even road worthy."

"We're not together anymore, you can't give me a car. It's just too much." I said refusing to take the key.

"I'm not giving you anything, I just found your car and I'm having it returned to you. It should be delivered here on Monday." He said quietly. "Please take it. Regardless of what you did or didn't do, I reacted horribly. I should never have treated you the way I did, and I would do anything to change it, but I can't. I can do this though. I had no idea what the best option was, and I frowned at him while trying to decide what to do. "Please?" He held out the key once more, gently taking my hand and folding the key under my fingers.

"Thank you."

"You're welcome." He replied.

CHAPTER 15

"So, will you ever tell us what happened between you two?"
Nicole asked. We were sitting at the kitchen table, while Mason
cooked them breakfast.

"No." I smiled back.

"Did he cheat on you?"

"No!"

"Ask you to do weird kinky sex stuff?"

"Nicole! Stop it." I glared at her.

"Nic. Leave her alone." Mason said in a warning tone. Since I had
broken up with Jackson, Mason had become even more brotherly
and was quite protective, while my best friend seemed to just
want to push us back together.

"It's all right Mason. Nicole will get the idea soon I'm sure." I
smiled at my friend. "It's in the past now, it doesn't have any
bearing on anything, so can you forget about it?"

"If it doesn't matter, why aren't you back together?" She said
raising an eyebrow. "You were talking for so long last night, and
when you walked back in together, I wondered if you were, but
then you sloped off and left him here moping around all evening
by himself."

"Nicole - please leave it." I said in a more exasperated tone.

"Here you go." Mason carried over two plates, each holding an omelette.

"Amazing, thank you." I said taking mine.

"You're welcome." Mason returned with his own and sat down at the table too.

"Listen. I want to talk to you both about something." They both looked up at me in between mouthfuls. "Last night, Jackson asked me to go back to work at the studio. I said no, but he was persistent, and I told him I would think about it." I stopped speaking, looking from Mason to Nicole and then back again. "Any thoughts?"

"Selfishly it would be great to have you back, because that woman we've had since you left is a nightmare." Mason said with a grin. "Would you find it awkward?"

"I don't know." I said truthfully. "I loved the job, but the idea of working everyday with my ex is a bit odd. Other people manage it though don't they?"

"I think you should come back too." Nicole said. "I think it would be good for you both. You never know, it might help you sort things out? You could get back together?"

"Nicole, please. Jackson and I aren't getting back together. Ever. In fact, I told him last night I was going back to England, and I still intend to, it's just I haven't been able to get another job yet and if this one is open it seems a little stupid to turn it down."

"Well, at the worst case, you can always change your mind Imogen. It's probably worth giving a go isn't it?" Mason asked.

"That's true." I nodded, "Does that mean I have to call him and tell him?"

"Yeah, I think it does." Mason answered. "In fairness Imogen, if you can't talk to him on the phone, you probably shouldn't be thinking about working with him again."

"You're right again. It's so annoying that you're always right!"

As soon as I made the decision to go back to work, I began to worry about talking to Jackson. I knew I had to do it as soon as possible, so straight after I had finished eating, I went back to my place to call him. I knew putting it off would make it worse. Having left my old phone at Jackson's house I'd bought myself a new phone, but seldom used it, and few people had the number, Nicole, Mason and Adam being my three main contacts. Eventually I dialled his number, wondering how it was that I still knew it off by heart. It rang a few times before I heard his voice at the other end.

"Hello?" Hearing his voice made me nervous all over again, and I paused almost unable to answer. After a second I heard him repeat his greeting, this time slightly less patiently.

"Hi Jackson." I said quickly.

"Imogen?" He suddenly sounded pleased.

"Yeah. Hi."

"I didn't recognise your number."

"No, you wouldn't, it's a new phone."

"Is everything okay?"

"Yes, I just wanted to call you about work." I paused, "Did you mean what you said last night? Do you really think we could work together? I mean, after everything?"

"Yes Imogen, I do." He stopped for a second, clearing his throat. "I know I made a hell of a mistake, and I get that you can't forgive me, but I'll back off at work. I won't make it difficult for you."

"Okay."

"Okay?" He asked, "Do you mean you'll come back?"

"If Eric is okay with it I will."

"Do you want me to call him for you? I can explain that it wasn't your fault that you left." He sounded hopeful.

"That would be great, if you don't mind?"

"I'm glad I can do something to help." He said softly. "I'll call him now, and then call you back."

"Okay, bye Jackson."

"Bye Imogen." He said and the line went dead.

I had only managed to put the kettle on for a cup of tea when my phone rang. I'd saved Jackson's number, knowing that he now had mine and saw it was his name flashing up on my screen.

"Hi." I said swiping the phone unlocked.

"Hey. He wants you back."

"Wow, okay. I wasn't expecting that."

"And he asked if tomorrow is okay?"

"Tomorrow?" I asked in surprise, I wasn't expecting it to seem so easy or so soon.

"Yeah. I told you, the team isn't the same without you. None of us are."

"Stop it."

"Sorry. It slipped out." I could hear a smile in his voice.

"Are you sure this is a good idea?" I asked him.

"I think it is. I haven't told anyone on the set about what I did, so no one knows why we split up. You can tell them as much or as little as you want. I won't say a word about it."

"Neither will I. It's no one else's business."

"Okay." He said quietly.

"Jackson, just so you know, I haven't told anyone. Not even Nicole or Mason."

"Really?"

"I mean, they know we broke up, but they have no idea why and I don't plan on telling them."

"Okay." He said slowly.

"Yeah, um also, I know you have this number now, but can you not give it out please?" I thought back to the messages his family had sent me. "I don't want anyone else to have it."

"No of course I won't."

"Thank you." There was silence for a moment. It seemed neither of them knew what else to say.

"Well, I guess I'll see you tomorrow."

"I guess you will." I replied. "Bye Jackson."

It was so strange being back at work. In fact, it felt like barely anything had changed. Everyone seemed to be pleased to see me, and welcomed me back, but it was like I had been away on a scheduled break, rather than coming back after quitting.

I got in early, wanting to familiarise myself again with my workspace before anyone else came in, mainly Jackson. I was nervous of seeing him, nervous of how to act around him and awkward about how to move on with this new way of life. There was a wireless sound system set up there, and I flicked it on, connecting it to my phone and starting a playlist. It might not make things any less awkward, but at least it could help to cover uncomfortable silences. Then I set about making coffee. The last thing I wanted was to feel like I wasn't busy.

By the time I began to hear chattering outside, I had already gone through my notes for the day to see what was expected. It looked like it would be a fairly straightforward day, with no injuries, which was a relief because it meant Jackson wouldn't be in the chair for very long. I knew I had to ease into this slowly. My tummy flip flopped, and I realised how nervous I felt. It was ridiculous! Sinking down in a chair, I tried to clear my thoughts before my day properly began, but the sound of the door disturbed me. Looking up, I saw Mason pop his head in.

"Hey, you're here!" He made his way up the steps and into the trailer. "I didn't see your car this morning at home, but I wasn't sure if you were here or not. Are you hiding?" He asked with a smile.

"Preparing myself." I said shaking my head.

"Well you can distract yourself with me, if you're ready?" He said gesturing to his face.

"Take a seat." I replied with a smile. Mason was so kind; he was great at making me feel relaxed.

Jackson came in a little later, saying good morning and taking a seat on the sofa at the back of the room. He looked a little on edge too.

"I'll be with you in a moment." I said, and once the words were out I realised how formal I sounded.

"No rush." He replied sitting back and watching me work.

Before long I finished up working with Mason and shooed him from the room. Leaning back against the work surface I looked coolly at Jackson.

"I'm not sure this is a good idea."

"It's a little weird, I'll give you that, but I'm sure it'll get easier." Jackson said, he hadn't moved from his position on the sofa. "It's just been a while."

"Yeah." I probably didn't look convinced, I certainly didn't feel it, but I was glad he was acknowledging the weirdness too. It must have been obvious as to how awkward I was feeling because after a moment he asked,

"Should we see if there's someone else available then? I don't want you to feel uncomfortable."

"No." I took a deep breath. "It's my job. I need to get over it or find something else to do. Come on over."

Trying to do a physically close job without being physically close to someone was hard. I felt tingly every time I touched him, and although I tried to maintain a distance, it wasn't really working.

"Imogen?" He looked up at me from his seated position. "I'm not going to bite, you know?" He added on a smile, but I thought he looked a little unsure and I wondered if he was just hoping to lighten the mood.

"I didn't think you were. I just worry that I'm going to cross a line somewhere." I turned my back to him for a moment, blinking away tears I hoped he hadn't seen. "I didn't expect it to be so hard to do this."

"Is there anything I can do to make it easier?"

"I don't think so." I turned back, pulling up a chair and scooting closer to him. "I just hope time will help."

***

Time did help a little. I couldn't say that I didn't feel on edge at all, but as the days turned into weeks I did manage to settle into a better routine, one where I was able to touch Jackson's face, almost in the same way I could touch Mason's. It wasn't like it used to be, but it was certainly a lot more normal. Things began to fall a little more into a routine, and I didn't feel so uptight before coming into work each day.

"Are you coming to the awards next weekend?" Mason asked as I tousled his hair into place. It was a hard job keeping his unruly hair in place. Although it was a wilder style, there was definite structure to it, and like the 'girl next door' makeup look, more time that you'd imagine went into it.

"No." I answered. I'd known the TV awards were coming up, but I hadn't realised it was so soon. Last year, the four of us had gone together. It had been my first awards ceremony, and I had really enjoyed it, although being photographed at the event with Jackson had made me nervous. I felt a bit of a fraud, like I wasn't supposed to be there, that someone would spot me and throw me out any moment. But they hadn't done, and of course, it had been lovely.

"Aren't you?" Jackson asked from the doorway. I jumped, looking over to see him standing watching me.

"No." I shook my head.

"Oh." He stepped into the room and made his way to the sofa. "Why not?"

"I just don't want to." I replied.

"But the whole team are going." Mason added.

"Well, it can't be the whole team, can it? Because I'm not going." I snapped, stepping away from Mason, hoping I could brush it off. "All done, off you go."

"Thanks Imogen." Mason said rising from the seat.

"Your turn." I told Jackson.

"Thank you." He said as he came to sit down before me. "It's a shame you're not coming. I thought you enjoyed it last year."

"I did, but things are different now." I didn't add that I was afraid of seeing him with someone else. I couldn't imagine that he'd go to an event like that on his own, especially when his co-star had a date.

"I know, I just thought you'd still come along."

"I'd feel like a hanger on. I'm not one of the cast, so no one will know I'm not there, so can we just leave it please?" I stopped as I realised how abrupt I'd come across. "Sorry, I didn't mean to be so short, I just don't want to go, and I don't want to have to keep explaining myself. I doubt you'd question anyone else on the crew about it like this."

"Yeah okay, that's a fair point and I understand." He nodded, "Although I can't say I'm not a little disappointed."

"I'm sure you'll have fun anyway." I said with a forced smile.

"Okay. What are we doing today?" I said turning my back on his to consult my notes.

I didn't want to tell Jackson that I was back in regular contact with Adam. I felt strongly that it was none of his business, and that it shouldn't matter, but something made me hold back from being too open, the last thing I wanted to do was hurt him. Texting Adam my new number had been a spur of the moment thing and I had no intention of starting anything up with him again. I hadn't thought any more about it than the fact that if he couldn't get hold of me when he wanted to, he would probably be put out. I knew I didn't have to answer to him, or to explain anything to him, but it was nice to think he was on side with me at least. Someone impartial that I could talk to. I really needed a friend. The text I sent him was simple, just stating my new number, yet it had opened a new dialogue with him. It was a distraction from everything else, it was nothing, but it was so nice to have someone to talk to. Someone that didn't want to talk to me about Jackson, like Nicole always seemed to, or try to push us back together. It was easy to talk to Adam about simple things, and to hear about what he was up to, it filled moments that otherwise would have been empty.

It was only talking to Jackson and Mason about the Television Awards that I remembered Adam said he would soon be coming to America for work. While I had the courage, I texted him, just asking where he thought he would be over the weekend of the event. Instead of a reply, my phone immediately rang in my hand. Swiping my phone, I put it to my ear.

"Why? He asked as I answered.

"Hi Adam." I said with a laugh. He was always so direct and to the point.

"Hi Princess. Why do you want to know?"

"I'm at a loose end that weekend, it's an award event, and I don't want to go. I knew you were over here, and I wasn't sure if we could meet up?"

"I'll be in New York."

"Oh. Maybe not then." I replied, realising he was almost as far away as he would have been if he had been at home in England.

"Imogen, I have a suite at a nice hotel. You could stay with me for the weekend. It would be lovely to see you."

"The flight though, it would be expensive. I don't have a lot of expendable cash right now."

"I'll take care of that, it's no problem." He answered quickly. There was an authority to his voice that made me feel he would eliminate any problem. I'd forgotten the way he dealt with things like that.

"Are you sure?"

"If you need to escape for the weekend then come to me. We'll have fun. I'll book some tickets for you and text you the times."

"Thank you Adam. It means a lot."

"No problem Princess. I'll see you soon." He replied before ending the call.

I put myself in his hands and luckily the flight he booked coincided with the end of the day. Leaving my car at work, I jumped in the car Adam had sent to take me to the airport. The flight arrived late in the evening and I made my way directly to the hotel. I hadn't even asked him the name of it when I agreed to come, but I knew that it would be high end because of the standards Adam had. He sent me a text telling me the room number and I made my way up, dragging my small wheeled suitcase behind me. It had been like this when we were together, I remembered. I never had to plan anything other than the clothes I would take. All I had to do was get in the car he sent, and trust that I would be delivered to the right location at the right time. When I'd been newly single after splitting up with Adam, it was something I had fought against. I wanted independence and I didn't want to rely on anyone. For a moment, now that I needed it, it was easy to let myself be taken care of.

I took a deep breath at the door. The last time I saw Adam I'd been in the hospital, but normally when we saw each other it was like no time had passed and we easily fell back into being comfortable and relaxed with each other. I knocked and two seconds later the door swung open. Adam was there in front of me, bare chested in low slung jeans that hung off his hips, towel in hand, hair damp from the shower. A strong believer in martial arts, his body was lean and toned, and I couldn't help noticing how much effort must have gone into keeping it the way it was.

"Hi Princess." He said pulling me straight into an embrace. "You look tired. Come in." He said taking my hand in his and relieving me of my suitcase. "Is this all you've brought?"

"Yeah. You know I travel light." I smiled. "It's good to see you."

"It's good to see you too." He led me into the living area, and motioned to the couch. "Have a seat. Can I get you a drink?"

"Yes please. Whatever you have." He walked away, towards a bar set up to one side. The room was vast and decorated opulently. I watched him go, he was entirely comfortable with himself, it didn't look like it had even occurred to him that he was barely dressed when he opened the door. He was certainly in no rush to put a shirt on now, although, I had seen it all before. I admired his physique, a body that I had once known well. Outside he portrayed such a suave exterior, coming across as such a competent businessman in his tailored suits, but at home and relaxed he was a different story. Tattoos covered the majority of his back, spreading across the tops of his arms and onto his chest. Some related to his family and gang connections while others were more decorative. Each one was exquisitely detailed, and I loved tracing the lines of them when we had been together.

"Here you go." He smiled in amusement, catching me watching him and handed me a glass of wine, keeping hold of another for himself. "It is so good to see you." He sank into the sofa next to me. The lights of the street twinkled in through the windows that lined the suite from the darkness outside. "So, are you going to fill me in on what's going on?" He asked softly.

We ended up staying awake well into the early hours just chatting. Adam had listened, but for once, not exploded when I'd explained what had happened between Jackson and me. To be honest I'd be worried about telling him, but he'd almost tried to justify it, telling me that I had to understand what it felt like to feel betrayed when family was so important. It made me smile to realise that Adam and Jackson actually had something in common, that they were more alike than I'd ever noticed. Seeing him like this was like seeing the man I'd fallen in love with again. He was relaxed and warm, almost vulnerable. It was a far cry from the man I'd left. He listened patiently, not rushing me or blaming Jackson. He was so easy to talk to and I ended up explaining that I hadn't wanted to go to the awards because I was afraid of seeing Jackson with someone else. I knew at some point he would move on; I just didn't particularly want to witness it. Especially while things were so raw. Adam understood, but then he questioned me, asking me if I was sure it was over. I told him it was, but he looked at me in disbelief and asked if I was really sure if I felt that strongly about seeing him with another woman. I was surprised when he urged me to work out how I really felt and told me I should before it was too late to fix the situation. I scowled at him, asking him when it was that he became a relationship guru. He smiled, slightly sadly I thought, and told me that sometimes life makes you realise your mistakes. He said he was trying to learn from his. We ended up falling asleep side by side in the same bed, no ulterior motive, just companionship and a strong bond that held us together more tightly than I had known.

On Saturday he took me shopping. I didn't want to buy, but browsing was amazing, and seeing the sights of New York with him by my side was an experience I wouldn't forget in a hurry. He was a gentleman, offering me his arm as we walked and generally taking care of me in a way that made me feel special for the first time since Jackson and I split up. After months of struggling to get through the days, it was good to feel a little glamorous, and like I had a purpose. I was surprised after so long at how relaxed and companionable things were between me and Adam. Our relationship was comfortable, like a pair of old slippers.

In the evening, after dinner in a lovely restaurant, we returned back to the hotel. After being dressed up for the whole day the first thing I wanted to do was kick off my high heels and it wasn't long before I shed my lovely dress too, pulling on a pair of pyjama bottoms and a cropped vest top. If I was spending the evening in, I decided I would at least be comfortable. Coming out of the bathroom I found Adam lying across the bed, head at the foot, watching tv. He too had removed his suit and had changed into a pair of jogging bottoms.

"What are you watching?" I asked joining him on the bed, sitting cross legged next to him.

"It hasn't started yet, but it's going to be live coverage of the awards." He said rolling onto his side to grin at me. "Forewarned is forearmed." He rolled back onto his stomach.

"Not everything is a war Adam." I couldn't help but smile. He tackled everything with the same method, believing knowledge was power.

"I wasn't saying it was. But don't you want to see if he is with someone?" I paused, unsure then slowly let out a breath.

"Yes, I guess I do."

"I thought so." He smiled.

The run up to the show seemed to go on forever and I lost a little bit of interest. There were so many people going that I wondered if I'd ever see anyone I knew, even if I waited all night. In the end, I stood up and stretched.

"I'm going to the loo, and to get a drink. Do you want anything?"

"Yes please. Wine?" He asked. I nodded and headed to the bathroom.

"I'll be right back."

Less than a couple of minutes had passed when from the bathroom I heard Adam calling me, telling me to be quick. I ran back in to see him pointing at the screen.

"He's with a blonde woman." He said, "Look." I sat back down next to him on the end of the bed watching the screen.

"That's Ashleigh." I replied with relief. Adam looked at me questioningly, "His sister."

"Ah. I see. She's pretty." He rolled to look at me, I was still watching as the couple posed for photographs and Jackson answered a couple of questions from the press. Mason and Nicole joined them and after a few minutes the four of them walked inside. "Relieved?" He asked.

"Yes. But it's annoying, because I really shouldn't care, should I?"

"You obviously still love the man. Much as it pains me to say it."

"I guess." I sighed and flopped down next to him. "Bloody feelings."

"Yeah. They are a pain." He smiled. "Did you get our drinks?" I shook my head.

"Sorry!"

"I'll go." He stood and once again I watched him walk away. I could see clearly the large cursive script running up his ribs on one side of his chest where my name was etched.

"You still have my name on your chest." I said taking the glass from him gratefully when he returned.

"We don't all go covering up our pasts Miss Dragon tattoo."

"Oh, you saw it?" I said sheepishly and he nodded. I immediately felt like I'd done something wrong and I pursed my lips together as I waited for a response.

"Yes, I did and while I can't say it didn't hurt a bit, I do understand. I'm keeping your name where it is though. You're still part of my family as far as I'm concerned. Even if we're not together." I nodded as he continued, "On that note, I wanted to say that I'm sorry."

"What for?" I asked with a frown.

"I know you lost me for a while back at the end of our relationship. I never meant for that to happen. I wanted to protect you, I wanted to fix the things that were going wrong and I realise now that I scared you and pushed you away. It was never my intention."

"It's okay Adam." I smiled, looking up at him, and seeing the honesty clearly on his face. His guard seemed to be completely down this weekend.

"No, it's not. We had something good, and I played a big part in ruining it. Now," He took my hand, "I'm not saying we should get back together; I don't think it would be the right thing for either of us, but I do want you to know that I am always going to be here for you. It doesn't matter whether you want to run away for the weekend, or have me get a flat tyre fixed for you, even if you want me to walk you down the aisle, I would do anything for you Imogen."

"That means an awful lot Adam." I was suddenly overtaken by emotion and came up onto my knees, reaching up to wrap my arms around his neck, feeling his arms slide around my waist as he did so. He dropped his head to my shoulder and nestled in. "Thank you."

"It's no problem." He murmured into my hair. "Like I said, you're very important to me, and although I can't say it wouldn't be weird walking you down the aisle, I would do it, if that was what you wanted." I pulled back to see him grinning at me.

"It would be weird." I laughed imagining what that wedding would look like, and sank back down on to the bed, letting go of him. "But I don't think we have to worry. I'm not getting married anytime soon."

"Well, for what it's worth." He started, sitting back down at the other end of the bed, back against the headboard, stretching his long legs out next to me, "I think you need to try to work things out with the actor."

"Are you always going to call him that?"

"Probably." He smiled.

"Why?" I stopped, "I mean, why do you think I should try again, not why do you call him that?"

"I saw the two of you together. You had something special. Yes, he fucked up. People do." He ran a hand through his blond hair. "I didn't realise what I'd lost until after you had left me, but then it was too late. It sometimes takes something big to wake us up. Losing our baby, losing you, losing my dad, all those things have changed me. I can't go back and fix them, but Princess, you could, maybe, before it's too late?" It was a shock to hear him mention the baby, it was something he had seldom spoken about. "Do you think?"

"I do. I wouldn't have said so otherwise." It was strange for me to be sitting this close, being this open with Adam. Especially about another man. We had never tolerated secrets when we were together, with the exception of some of his work, but it felt wonderful to be able to chat this freely with him again. It was only then, as I listened to Adam and saw the honesty in his face that I realised how lucky I was to have him in my corner. Our romantic relationship might have been over for a long time, but I realised our friendship was still very special and for that I was really grateful.

On Sunday Adam had a couple of meetings, but before he went, he told me he'd booked me into the spa to keep me out of trouble while he was gone. His words made me smile, but he told me that he wanted me to relax and indulge myself. It was so selfless of him, it almost made me cry and I was lost for words. While I enjoyed the relaxation of a massage, I reflected his behaviour and our relationship and wondered if I had misread him. Before, I would probably have thought he was trying to keep tabs on me by arranging something to keep me busy, possibly trying to keep me out of the way. The more I thought about it now, the more I realised I was wrong, and his actions had been rooted in an intention to be kind to me. It made me wonder how many other things I had also misread.

At the end of the weekend Adam came with me to the airport. He told me to stay in contact, and that he was always there for me, if ever I needed him. Reassurance like that made me feel safe and cared about and set me up for the journey home.

***

My flight was delayed, and I arrived back at work late on Monday morning. I rang ahead to forewarn the team that I was on my way but wouldn't be there on time and then relaxed, there was nothing I could do about it and worrying wasn't going to help me. I felt more relaxed and peaceful than I had done in weeks. The idea of going into work wasn't even worrying me in the least. The taxi delivered me back to the studio and I hurried to drop my bags in my car before heading to the hair and make-up trailer.

"Sorry I'm so late! Did you get my message?" I called as I walked in. Jackson and Mason were both sitting on the sofa chatting and when I looked further, I realised Ashleigh was also there. I blinked in surprise, and then looked down. I had no idea why Ashleigh was there, in fact her presence was really confusing, but I hoped if I carried on as normal things would be okay.

"Yeah, we did, something about a flight being delayed? Where have you been all weekend?" Jackson asked not moving from his spot.

"New York." I replied. "Yeah, I would have been on time, but the plane got held up. Who's first?"

"I'll go first, then I can get out of your way and leave you three to catch up." Mason said scooting over into the chair. "You need more work this morning anyway don't you?" He asked Jackson.

"Yeah. I've got to save some hostages and run out of a burning building today. I'm a hero. I need some damage." Jackson replied with a smile.

"Okay." I looked at Ashleigh warily, but again didn't speak to her. I didn't feel I had the right to, after all, however threatened I felt by her, she was Jackson's sister, and as the star of the show, he had the right to have pretty much whoever he wanted on the set.

"So, New York?" Mason asked as I got started. "I didn't know you were planning that?"

"It was a last minute thing really." I said cagily.

203

"So last minute you left your car here all weekend?" Jackson asked.

"No. I planned to do that."

"Oh?" It seemed Jackson had no intention of making this easy for me.

"Yes, because it was easier than getting a lift to the airport, and cheaper than leaving the car there." Jackson nodded, but still looked put out.

"What did you do there?" He asked.

"Does it matter?" I replied, biting my lip nervously.

"I was just interested, that's all." He said looking a little hurt and I immediately felt bad.

"Oh, well not a lot really. Chilled out in the hotel room, saw some sights. Had a spa day. It was a nice change." I leaned over Mason, "You need a haircut. It's going to affect continuity soon. I'll talk to your hair stylist." I said trying to change the subject. After Mason was finished, he left, and Jackson moved into the chair. I reached for my notes before I began work, checking there was nothing I had missed. Normally I was completely on top of everything, I knew which scenes were coming up and what was needed, normally before the actors themselves did, but lately, I didn't trust myself quite so much.

"Imogen?" Ashleigh's voice was uncharacteristically timid and I looked over at her impatiently. "Can we talk?"

"No disrespect, Ashleigh, but I think I've heard everything you had to say. You certainly left me enough messages." I knew I sounded sharp, but I felt ambushed.

"I just need to tell you how sorry I am." She continued as if she hadn't heard my dismissal.

"Okay. Thanks." I pulled a stool up next to Jackson and consulted the set notes again. "So, a bit of bruising, some ash and a nasty gash over your left eye." I said. "Let's get going." Working delicately at speed took my attention and I was glad that I had a distraction so I could appear too busy to chat. I could feel Ashleigh's eyes on me, but out of principle I didn't look up or make eye contact. I got increasingly uncomfortable as time went on, and I was glad once I had finished. I was so distracted that I didn't jump as I usually did when my knee brushed Jackson's thigh, and I was so caught up in my thoughts that I didn't immediately move away.

"Are you okay?" He asked quietly, catching my hand to get my attention.

"I was." I replied, knowing how grumpy I sounded. I didn't want to take it out on him, but at the same time, I felt my space had been invaded by his sister and I wasn't comfortable at all with it. "I'll just tidy up here, and then I'll be out if you need any touch ups." I told him once I had finished. I often hung around on the side of the set, in case I noticed anything out of place. I'd heard jokes about me, about what a perfectionist I was, but I also knew that it was my attention to detail that had got me to where I was.

"Okay, thanks Imogen." He pushed back his chair and got to his feet. "Ashleigh, shall I show you around?" He asked as he walked towards the door.

"You could." She said hesitantly, before looking at me. "I was kind of hoping that Imogen might be able to."

"Me?" I exclaimed, "Oh no, I don't think that's a good idea." I was dumbfounded. It seemed like a joke, and I couldn't believe Ashleigh was serious.

"Oh. I was hoping we could clear the air." Ashleigh replied looking straight at me. She didn't seem to be able to hear what I was saying, and I was sure I was being quite obvious about my feelings towards her. "It would mean a lot to me."

"Well, that may be, but it would have meant a lot to me if you had tried to find out the truth before you started leaving hateful messages for me."

"I'm sorry, I was hurt! I didn't know!" Ashleigh said quickly.

"I understand you were hurt, but I didn't do anything. You and your family said you cared about me, but not one person even asked me for my side of things, you just all assumed the worst. I had no one Ashleigh. Why should I give you time now, when no one would give me time then?"

"Imogen." Jackson spoke from the other side of the room. "This whole mess is my fault. If you want someone to be angry with it should be me. Ashleigh was only acting on what I told her and we all know I was completely wrong."

"You're right. It was your fault Jackson." I said slowly, meeting his gaze. "But although you thought you had the right to be angry and threw me out, you didn't once call me names or leave nasty messages for me. That was no one's choice but Ashleigh's, and she can't blame you for that. For someone that was supposed to be my friend, she turned very quickly when she thought she could blame me for something." It didn't look like he knew what to say to that.

"But..." Ashleigh went to speak again, but Jackson waved his hand, telling her to stop.

"The two of you were so close." He said.

"We were, but I'm all about trust, you know that. It took me a long time to trust you, but when I did, I was all in. When you broke that trust, that was it. There's no coming back from that. Ashleigh it's the same for you. I work with Jackson, so it's got to be a little different, but I don't have to force a relationship with you, so I'm not going to." I rolled my shoulders, feeling the tension tightening in my neck. "Now if you'd excuse me, I'd like some space to work."

It was awkward for a good few days after the blow up between me and Ashleigh. Jackson seemed more guarded around me, and although I didn't necessarily like it, it did make things easier. There was a lot less small talk, and although he'd tried to apologise for bringing Ashleigh into my space, I was struggling to let it go. I'd promised Adam I would try to work out how I felt about Jackson, and yet all I seemed to be able to do was push him further away. I tried to talk to him when the silence had got too much to bear, but he always stopped himself before he said too much and I realised that things were probably going to be awkward for the foreseeable future. It was weird. Spending less time with him meant there was less for us to chat about, and while that was fine with me it meant we spent a lot of time working in silence.

On Friday I drove home feeling preoccupied and distracted. I knew she wasn't paying as much attention as I should to driving, but it was hard to keep my mind on the road. Once I got home, I headed straight down to the beach, knowing the cold water would help clear my mind, but I also knew that something was going to have to change. Things couldn't keep on like this.

Back at the cabin I dried off and snuggled in an armchair with my book when a knock at the door interrupted me from reading. Before I had the chance to get up, Nicole let herself in.

"Hi Nic."

"Hi babe."

"What's up?"

"We're having an impromptu get together. Can you come over? I don't want it to be all of Mason's friends and no one else." Nicole said as she made her way to my hanging rail of clothes.

"I don't think I'm in the mood." I said honestly.

"Imogen, you're never in the mood. Not anymore, and you can't sit here moping all the time. It's not good for you." She pulled out a skirt and top and held them against herself, before putting the top back and pulling another one out. I didn't know if she was looking to help me out, or for something for herself to wear.

"It's been hard." I sighed. "I know you're right, but it's hard."

"I know. But it will only get easier if you try to push yourself."

"I know. Will Jackson be there?" I asked.

"Yeah, probably. I don't know about his sister, is she still around or has she gone home?"

"I don't know Nic. I hope she's gone."

"It's a fairly open invitation, so you might meet a man." Nicole said with a grin, "Although, I still don't know the details of what you got up to last weekend!"

"Not a lot. I just went to see Adam." Nicole's eyebrows jumped up. "Don't look at me like that, he was staying in New York. We had a lovely weekend." I smiled, for once it was a relaxed and genuine one.

"Where did you stay?"

"With him, at his hotel. It was nice. We did some sightseeing, watched the awards on TV and I went to a spa."

"That sounds lovely." Nicole said.

"It was. But don't tell Jackson or Mason that I saw him, I don't want them getting the wrong idea." Nicole nodded.

"Why? Did you sleep with him?"

"In his bed, but it wasn't like that, we didn't have sex or anything. It was just nice to be close to someone." Nicole nodded, "He noticed I'd had his name covered up, he seemed a bit hurt and it made me feel bad."

"Ouch. Yeah, I bet that did upset him. Can't be nice to see someone you care about moving on." I nodded, but didn't say anymore. I wasn't sure how much I really wanted to share with Nicole, even though she was my best friend.

"So..." Nicole said her eyes twinkling after a moment had passed, "Are you coming?"

"Okay, wait for me to change and I'll come with you now. I hate walking in to places full of people on my own."

Once I was dressed and had done my makeup I went over to the main house with Nicole and followed her up to her room. I crashed out on their massive bed while Nicole tried on outfit after outfit. Music was already playing from downstairs and after a while we began to hear voices and the sound of cars from outside.

Once downstairs I found a spot in the outdoor seating area and snuggled in with a glass of wine. I had no intention of socialising too much, and was quite content to just be. I felt I'd done my part by at least making the effort to come, although I was a little annoyed that Nicole had disappeared so soon.

"Hey." Mason settled in bedside me.

"Hi." I couldn't even see Nicole, but knew she'd be mingling somewhere.

"How are you doing?"

"I'm okay thanks. What about you?"

"Good. I'm good. Enjoying the evening, you know, good friends, good music, good times." He said, adding after a pause, "I came to warn you to be careful, Nicole is going to try to set you up."

"Oh really?" I asked. "No wonder she was so insistent I came."

"Yeah, sorry." He looked a little sheepish. "She's a pain in the ass for trying to matchmake."

"She really is. Do you know who?"

"I'm not sure. I just know it's part of her grand scheme tonight."

"Well, thank you for letting me know."

"Also, have you seen Jackson?" He asked.

"Not tonight, no."

"Okay, well, just so you know, he isn't here alone."

"Oh?" I tried not to seem too interested, or too upset by the news.

"I'll point her out if I see her." He looked across the patio, towards the hot tub and pool, but couldn't see Jackson.

"Thanks. Do you know her then?"

"A little, not as well as Jackson obviously." He grimaced as he realised how that sounded, "But yeah, she played a small recurring role on the show a couple of years ago. I think they dated for a bit, but it wasn't very serious."

"Oh." Now I was disappointed. That meant she would be beautiful.

"Ah, there they are." Mason nodded towards the house, trying to point them out without drawing attention to himself. "They're just coming out of the door." I found myself looking in the right direction, and once I'd seen them, I felt unable to look away. It was like driving past a car crash, when all you want is to look away and yet you can't. The couple were close but not touching, but then not many of the couples at the party were.

I wished Mason hadn't pointed them out, and watched as they walked hesitantly through the wide doorway and onto the deck. The woman was beautiful, perhaps in a slightly removed way. It was a refined beauty, but she looked like she was putting on a show, unlike me who preferred to be more natural these days. It was no wonder he was with her though, they made a stunning couple. She was clearly the sort of person he was meant to be with, not someone plain and normal like I was. Without even meeting the woman I felt in her shadow.

"If you lean forwards a little, I can tuck in behind you and they won't see me." I said awkwardly. I was only half joking.

"I'm not hiding you Imogen." He sounded amused.

"Okay."

"Why don't I introduce you? At least then it's done."

"Yeah maybe." Jackson and the woman had stopped and were leaning into the outdoor bar as they surveyed the outdoor area. She was dressed in a long maxi dress, but you could see there were no curves to be hidden beneath it. Long, white blonde hair fell down her back, and she looked perfect. It was as if she were a sculpture, rather than a real person. I tried to remember that she too was just a person really, but it was hard when she looked that good. Jackson was casual in jeans and a polo shirt and while I hated to admit it, he looked great too. As I looked, he turned and caught my eye, and his face broke into an immediate grin. Much to my confusion he looked genuinely happy to see me. "What's her name?" I asked Mason, seeing Jackson make his way towards them.

"Indigo."

"What sort of stupid name is that?" I asked him, faking a smile for the benefit of those watching them.

"Be nice." Mason said with a laugh, "She's okay actually. I think, under different circumstances, you two could have been friends."

"Haha that's funny." I said smacking him lightly on the arm, as we both stood up as Jackson arrived by us.

"Hi Mason, Imogen." He leaned in gently, one hand going to my waist, planting a kiss on my cheek. I was taken aback; I hadn't been expecting a warm greeting like that. Lowering my gaze, I replied,

"Hi Jackson."

"This is Indigo. We used to work together for a bit, she's an actress. We ran into each other again at the awards after party." He turned to the woman, "Indy, this is Imogen. She's our lead make-up artist and we used to…" He trailed off.

"I'm his ex." I finished for him.

"Oh." Indigo said, looking me up and down. As if I needed to feel judged on top of everything else! I tried desperately to think of an excuse to get away, but everything seemed too obvious. Just as I thought I was out of luck I saw Nicole running towards me, dragging a man along behind her by the hand.

"Imogen!" She squealed and as much as I didn't want to be set up, I was grateful for a way out of the awkwardness.

"If you'll excuse me, I think I'm wanted." I said bowing out of the conversation. "It was nice to meet you." I told Indigo, "See you later Jackson."

Nicole introduced me to Travis, a young actor. He was handsome, but I didn't feel a connection with him, and we didn't seem to have anything in common. He seemed nice enough, but just a bit shallow, no, I corrected myself, he was a lot shallow. He seemed to be more focused on his looks than anything else and was constantly on the lookout for what was going on around him. It made me wonder if anyone would ever meet up to the expectations I had for my relationships, but both Adam and Jackson had been very special in their own ways. Travis and I danced though, and that was fun. It took my mind off Indigo and Jackson, and I found myself relaxing a little. Towards the end of the evening I told him I was going to call it a night, that I was tired, but he was insistent that there was plenty more of the evening left. I said I wanted to go home, said goodbye and began to walk away, but he tried to discourage me. Trying to stop myself from panicking, I remained firm, told him goodnight again and began to walk down the path towards my cabin. I thought I had finally made my point and had just rounded the corner when a hand grabbed my arm from behind, pulling me roughly into the shadows. Travis had caught up with me. We were already largely out of sight of the rest of the group and he pushed me up against the wall beneath the trees, trying to kiss me.

"No!" I spat out, trying to push him away. He was much stronger than he looked.

"You know you want it. Just relax." He said, his breath stank of alcohol but I couldn't get away.

"I don't. Get off!" I shoved him as hard as I could, but he barely moved, and then suddenly he did, shooting backwards and falling to the ground. Looking up I saw Jackson towering over the cowering Travis, a look of pure anger on his face. Mason was approaching fast too, and as he reached me he asked softly,

"Are you okay?" I nodded, unable to say a word for fear of tears coming. Mason must have noticed because he instantly pulled me into his arms, cradling me against his chest, stroking my hair with one hand. I'd never seen Jackson so angry. He very rarely lost control, but on this occasion it looked like he was nearly there. Bloody Nicole and her matchmaking. If only she'd left me alone. I knew she was trying to help, but this was not the sort of help I wanted.

"When a lady says no, she means no!" Jackson growled, grabbing the man's collar and dragging him to his feet, drawing his arm back before releasing the full force of his fist into the other man's face. Travis stumbled backwards holding his nose but Jackson caught him again and before he knew what had hit him, he had been propelled through the garden and into the driveway out of sight.

"Thank you." I muttered, more into Mason's chest than anywhere else.

"You're welcome. I'm so sorry that happened." Mason said in a low voice near my ear. "Are you sure you're okay?"

"I'm fine, just a little shaken."

"That's good to hear."

"Of all the ways to end the evening…" I stopped, watching as Jackson returned. He was looking carefully at me as if trying to assess my condition. I could see him cradling his hand, and wondered if he'd hurt it badly.

"Let's get you into the house." Mason said, "I think you could do with a drink, and I'm going to have a word with my girlfriend about the type of guys she's inviting to our house."

Later on I spoke to Nicole and asked her to please stop trying to set me up, and just leave me to get on with things in my own way. She was so apologetic, but I was actually quite angry with her. I knew she meant well, I just wanted her to keep out of things and stop trying to push me. On the other hand, it did seem to settle things somewhat between me and Jackson. The air between us wasn't so tense, and it felt like neither of us was quite as on-edge as we had been.

CHAPTER 16

"Thank you for the other night." I told Jackson one said one morning during makeup.

"Forget about it."

"Jackson, if you hadn't been there…"

"What stalking you?" He said with a smile.

"I'm serious! I just couldn't get him to leave me alone, and then when I thought I had…" I trailed off. "Thank you. I'm glad you came when you did."

"It was just lucky really that Mason and I were talking and saw him follow you. Anyone would have done the same thing." He said with a shrug.

"That's not true. Some people would have turned a blind eye." I sighed, "Anyway, I just wanted to say thank you."

"You're welcome."

"Is your hand okay?"

"It was a little sore, but it's okay now thanks."

"Good. I was worried you might have broken it."

"No, I don't think so, just bruised it a little." He said holding up his hand and wiggling his fingers at me to show he could.

"That's good." I managed a small smile as I went back to work, continuing quietly for a few minutes. It was strange when I thought how close the two of us had been, and now a conversation like this was as intimate as it got. It made me feel sad to think of what we'd lost.

"Imogen?"

"Yeah?" I stopped what I was doing to look at him properly.

"There's nothing between Indigo and me."

"Hey, it's none of my business." I answered softly, feeling a little embarrassed that he would bring her up.

"It is, because I want it to be." He caught my hand so I couldn't escape. "A few years ago she had a small role with us. We got on and we went out a few times, but you couldn't have called it anything serious. She certainly wasn't my girlfriend." He relaxed his grip letting me pull my hand gently away from his.

"You don't have to explain yourself to me."

"I don't want you to get the wrong idea." He looked down momentarily. "I don't want you think I've moved on, because Imogen, I haven't." Biting my lip I looked at him in shock. I hadn't expected to hear those words from him but as I looked at him I saw the honesty in his eyes.

"Neither have I." I told him after letting what he has said sink in for a moment.

"Really?" He said sounding a little bit hopeful. "I thought you going to New York was maybe something."

"Nothing romantic, just visiting a friend." I said and I could have sworn he looked relieved.

It wasn't as if the past was swept away, but it did feel like the tension between us had been. I realised that the anger I'd been holding on to had slipped away and we were both just a little kinder to each other. The more we spent time together, the more we both relaxed, and while it wasn't like it used to be, it was better than it had been. I for one thought that was a good start. While things were better between Jackson and me, the chatter behind my back was beginning to annoy me. Not only did it annoy me, but it was actually quite upsetting. I knew I shouldn't let it get to me, but to hear people that didn't know me or Jackson have an opinion on the end of our relationship was difficult. Especially when I didn't feel I was able to correct them. I was pretty sure that this particular group of girls, extras on the show, felt they had superiority of me because they were actors and I was ultimately one of the crew, but I hated to think they thought they were better than me. It seemed that one at least of them had their eye on Jackson, and were keen to have me overhear their plans. Hurriedly I threw the few brushes I'd had out back into my kit box and closed the lid. My movements were harsher than normal, but the only way I seemed to be able to vent my frustration was in throwing things around. Albeit in a controlled manner that drew no more attention to me. It's not like I would throw something at the girls.

"What's wrong?" I had been so preoccupied that I didn't see Jackson watching me. He looked concerned as he approached.

"Nothing." I shook my head lightly as I spoke.

"It doesn't look like nothing." He gently reached out and touched the side of my face, brushing my cheek with his fingertips. My tummy fluttered a little at his touch, and I tried not to give away how much it affected me. "In fact, I'd go so far as to say you look quite upset."

"I'm just being silly." I replied looking up at him, "Don't worry about it."

"I'm already worried. You know you can talk to me."

"It's just, well, it feels like some of the new female cast members are talking about me."

"About you?" He asked with a frown.

"About us." I blinked before looking up at him again. "It just makes me feel judged, like everyone has an opinion on what I'm doing or who I'm with. I know it shouldn't matter, but I hate that they think they can discuss what they think happened between us."

"I hate that you're feeling so sad and that it's my fault." He said softly, his voice low. "I wish I could do something."

"It's okay Jackson." I said once again seeing the girls walking past them. I'd never worked with a group of girls that I disliked so much. The only reason I hadn't said something so far was because they were extras and although I had to keep reminding myself of that fact, I knew they wouldn't be around forever. He must have seen my eyes follow the girls because he turned to see what had attracted my attention.

"Hey, come here." Suddenly Jackson had grasped my hand and was pulling me along behind him.

"What are you doing?" I asked as he led me quickly past the other girls to a quiet corner of the set.

We reached a corner which wasn't used, out of the way and Jackson stopped, spinning me around. I had no idea what he was doing. Gently placing his hands on my waist he lifted me onto the counter behind me, stepping forward to stand between my legs. He left one hand on my waist while the other slid up to the back of my neck. I held my breath, unable to be sure what he was planning or even what he was thinking. Slowly he dipped his head to mine, closing the gap between us, and before I knew what I was doing, I'd reached up and laid my hands on his shoulders. It was strange being so close to him. It was so familiar, and yet so different, and I still had no idea why he was so close to me.

"I just thought, if they want to talk, let's give them something to talk about."

"But…" He stopped me, but all I could think about was how close he was to me. It would be so easy to wrap my legs around him and hold him closer…

"All you need to do now is slap me and shout something like, 'Jackson I told you it was over!'" He said with a smile.

"What if I don't want to slap you?" I said softly.

"Well then I guess they'll think we're over here kissing which will give them the impression we're still together. Either way, I think they'll stop bothering you."

"You're crazy." I said, but I smiled at him. It was sweet that he cared so much to try and stage something like this.

"So I guess we're going with the kissing option?" He said, and just for a moment I contemplated it. He was so close it wouldn't have taken much to reach his lips with my own. I could even feel his breath on my face. His hand left my waist, sliding down and coming to rest on my thigh and I realised I was feeling nervous. Not of him, just of where this was going. It was so unexpected. He hadn't broken the eye contact we had, and I felt like he was trying to read my mind. I was only afraid I'd give something away that I wasn't ready to.

"Jackson!" Came a shout from the set. "Hey, put the poor woman down and get back on set! We've been looking for you." I looked over Jackson's shoulder to see Mason grinning at us. "Hi Imogen." He said with a wave before walking away.

"Well, that was loud." Jackson said with a smile, "Trust Mason."

"How embarrassing." I groaned, dropping my head without thinking to Jackson's shoulder and closing my eyes. "Now everyone will be talking."

"Don't worry about it. No one that cares will be listening." I raised my head and he stepped back, gently sliding his hands back around my waist and lifting me down. "And it was nice to see you smile again."

"Well thank you." I said looking up.

"No problem, just remember I'm always available for light relief and comedy value." He grinned as he turned away, "Or anything else you can think of. I'll see you later." I couldn't speak. My words just stuck in my mouth, but I managed a smile as he walked away. It felt like a lid had come off and every feeling I had tried to pack away about the way I felt about him had been set loose. For the rest of the day, every time I remembered him picking me up I got butterflies. I just had no idea what to do about it.

CHAPTER 17

On Saturday evening I had an invitation to Nicole and Mason's for dinner. Mason said he and Nicole had something to talk to me about, but I had no idea what it could be. Even though I lived in their garden, I tried to give the couple as much space as I could and so I waited until the last minute before going over. As I walked I wondered what it was that they wanted to talk about. Briefly I considered it might be that they were hoping I was ready to move out. It was likely that they wanted more space, and with that thought in my mind I raised my hand to knock on the door. Mason answered the door to me.

"Hey come on in." He said, stepping back to let me in. "We're in the kitchen." I walked through with him to see Jackson sitting with Nicole at the table. If I had been paying attention outside I would have seen his truck in the drive as I approached from the garden.

"Oh hi." I said in surprise looking from one to the other of them.

"Sorry, we're not ambushing you." Mason said sliding into the seat next to Nicole, leaving the one next to Jackson for me.

"I feel like I'm in trouble with the headteacher." I smiled looking across the table at Nicole and Mason.

"I feel like I'm at a job interview." Jackson said, leaning back in his chair. "What's going on?"

"Is this an intervention?" I asked.

"Wow, they are a suspicious pair aren't they?" Nicole joked. "Hey, would you like a drink Imogen?"

"Yes please." I replied, noticing everyone else had got one.

"Stay there, I'll get it." Mason stood up, dropping a kiss on Nicole's head, and walked to the fridge, pulling a bottle of wine from inside before filling up a glass from the cupboard. He returned to the table, placing it down in front of me.

"So…?" I was intrigued.

"Well, firstly, a cheers to you guys, for not killing each other at work. I know it hasn't been easy, but you know, we're friends with the both of you, and it's so good for all of us to be able to be in the same room together again." Mason said with a grin, raising his bottle and holding it in the middle of the table. I lifted my glass, gently clinking it with the others. "Secondly," He took Nicole's hand, "We wanted to tell you both together, because you are our best friends, and we care about you. It's hard for us because we want to be happy, but we don't want to upset you guys."

"What is it?" I said feeling excitement at the way they were acting and hoping some good news was about to be shared with us.

"We're getting married!" Nicole squealed.

"Nothing like telling them gently." Mason said rolling his eyes at Nicole. The way they were with each other made me smile, it was endearing, and there was never any malice in the actions between them, even when they were laughing at each other.

"That's amazing!" I said standing up and going to hug Nicole. Nicole was already on her feet, ready to wrap her arms around me too.

"Congratulations man. That's awesome news." Jackson said smiling at Mason and clapping him on the back.

"We weren't sure when to tell you, but now you're getting on all right we thought it would be okay." Nicole said letting go of me and looking me right in the face. "I'm sorry if it's weird for either of you."

"Weird?" Jackson asked as I returned to my seat next to him.

"We didn't want to make it harder for you both since you called off your engagement." Mason replied diplomatically. "We thought it could be strange considering that we are getting married instead of you two."

"Just because things are different for us now, doesn't mean you can't be happy. Honestly, and I know I'm speaking for you too Jackson, but we are happy for you. Really happy." I said and Jackson nodded.

"Yeah, I totally agree. Just look after her and don't screw things up like I did." Jackson said quietly without meeting my gaze. Before I had thought about it, I reached out and gently laid my hand on his forearm, wanting to reassure him. He looked up in surprise at me, frowning slightly before relaxing again and gently covering my hand with his own.

Much later that night I stretched my arms above my head, arching my back and rolling my neck. After dinner we'd moved to the sofas in the living area and had chatted late into the evening. It had been a long time since the four of us had spent a relaxed evening together, and it had been lovely. I had been asked to be maid of honour and Jackson the best man, another reason the couple had been nervous to ask us I think, they weren't sure how we'd react to being asked to so close at the wedding. I was happy to do it, but I had to admit, it was going to be a little weird. Mason and Nicole told us they wanted to have a small wedding, with just their closest friends and family, and didn't want to wait long for it. They were hoping to be married within six months and were keen to have us, their best friends heavily involved. After an evening of talking, I was exhausted.

"It's been a really lovely evening, but I am going to go now, before I fall asleep here." I said standing up, and sliding my feet back into my flip flops.

Nicole was intertwined with Mason on the other sofa and it was hard to tell whose limbs were whose. It didn't make me feel uncomfortable, rather, I was pleased my friends were so happy together. I hadn't ended up entangled in Jackson's arms like I would have done in the old days when we were still together, but I had relaxed and stretched my legs out along the length of the sofa we shared, so my bare feet almost reached his leg. At one point he shifted in his seat, brushing my foot with his leg, and I jumped, apologising and pulling my legs back to give him space. Gently he had caught my foot in his hand and replaced it on the sofa, telling me not to worry. His hand had remained there resting on my foot just a little bit longer than necessary, which made me wonder if I was reading too much into it. It seemed just a little bit like old times.

"I'm going to make a move too." Jackson said also standing. "Thanks for tonight, it's been great." He followed me to the door as we said our goodbyes and I pulled my cardigan over my shoulders, "I'll walk you to your door Imogen. You never know who is lurking in the bushes in these private homes." I knew he was joking, but it was nice after the way Travis had followed me, to know that I wasn't on my own.

"Thank you." I smiled at him, thinking it sweet of him to offer to walk with me.

"Any excuse!" Mason said with a grin, standing in the doorway. "Night guys."

"Night." We both called.

"That was nice." I said, walking down the steps. Between the trees a small pathway led through the garden to my cabin. I knew it was safe but given the darkness it was nice to have Jackson's company.

"It was like old times." He said. "Well with less touching." I laughed.

"Yeah, that's what I was thinking too." The path ended as we came to the cabin, lit from the outside by fairy lights to help me find my way back in the dark. "Well, this is it." I said unlocking the door and pushing it open.

"It's pretty with the lights."

"You should see the view from here when it's not dark. I love seeing the sea first thing in the morning." I leant against the door frame, looking up at him.

"I bet it's beautiful." He agreed. He was standing just a little bit too close to me, but almost not close enough. I'd forgotten how intoxicating his presence was and I realised I was holding my breath again. "Are you okay?" He asked coming a little closer still, and looking down at me with concern in his eyes.

"Yes." I murmured, "Just remembering." He tilted his head down until he was almost close enough to kiss me. His hands were in his pockets, but I realised I wanted them on me. I wanted him to touch me, I wanted to be held by him and I wanted to touch him too. I bit my lip, tilting my face to his and momentarily closing my eyes. I might have looked crazy, but I didn't care. I could feel his breath on my face, but I didn't know what to do. If I could, I would have frozen time right there, with just the two of us, in our own little bubble. Just as I thought he was going to kiss me, he took a step backwards, breaking the spell. "I should go. It's late." It sounded like the last thing he wanted to do.

"You should." I agreed letting out a sigh. "Or, you could come in for a coffee before you go?" The words were out of my mouth before I could stop myself.

"A coffee?" He asked raising an eyebrow.

"Yeah, you know, warm liquid, comes in a mug?"

"Yeah, okay." He agreed.

"Come on in." I stepped back, flicking a lamp on as I walked into the room, beckoning for Jackson to follow me.

"Well, it's certainly cosy." He said with a smile.

"It is, but it's nice. It's all I need." I kicked off my flip flops, shoving them into the corner and nodded to the sofa, "Take a seat." I was desperate to seem relaxed, to seem like his presence didn't give me butterflies. It shouldn't, it wasn't like we were strangers or I was trying to impress him. Jackson sat down, dropping his car keys and phone onto the coffee table in front of the sofa. I knew he could see me in the small kitchen as I busied myself making the drinks. I imagined he was assessing the space around him. Beyond me was a door leading to the bathroom while everything else was in the same room, with a TV opposite the sofa and a bed at the back and then this little kitchen area to one side. It was compact and very different to the home we had shared. Stacked in one corner were the suitcases Jackson had given me, it was fairly obvious from the stretched seams that they were still as full as they had been when I moved out. On top of them were the boxes of jewellery he had insisted I took. I hadn't put any of it away, instead leaving it there, hoping one day it would suddenly be obvious what I should do with it all.

"Thank you." He smiled, taking the mug I was offering to him. I sank down on to the sofa next to him, drawing my legs up underneath myself.

"You're welcome."

"Is that all the stuff you packed from our place?" He pointed to the suitcases.

"Yeah. I just don't know what to do with it all." I shrugged.

"Just throwing it out there, but you could, I don't know, wear it?" He said with a smile.

"I'm not really in the habit of wearing clothes and jewellery like that any more. I'm more of a jeans and t-shirt girl." I looked up at him, and saw him nod. "Or shorts." I added with a laugh, gesturing to my bare legs.

"I like your shorts."

"Thank you." I replied shyly.

"They do your legs a lot of justice."

"Stop it, you're awful!" Trust him to lower the tone.

"You've always had good legs though. It was one of the first things I noticed about you." He continued, ignoring my complaints. "I still remember those little skirts you used to wear to work before we were together…"

"Jackson!"

"Okay, sorry!" He grinned and drank a little of his coffee, his eyes not leaving mine.

"Can you believe they're getting married?" I asked attempting to change the subject.

"It was a surprise, but not completely unexpected and it's good news. I'm happy for them."

"Yeah, me too. I thought they were going to ask me to move out of here."

"Did you really?"

"Well, when Mason asked me to come over, he said it was because 'they needed to talk to me,'" I said making air quotations with my fingers, "It sounded so serious. I didn't know what else it could be." I smiled, realising in hindsight how daft it sounded, "But it's good and I am pleased for them. It is a bit hard though you know? I'm not jealous, but I suppose a part of me wishes I still had what they have." I said thoughtfully. I think I was making sense of my feelings by expressing them.

"I know exactly what you mean. It's so good to be able to talk to you again though. I thought I'd lost that too."

"It is. Can you believe we're going to have to dress up and dance together at someone else's wedding? It's ridiculous!" I laughed.

"Yeah, but we'll have fun. There's no one else I'd rather dance with." He said leaning over and placing his mug on the coffee table. He turned and looked at me thoughtfully.

"What?" I asked looking at him suspiciously, tilting my head to one side and raising my eyebrow.

"Do you have any idea how hard it was for me not to kiss you outside earlier? I'm going to be a mess at the wedding. Maybe you should take out a restraining order beforehand?"

"I probably didn't help." I admitted, blushing a little. "I was kind of hoping you would, and that's not really helpful is it?"

"You were hoping I would kiss you?" He asked doubtfully, his brow furrowing.

"Yeah. You were just standing so close, it gave me butterflies."

"Are you drunk Imogen?"

"No. I only had a couple of glasses of wine. I just… I'm not sure, I guess the evening, spending time with you like that, it's just been so nice. It made me reminisce. And then when you were standing there looking at me like you used to, and…" I stopped. "Yeah, maybe the wine went to my head." I smiled at him.

"Oh that's a shame, if you weren't drunk, after saying something like that, I'd definitely try to kiss you."

"Oh would you now?" I asked, turning a little more towards him, before reaching down and putting the mug I was holding on the floor beside me. I didn't know what I was doing. I'd given up trying to analyse my feelings, I was just there in the moment, enjoying it for what it was. "You really hurt me Jackson, but that doesn't mean my feelings for you just went away."

"I understand that." He said before asking, "Would you want me to kiss you?"

"Do I have to answer that?" His directness embarrassed me.

"I find it easier to hear what you're thinking than trying to read your mind. We both know from past experience that doesn't always work out so well. I also don't want to do anything to ruin whatever this is that we have now. I like being able to talk to you and I don't want to make anything worse. I'd rather have you in my life as a friend than not at all."

"That's true. It's the same for me." I sighed. "The thing is, what I want to do and what I should do are probably two completely different things."

"Do you know how much I care about you Imogen? I made a

mistake, a big, huge, massive one, but it was a mistake and I regret it every single day. I miss you so much." He looked so sad that it hurt.

"Jackson." I almost whispered, dropping my head, "I don't know that we could ever go back. Not now. Not after everything." He reached out and cupped my jaw with his hand, gently tilting my face up to his. I felt a tingle down my spine.

"I know that. I don't expect you to just forget what I did sweetheart, but maybe we could find something new. Together." He looked hopeful. Without thinking I placed my hand on his arm, sliding it up and over his shoulder coming to rest at the nape of his neck, my fingers moving up into his short hair.

"It would have to be super slow." I said doubtfully.

"Snails pace." He replied nodding.

"I don't know whether it will work. I don't know if I want it to." I said honestly. It was all so complicated.

"You," He corrected himself, "We, won't know, not unless we try." He slid his arms around my waist, pulling me closer to him. "But, at least we would have given it a chance."

"No relationship. Just two people, getting to know each other again." I whispered, as he lowered his mouth to my neck. He looked up in surprise.

"No relationship?"

"No. I don't want to put any more pressure on either of us until we know if this is even possible or if we even want it, and I think it should just be between us, I don't want anyone else to know."

"If that's what you want?" He sounded doubtful so seizing the moment I climbed astride his lap, gently tugging his head down to meet mine.

"It is, but for now, you can kiss me."

"Oh can I now?"

"Yeah, you can." I replied before he did exactly that. He kissed me tenderly though I thought he was very restrained, his hands moved up and down my legs and back, but didn't venture under my clothing. I slid my hands down his chest from his shoulders, feeling the hardness of his muscles beneath his shirt and round his waist before moving them up his back underneath his shirt. His skin was smooth and warm, I'd forgotten what it was like to touch him. As he nuzzled my neck I gently caught the bottom of his shirt and tugged it upwards. Jackson stopped, his hands covering mine and looked at me quizzically. Sitting on top of him as I was, I began to doubt myself, wondering if I was throwing myself at someone who didn't really want me like I thought he did. Pulling back I bit my lip and slid off his lap onto the sofa. I hadn't expected to add rejection to my list of relationship failings this evening.

"What's wrong?" When I looked up I saw that he actually looked a little confused.

"It feels like you don't want this as much as I do."

"Are you serious?"

"You're barely touching me."

"I was trying to be a gentleman. I don't want to rush you." He said coming up to kneeling and gently pushing me backwards. Gradually I let him guide me back, lowering myself down, until my head reached the arm of the sofa. I pulled him down on top of me, opening my legs to let him closer. He stroked my thigh with one hand using the other to hold himself up, catching his weight before he squashed me. I heard his breath catch as I pulled my other leg up, hooking it around his waist, my arms wrapping around his shoulders. Gently he dropped his lips to mine and I softened, moaning slightly against his lips.

"You are so beautiful Imogen." He said breaking away for a moment.

"Did I mention that I haven't had sex in like forever?" I said returning my hands to the bottom of his shirt and gently pulling it up. Jackson stopped again, pulling back from me to tug his shirt up and over his head, revealing his sculpted chest and stomach. Keeping the space between us he looked down at me as if trying to assess what I was thinking.

"Is this really what you want?" He asked kneeling up to put a little more space between us and looking down at me carefully.

"I want you." I said quietly, before asking, "Why?" I felt the nervousness creep back, and I wondered if he could see it. "Don't you?"

"Hey, please don't ask me that sweetheart. I thought it was obvious how much I want to be here." He smiled, and leaning back over me, he kissed me once again.

"Then will you please take me to bed?" I asked him softly, and before I had a chance to think any more, he was standing up, swinging me into his arms. As he carried me to the bed he made me feel as light as a feather.

CHAPTER 18

"Did Jackson spend the night with you?"

"You are so nosy."

"He did, didn't he?" Nicole asked, and I pretended I hadn't heard.

"Imogen, why was his car still outside this morning?"

"Because it wouldn't start?" I said not meeting Nicole's eye. It was bad enough that Nicole loved sticking her nose in where it didn't belong, but it was made worse by the fact that she lived so close. There was no such thing as secrets any more.

"Bollocks Imogen. If you're going to lie, at least make it believable." Nicole said scowling.

"Okay. Yes he did. But I don't know what it was. Just sex probably. Can you keep it to yourself please?" I didn't bother trying to disguise the annoyance in my voice.

"Do you want to talk about it?" Nicole said more carefully, she'd obviously heard my tone.

"No I don't thanks, and I don't want anyone else to know about it. Not even Mason." I definitely didn't want to talk about it. I wasn't sure what 'it' was. I just knew that it had been wonderful. I hadn't asked Jackson to stay, but we'd both fallen asleep, and he had.

When we woke up, the soft morning light had been streaming through the open curtains. It felt so good to wake up in his arms again, and if I could just push away the hurt that I still felt, it would have been perfect. For a moment, it felt like I'd gone back in time, to when we were together and happy. He'd joked about the lack of privacy, and I told him it was all right because I knew the neighbours, and the view of the sea was worth it. We'd made love again, more slowly this time in the early morning light, and then stayed wrapped together in each others arms until eventually we'd got up. I wasn't sure what rules I was following anymore. I didn't know whether to ask him to stay, and so when he said he'd better get going, I nodded, walking him to the door and letting him kiss me goodbye. It was a long lingering kiss that made my tummy flip, and made me want to drag him right back to bed again. It didn't feel like a one night thing and that worried me because I didn't know what it was. I wasn't sure if it was reassuring or worrying that it actually felt like the start of something. And now my best friend was on my doorstep trying to dig for dirt.

"Okay. Are you going to be okay being with him for the wedding?" Nicole asked, and before I knew it, I was being swept up in wedding planning.

The week passed slowly and things weren't necessarily awkward between me and Jackson, but I did feel a little on edge when I was close to him, unsure of how to behave, and I could tell from his body language that he felt the same. Part way through the week a gorgeous bouquet of flowers was delivered for me, getting the attention of a lot of the cast. Flipping open the envelope I found a little card that read simply, "Can I see you again?" The message was followed by a kiss. My heart skipped a beat and I hid my smile, putting the flowers in water. I denied knowledge of who they were from to anyone that asked, but I was sure Mason gave me a knowing smile.

"I don't feel like I've had a minute alone with you this week." Jackson said quietly to me as I concentrated on creating some accident damage to his cheekbone. He moved his leg slightly rubbing his knee against my thigh as I worked.
"It's been a busy week." I agreed. "Thank you for the flowers. They were beautiful."
"I'm glad you liked them."
"What are we doing?" I asked after a moment.
"I'm pretty sure you're doing my makeup?" He said with a grin.
"Funny." I slapped his arm playfully and he responded by catching my hand in his.
"I don't know Imogen, I'd like to think we're working out a way to be together again. If that's what you want?"
"I haven't quite worked that out Jackson." I said pulling up a stool and rolling towards him so my legs slid around one of his. It was probably unprofessional, but the easiest way to work closely to him. Not that working so closely helped anything. "If we could just erase the past, then yes of course I'd like to try again, but it's all just so much. I'm not saying no, but, well it's hard."
"I get it." He said he said cupping my face with his hand, gently stroking my cheek. "I don't like it, but I understand." He dropped his hand to my thigh. I put down my brushes, and reached up to him, linking my hands behind his neck and softly pressing my lips to his. He slipped his arms around my waist pulling me closer. "If this helps you work things through, just remember I'm available

whenever you need me. Just give me a call, day or night." He smiled and I planted one last kiss on his lips.

"You're a distraction, you know that?" I raised an eyebrow at him.

"But you love me." He said without thinking.

"Yeah. I do." I replied and he grinned.

"Have dinner with me tomorrow?" He said, then added, "If you're worried about people seeing us together and asking questions then come to my place. I'll cook." I looked at him, trying to decide if this was a good idea or not, before nodding.

"Okay."

I hadn't intended to go to bed with Jackson again, not until we'd at least had the chance to talk things through properly. I really felt strongly that we had things to address before we moved in any direction, but my thoughts changed the moment he answered his door to me. Before I knew what I was doing had launched myself at him, arms around his shoulders, fingers in his hair. If he was taken aback he didn't show it, instead catching me and lifting me up. I wrapped my legs around his waist as he kicked the door shut behind us.

"Dinner is going to be ruined." He told me sometime later as we lay together in the bed that had been ours. He held me snugly to his side as I ran my hand across his stomach.

"Yeah. I don't know what you were thinking seducing me like that." I said with a smile.

"Me? I believe I was the innocent party here tonight." He propped himself up on his elbow, rolling me onto my back so he could look down at me. "You nearly took me down, you tackled me with such force." He kissed me on the lips, "Not that I'm complaining, but have you thought about playing professional football?"

"Oh haha." I smiled, "I didn't plan it. I just couldn't help myself." I added shyly, stretching my hand out to the side of his face, stroking his cheek with my thumb.

"You are beautiful Imogen." He lowered his lips to mine, "I've missed you so much."

"I've missed you too, but how do we know things will be any different this time?" I said softly. "Being with you again scares me."

"I'll do whatever it takes to prove it to you. I've changed Imogen. I know I hurt you. I rushed in and made some terrible assumptions when I should have stopped to think. I should have spoken to you. There's no way I would ever let a situation get out of hand like that again. What can I do to prove it to you?"

"I'm not sure Jackson." I said laying my head down onto the pillow. "This, you know, us in bed, was never a problem, but I can't live waiting for the next blow up. It was scary having nowhere to go, and I can't live like that, waiting for the next thing." Meeting his eyes I whispered, "I've never been so hurt."

"I know, and I wish I could make it better. I wish I could change how I did things, but going over them won't change how I acted. All I can tell you, no, I mean all I can promise you, is that nothing like that would ever happen again."

"But how do I know that?"

"You're going to have to trust me a little bit baby, if you want to give us a second chance." His eyes found mine again and it felt like he was searching my soul.

"I know. I'll try." I whispered. It was all I could do. I just hoped it was enough.

CHAPTER 19

It started so slowly that I didn't notice at first, coffee tasted weird, my sense of smell was off, and boy, did my boobs ache. It was only when the sickness started that I began to suspect that I was pregnant. Everything seemed the same as before, except of course the last time, I had been expecting it, hoping for it, after all Adam and I had been trying for a baby. This time, it caught me by surprise. Even still, I didn't quite believe it until I'd seen the test results, and then I had to do more than one, just in case, but they all said the same thing. They were all positive.

For a long time I just stayed in the bathroom, head in hands. I had no idea what to do. I worried that if I told Jackson, he'd stay with me out of obligation. He was a good man, but I didn't want that. The more I thought about it, the more I knew I wanted to keep the baby. Having had one miscarriage, I just wasn't sure I could cope with losing another.

The thought occurred to me that I could just move on. I knew Adam would help me if I asked. I could just disappear and not bother Jackson or his family again. He could move on and start afresh, and he'd never need to know about our child. I kicked myself for being so stupid, it felt like it was my fault and in a lot of ways it didn't seem fair to tie him down if he didn't want us.

All at once everything seemed too much, the wedding was coming up in only a couple of months. Nicole was so impatient she had moved it forward again and again. Before that, in only a couple of weeks I was supposed to be going away to film with the rest of the team on location and I'd been looking forward to it, but now, knowing nothing really had changed between me and Jackson, as well as bringing a baby into the mix, everything was just confusing. I tried to carry on, I wanted to keep everything as normal, but with the morning sickness and a couple of people commenting on my paleness, I felt so awkward and obvious that I called in sick for a few days, saying I had a bug. I wasn't planning on hiding so much as just giving myself time to get my head together, without input from anyone else.

The first morning I didn't go to work I had a text from Jackson almost straight away asking if I needed anything, if he could help, but it just felt like more pressure. Instead of accepting his offer, I replied with a short message telling him I okay and just needed to rest, and turned my phone off, climbing into bed and pulling the covers up and over my head. Even then I was on edge all day, knowing Mason and Nicole could pop by anytime they felt like it. It wasn't peaceful and I knew I had to get away for a bit. Texting Adam was my last resort, it didn't even seem like the best idea, but I didn't know what else to do. Of course he told me, as I'd known he would that I could come to him, to stay with him in London for as long as I wanted. I didn't tell him I was pregnant, it didn't seem fair to tell him about the baby over the phone, so I didn't, instead just telling him that I had a lot on and I needed to get my head together. All I had to do now was tell Jackson that I was going away for a bit.

"Imogen?" There was a tap on the door. "Are you okay?" Mason's voice came from outside the bathroom. I'd been back in work for a few days, still trying to hide my symptoms while I tied up a few loose ends. This morning, sickness had caught me out.

"Yeah give me two minutes." I stood and washed my face as best I could, without damaging my eye make up too badly. Opening the door I was confronted with Mason sitting on the sofa waiting for me. I looked warily into the room to see if he was on his own. "It's just me. Are you okay?" He said with concern, holding out a glass of water to me.

"Yeah, better now thanks." I sank down next to him and sipped some water. "Thanks for the water."

"You look very pale." He said still looking concerned.

"Can you keep a secret?" I asked and he nodded I wanted to have someone to confide in, and I didn't really want to lie to Mason.

"Of course I can. Is everything all right?"

"I'm pregnant."

"Oh!" His eyebrows showed his shock.

"Yeah." I nodded.

"Is it Jackson's?" He asked cautiously.

"Yes. There hasn't been anyone else."

"Hey, that's none of my business, I was just wondering."

"It's a really stupid accident. I just didn't think. I was on the pill, and when we split up I just stopped taking it. There's been a few times recently, and I just didn't think. I don't know what to do." I said quietly.

"What does he think? Have you told him?"

"No." I shook my head, "And I don't want him to know just yet, so please don't say anything to him."

"Of course I won't. Look, the first thing to do is to find out for sure." He said firmly. "You can't make any decisions until you know that much at least. I could ask Nic to pick a test up for you? Would that help?"

"It's okay Mason, I do know for sure, I've done a lot of tests."

"Oh! Right, okay." He couldn't cover the surprise on his face. "Why didn't you tell us? We could have helped you."

"I suppose I just wanted to keep it to myself. I've been pregnant before. This feels just the same, especially with the sickness now too."

"What do you mean, when?"

"It was a long time ago, before I knew you Mason. It wasn't Jackson's baby, it was Adam's." I laid my hand on my tummy. It was unbelievable to think a new life was growing there. "But it was different, it was planned and we really wanted it. It wasn't the surprise this one was."

"What happened Imogen?" He asked me gently.

"I had a miscarriage. So now, I'm terrified that could happen again, especially if I tell anyone." I was being honest, the thought of telling anyone made it seem all the more real too.

"I'm so sorry, I feel like I've really put my foot in it." He said running one hand through his hair, "I had no idea. Nicole never told me. I'm sorry if I upset you."

"No you haven't, it's okay. Actually, Nicole didn't know, so please don't tell her. Not now." I sighed. "Or Jackson. I will tell him. Just not yet."

"I won't. Did he know about your miscarriage?" He asked and I nodded. "Would you keep it?" He asked.

"What living in your cabin? It's not ideal is..." Before I could finish, the trailer door swung open and Jackson walked in.

"Hey." It was obvious silence had just fallen and I'm sure he could feel the tension in the room. He stopped and looked at us both, "Sorry, am I interrupting something?"

"No. I was just asking Imogen for some advice. I wanted to get something special for Nicole as a gift when we get married, and I need some help from her best friend." Mason smoothed over the silence with ease.

"Ah, jewellery? That always seemed to work for me." He swung my make up stool round and sat on that, turning to face us.

"Yeah, and now I have an expensive box of jewellery and several suitcases full of clothes I don't wear stacked in the corner of my living room. It's such a waste." I added. "Don't buy her jewellery. Do something with her. Take her somewhere. Make some memories."

"That's a good idea." Mason said nodding.

"She loved India. Well we both did. You could take her there for your honeymoon. Or do lots of places. You could do a long trip across Europe." I knew I was probably being overly enthusiastic but it seemed to make Jackson smile. "Oh, take her to some new places, but let her take you to some of her places too. That would be lovely."

"I forgot how much you loved travelling. I should have taken you away more." Jackson said. "In hindsight, there is a lot I would do differently now."

"Don't say that." I said softly, "In the grand scheme, we weren't together that long though really were we? I mean, not long enough to go to lots of places together, and you showed me some beautiful sights when we were in Texas." I smiled at him and he returned it. It was so nice now that there was less tension between us now. Things were so much easier, but I knew it was about to get a lot more complicated and the last thing I wanted was him feeling tied to me because of the baby.

"Well we've got the trip to Vancouver, you're coming right?" Mason said, "It's beautiful there and filming is always fun. That'll be like a nice holiday. Admittedly it's a holiday with work, but it's nice, especially if it's the four of us."

"Actually, I'm not." I said quietly. "I was going to tell you." I looked worriedly at Jackson, "There just hasn't been the right time." I bit my lip, this was not how I'd planned to tell him I wasn't coming.

"Why not?" Jackson asked, a frown playing across his brow.

"I have some things…" I trailed off. I hadn't planned what to say and didn't have an excuse for why I wasn't going. Trying to cover my mistake I carried on, "I've spoken with Eric, and I'm going to get one of my team in here working with you both beforehand so the transition should be smooth."

"Oh." He looked disappointed, but didn't say anything else.

"Are you feeling better?" Jackson asked when Mason had left and he was alone with me.

"I am thank you." I sank down on to the chair next to him.

"Good. I have to say, you're looking a better colour than you did the other day." He smiled, gently touching my face. "And with that in mind, can I take you to dinner tonight?" I didn't know if it was a good idea, and wondered if I should say no. I didn't want to lead him on now there were so many complications, but at the same time it would be nice to spend at least one more night with him, pretending things were normal, even if they weren't. "It's not a trick question." He said looking at me with amusement in his eyes.

"Sorry." I shook my head and gave him a smile. "Yes, that would be lovely."

"If I'm not pushing my luck, you could jump in my truck with me, and leave your car here. If you wanted to stay at my place tonight, I mean?"

"Okay." I nodded.

"Yeah?" He looked relieved, and happy.

"Yes." I leaned over to him and brushed my lips across his. "But for now, you'd better hush up, we need to get on."

"Yes ma'am." He said with a smile.

Much later we left the studio together. I felt safe nestled into the passenger seat of Jackson's truck with him. Before I knew it I was dreaming of telling him about the baby, and imagining how he'd be with his own child. I knew he'd make a good father, I'd seen him with Theo often enough, and that had made my heart melt. But then, I reminded myself, that was before, when everything was good between us. Now, he might think I'd got pregnant intentionally, maybe to trap him, and the idea of that scared me. I seemed to always see the worst case scenario in any situation, rather than the possibility of any good. But then for some reason it always seemed that others thought the worst of me too, so maybe I just preempted it, before it happened? All I wanted was for him to be happy and excited, but the thought that he might not be filled me with dread. I didn't want to even think about how his family would react to the news and the conclusions they'd jump to.

"Where are you Imogen?" He reached over and lay his hand on my thigh, pulling me from my thoughts. "I mean, I can see you, but it's like you're somewhere else."

"Sorry." I covered his hand with mine, "I've just got a lot on my mind."

"Do you want to talk about it?"

"No, I don't. But thank you." I replied without meeting his gaze.

"I feel like you're keeping me at arms length sweetheart. Not when we're in bed obviously." He grinned, "But a lot of the rest of the time." I glanced up again and saw him looking over at me.

"I don't mean it to be like that. This is all so weird, I'm trying to work it all out. I mean, what are we doing?" I gestured to the both of us. "We split up and now we're sleeping together. It's crazy."

"I'd hope it's a little more than just sleeping together." He said in a low voice, "It certainly is for me." He seemed hurt by my words.

"Oh I didn't mean it like that. I just mean, we're not together. It's so complicated." I pressed my lips together. "I really enjoy the time we spend together, I'm just trying to work out where we go from here. I need to protect myself better than I did before. So if it feels like I'm keeping you at arms length, maybe subconsciously I am."

"What can I do? There has to be something?"

"I just need some time to clear my head. I was going to tell you tonight, but I suppose now is as good a time as any, I'm going away for a bit. I think it will do me good."

"When?"

"Next weekend."

"Right. Is that the reason you aren't coming to Vancouver?" He asked and I nodded, "And just how long are you going away for?" He asked warily.

"I'm not sure yet. I haven't told Mason and Nicole I'm going yet either but I'll be back for their wedding."

"But that's weeks away." He said in surprise.

"I know." I twisted my hands in my lap, feeling uncomfortable, "I'm just so confused Jackson, I don't know what to do. It's not easy."

"It could be." He took his eyes off the road to look at me, "This isn't the ideal place for this conversation really is it?"

"No, probably not." I smiled.

"The restaurant I was thinking of is only about five minutes from here. We'll soon be there. Maybe we can continue inside, when I'm not thinking about driving?"

"Of course."

Once we were seated, we were quick to order, although Jackson seemed surprised when I refused wine, asking for water and telling him I just wanted to keep a clear head while they were talking. I hoped it was believable, I rarely avoided wine with a meal.

"So. Where were we?" He asked me after the waiter had left them.

"You were telling me that things could be easier." I told him looking at him across the table. They were sat away from the door in a back corner of the restaurant. There was a lovely atmosphere to the place, with subtle lighting affording them a degree of privacy.

"Yeah, well they could be." He started, "I've told you before, I know what a mistake I made, I know I was an idiot, but Immy, I really don't want to lose you. You could move back in with me.

We can start over." I smiled at the endearing way he'd shortened my name and struggled to keep my resolve.

"But if we just go back to how it was then nothing changes really does it? I'll just be living in your house again, and if things do go wrong… Well, even if they don't, I think I'll feel like I'm walking on egg-shells making sure you don't misunderstand anything."

"I promise I would never react like I did back then. I was wound up, and my family were angry. I let them get to me, when I should have spoken to you first. I see that now, but I would never let anything like that happen again." Our eyes met and we held the gaze for a moment before I looked away.

"I am so scared Jackson."

"Scared of what sweetheart? Let me help."

"I don't think you can. I'm scared of what we have, of losing you again. I can't do that." I felt tears prickling my eyes and looked upward trying to blink them back. He reached over and took my hand, holding it gently across the table.

"I made a mistake Imogen, I can't say it enough, but I'm so sorry. I know I would never do anything like that again. It hurt so much losing you, even when I thought you'd really sold those photos. I've never loved anyone like I love you." He looked lost, but I barely could take in his words before he added, "You can have whatever you want. I'll sign the house over to you if it gives you more security. I'd do literally anything for you."

"No!" I softened and laid my hand on top of his wanting to reassure him. "I mean, that is very sweet of you, but I don't want to do anything else to make your family think badly of me. Do you understand?"

"Yes unfortunately, I do." He sighed. "You have to understand that although it's not your fault, those photos still got out, and it's the one thing Ashleigh didn't want to happen. She jumped to conclusions, so did my parents and so did I. That being said, it doesn't mean we can't work through it. You know, I haven't told you, but my Mom and Dad, they want to see you sometime. They want to apologise, if or when you are ready." I nodded, unsure of how to answer that, and what felt like hours went past while we just looked at each other.

"Look, just let me have some time. I need some space to clear my head."

"I don't want you to go." He held onto my hand, grasping it between both of his.

"I need to." I said quietly.

"What if you don't come back?"

"I will." I took a breath. "And I was hoping you'd take me to the airport."

"Of course I will, if that's what you want? But then I'll know where you're going. Does that matter?" He asked.

"It's okay - I think you've probably got a good idea anyway."

"London?" He asked and I nodded, "Back to Adam?"

"Not back to him, but I'm going to stay with him. I don't have anywhere else to go. I'll just move from Mason's spare room to Adam's."

"So you're not… There's nothing between the two of you?" Jackson asked cautiously.

"No Jackson, of course not, but he's still my family if that makes sense." I replied surprised that he would still wonder about me and Adam.

"Does he know that?"

"Yes. Please stop worrying, you've got such a frown." I lifted one hand to his face, and lay it on his jaw. He laid his hand over mine, interlinking our fingers. We broke apart as the waiter approached our table, bringing over two plates and laying them carefully down first in front of me and then Jackson. Once he had gone I continued, "In fact, just between you and me, he told me that he thinks I should try to work things out with you."

"Really?" Jackson looked at me in surprise.

"Yeah, and would you believe, that was after I told him everything. So now he knows you kicked me out, and yet he still thinks I should try again with you. I thought he'd be trying to hunt you down. Weird huh?" I smiled, trying to seem as relaxed as I could, when in reality, nerves were eating away at me.

"When did he say that?" A frown played across his forehead and he sat back, running a hand through his hair, gently ruffling it. I had noticed it was a habit he often did when he was nervous or unsure.

"The last time I saw him." I picked up my knife and fork.

"When you went to New York?"

"Yeah."

"I didn't know you saw him then."

"Oh, well yeah. He was there on business so I went to stay with him for the weekend." I stopped, looked up at him and then continued, "But before you get any ideas it was nothing other than friends. We went shopping, he had some meetings and I went to a spa. We had dinner together, he made me watch you at the awards on TV, mainly because he knew I wanted to know if you were with someone, and we talked. I slept in his bed, but it was just because we were talking so late, and it was more comfortable than the sofa." I caught the look on his face and added quickly, "We both wore pyjamas! Jackson, nothing happened between us. At all."

"Well I can't pretend I'm happy about thinking of you in another man's bed, but okay. Thank you for telling me and for being so honest."

"It's okay. I know how it feels. When I saw you and that India girl…"

"Indigo." He smiled.

"Whatever." I shrugged. "I know girls fancy you, I mean, how could they not? But having it paraded in front of me makes me feel a bit sick. I imagine you did it for a reaction though didn't you?"

"It might have crossed my mind." He said slowly and I scowled at him.

"Low blow."

"Just seeing if I could make you jealous. I wondered if you'd go a bit crazy and try to mark your territory." I laughed.

"So you're my territory now?"

"Always." His voice was low and he didn't smile. "So when is your flight?"

"Do you want me to take you home?" He asked as he helped me into the truck after we left the restaurant.

"Oh, I thought I was coming back with you?"

"I just didn't want to assume."

"Well I thought I was, but only if you still want me to?"

"You don't need to ask me if I want you to stay the night. The answer would always be yes. I'd prefer to have you back with me permanently, but I also want you to know you have the choice, and we don't have to do anything, I just want to be close to you."

He dropped his lips to mine, pulling away after a few moments before gently shutting the door for me. "It's going to be so weird without you here." He said after climbing into the drivers seat.

"It's going to be weird going home, but hopefully it will help me get my mind clear."

"I hate that you still call it home, I thought our place was your home."

"It was when I lived there. Now I'm practically a sofa surfer." I smiled, but I knew the smile didn't reach my eyes.

"I just hope going there brings you back to me." He let out a sigh.

"Stop it." I swatted his arm, "I don't need any more pressure."

"That wasn't my intention. I just wanted you to know that I want you, and we can work this out." He looked at me, "We can Imogen, as long as you talk to me. We can overcome anything."

CHAPTER 20

Jackson had offered to pick me up early from my cabin on the morning of my flight. I'd packed lightly choosing to leave most of my things behind, partly because I didn't need them and partly because I wanted to reassure him that I was coming back. I also didn't want to carry too much considering I was going to have to manage everything I took by myself.

I was just washing up the last of my dishes when there was a knock at the door.

"Hi." I smiled to see Jackson waiting there for me as I dried my hands on a towel. "What are you doing knocking? You could have come in."

"Hey, I didn't want to intrude." He dropped his head gently kissing my cheek then stopped and pushed his hands into his pockets. "I wasn't sure if you would be ready."

"Are you okay?" I looked up at him.

"Honestly?" He met my gaze, "No, not really, I'm finding the thought of saying goodbye to you really hard."

"I'm going to come back." I reached up, slipping my arms around his neck and holding him tightly. "Please don't make me feel worse about going."

"Sorry sweetheart, I don't mean to, I just can't get excited about putting you on a plane." He pulled me closer to him, wrapping his arms around me tightly.

"It'll be good for both of us." I said into his neck as he held onto me. "I think we both need some clarity."

"If you say so." He didn't sound convinced.

"I do." I pulled back. "Okay. I just need that bag there, and I'm good to go."

"That's all you're taking?" He said looking at the small suitcase.

"Well, yeah, and my shoulder bag. I told you, I like to travel light."

"Okay. I'll take it to the car."

Mason and Nicole came out of the house as Jackson closed the boot of his truck down.

"You'd better not miss our wedding." Nicole said in mock seriousness as she hugged me.

"You know I won't. I'm so looking forward to it." I laughed, "And of course, to saying goodbye to Bridezilla. I had no idea how controlling you could be!"

"Well thanks! It's a good job I know you're joking, but I bet you would have been exactly the same." Nicole stepped back, "Travel safe and hurry home."

"I will." Mason swooped in for a quick hug, whispering into my ear as he did so,

"Have you told him yet?"

"No." I replied, "You're the only person that knows, so please don't say anything." I stepped back and looked up at him, my eyes pleading. I knew I didn't have all that long until I began to show, but I still just needed some time to think, to separate myself and be alone. His gaze was intense, and I felt like he was trying to decide what the best thing to do in this situation was.

"You're going to have to soon." He said finally as he let me go.

"I know, and I will."

"Imogen?" He said taking a step back but keeping his voice low enough that he couldn't be overheard.

"Yeah?" I looked back at him warily, conscious of Jackson and Nicole standing near the truck.

"You are coming back aren't you?"

"Why do you ask that?"

"It just suddenly crossed my mind and I wondered if you were leaving him?" He held my gaze, looking at me inquiringly, "Because if you just disappeared, you'd break his heart. You know that, right?"

"I'm coming back Mason." I said firmly.

"Good. I'm glad. I know it's none of my business but I think you two are made for each other."

"Imogen! We need to go." Jackson called and with a final wave I walked the remaining distance to his truck and got in.

It was a longer flight than I remembered. Long and boring and I couldn't focus on anything. I had turned down the first class tickets Adam had tried to insist on, but given the noise in the cabin, I was now wondering why I had been so keen to say no. Saying goodbye to Jackson had been harder than I imagined too. He stayed with me right until the last moment he could and then took me into his arms, holding me tightly. He told me he loved me and told me he'd wait for me. For as long as it took. I didn't think he was going to let me go and I didn't do a great job at hiding my tears then, for a second wondering if I should just stay and tell him the truth. Autopilot took over and I found myself stepping away from him and walking towards the gate to the plane.

On the flight I lost count of the amount of times I opened and closed my book, but whatever the number, I knew I hadn't managed to get past the page I had been reading.

Finally the plane descended over London and I was able to disembark, making my way through the airport with ease due to my lack of bags. I was really grateful I'd only brought carry on luggage. Adam wasn't waiting, but had sent one of his men who recognised me at once, and led me to a waiting car before driving me back to my old home. I was let in by a doorman and whisked up to the seventeenth floor, the penthouse. It was the nicest apartment in the building, but then it could afford to be as Adam owned the rest of the building too, as well as many of the neighbouring ones. His investments in property were some of his less shady business dealings.

The apartment hadn't changed much in the time since I'd been gone. There were a few additions here and there but the general feel of the place was the same. It was very much an elegant bachelor pad, it's just that once I had lived there. It seemed like that was another life now, and although it was familiar, the memory seemed very removed. It was breezy so I didn't go onto the balcony, but standing at the full length windows that ran the length of the living area I admired the view of London below. I'd always loved the view from here, in the daytime you could pick out landmarks like The Shard and Tower Bridge, but at night, the whole city sparkled below like fairy lights. Having been told that Adam would be out for another hour or two

I made a cup of tea and settled on the sofa. The flight had worn me out.

Voices drifted into my subconscious, pulling me from sleep. No, I realised, it was just one voice talking with silences between. Adam was on the phone. I sat up slowly and stretched, it was a comfortable sofa at least, I had definitely slept in worse places.

"She's awake now. I'll let you know if there's anything else." Another silence followed by, "You're welcome. Bye." Adam walked over to me, sitting down on the coffee table in front of me. "Hello sleeping beauty." He said with a smile. "Tired?"

"Yes. I thought I'd just sit down for a minute, but that's the last thing I remember." I still felt groggy from sleep. "It's good to see you." Slowly I rolled my neck, stretching my arms above my head.

"And you Princess. But, before you ask, that was Jackson I was talking to on the phone just then."

"What? Why?"

"I thought it would be nice to let him know you arrived safely."

"Oh, yes, I probably should have done that." I said sheepishly.

"Yes, you should have. He was worried but said he didn't want to seem like he was hounding you." He frowned at me, "To make up for it, I sent him a photo of you sleeping on the sofa and rang him to tell him I'd just got in to find you asleep here. I think he understands that you're tired, but at least now he won't worry."

"Thank you Adam."

"No trouble. I would worry, knowing my other half was half way across the world on her own." I went to open my mouth but he stopped me. "No, I don't want to hear definitions about what your relationship is or isn't. I know you're here to work it out, so I'm here if you want to talk, but don't stress out about it."

"Thanks Adam."

"Like I said, no problem." He stood up, "Ah, one other thing. I told him if any pictures surface of you and another man while you're here, that it's one of my men. I told him you'll have a minder at all times if you leave here without me, and I didn't want him jumping to the wrong conclusion."

"That's good of you."

"I know." He afforded me a small smile. "Now, are you hungry?"

***

Adam worked a lot. I'd almost forgotten how much, but then he was running several large businesses and had a hand in the goings on of the London underworld, so it was likely he would be. I'd just forgotten. I hadn't anticipated spending so much time alone, but I didn't really mind and it gave me time to think. Ultimately that was what I was there for, not socialising.

I was out of the habit of going everywhere with a minder in tow, and it seemed excessive in some ways, but it was nice to know there was someone nearby if I needed it. I thought I'd be able to fly under the radar, that no one would recognise me, but after only one trip to a restaurant photos appeared online of me with Adam. The captions amused him, claiming that businessman Adam Carter had reunited with me, his old flame, but they made me nervous. I didn't want Jackson seeing them, especially when I knew how they looked. In one, I was wearing a fitted purple cocktail dress, with killer heels, holding onto Adam's arm as we left the venue. He as ever looked smart in his tailored suit and I knew we made an attractive couple, but it wasn't what either of us wanted anymore. It had been innocent, and he had only offered me his arm to steady me going down the steps. I knew the photo itself could be misconstrued though.

One thing I was grateful for was the swimming pool in the basement of the building. It went hand in hand with a gym, but in my condition I had no intention of making use of that, I just enjoyed a swim somewhere I wouldn't be bothered.

Adam didn't push me either, well, at least not to start with. He asked few questions and yet listened when I wanted to talk to him, although even that was rare.

"You seem to have become a permanent fixture on my sofa Imogen. When I want a new one, will I have to have you removed with this one, or do you think you will be able to detach by then?" Adam had walked in and removed his jacket and tie as he spoke, coming to the end of the sofa where my head was, gently lifting it so he could sit down, letting me put my head back down in his lap. Absentmindedly he stroked my hair.

"It's comfy, and I don't have a lot else to do." I laughed.

"Oh God Imogen, don't say that to me. I'll give you some money. Please go shopping or something." I could sense him rolling his eyes at me even though I couldn't see him.

"I didn't say I wasn't happy. I just like the peace and quiet."

"Okay, but there will be some point in the future when I want to sit here with someone else. It's been a week, and you've barely moved."

"I do, in the day, you just aren't here to see it." I rolled onto my back so I could look up at him. "I swim and everything!"

"That's good to hear. I was concerned we might have to have you surgically removed. Or I'd have to have removal men fly the whole sofa back to the States when you go home."

"Stop being so mean. I came here for support, not to be picked on."

"Well you've not spoken to me about anything, so how am I supposed to support you exactly?"

"Well, I don't know where exactly I should start. I just want a magic wand to wave and make everything work out."

"I don't know what you're so scared of. Your actor loves you, he's told you that, he's told me that." He looked down at me, "Have you told him you're pregnant?" I couldn't believe he knew.

"What? How do you know? Did Mason tell you?" I sat up and came to face him properly, crossing my legs in front of me.

"Imogen, no one told me. I know you so well, don't forget, we lived together for a long time. I saw your body change when you were pregnant before, so unless you've had a boob job, and have coincidentally given up alcohol then I'm assuming you are. I was just waiting in the hope you'd tell me yourself."

"God you're annoying."

"Also, you sleep a lot. It's kind of obvious. You can't be that far along though?"

"No. I guess about fourteen weeks, and no, I haven't told him yet. It will just complicate things. I don't want him to feel trapped."

"Imogen, from the conversations I've had with him, I think he would happily be trapped by you."

"I'm not sure."

"I don't know why you're pushing him away."

"He dumped me Adam. For something I didn't do."

"We've covered that. It was a misunderstanding where he over-reacted. You may not like me saying it, but I think you have a choice to make, either you forgive him and move on, or you stop sleeping with him because it isn't fair on either of you." I listened as he spoke, and realised he was making a lot of sense. "If you don't want to be with him anymore then have the decency to tell him so he can move on and try to get over you. You really need to be honest with him."

"You're right." I said softly. "I hadn't really thought of it like that. It didn't feel like I was being unfair to him, but I am."

"You know, and even though you don't seem to believe it, you're a hard act to follow Miss Cole. Credit both of us with something, we both have good taste. Neither of us went rushing out to replace you did we? Whatever you think, the truth is you're not so easy to replace. So try to believe it when he or I say we care about you, because neither of us are in the habit of lying or telling you things you might want to hear. Without being crass, I don't have to go looking for it, so why would I waste my time if I don't have to? I think it's the same for him. I just don't want you to leave it too late."

"You're right Adam."

"Other than the 'dumping'", he moved his hands in air quotations, "Has he ever done anything to hurt you?" I shook my head, "And you love him?"

"I do."

"Well it's clear that he loves you, so you already have a lot more than a lot of couples. Especially now with this little one." He gestured to my stomach.

"I know. Thanks Adam. Sometimes space and someone pointing things out really helps, you know?"

"I know." He agreed, "What do you mean about guessing how far along you are though? Haven't you had a dating scan yet?"

"No. Healthcare is expensive at home, and I didn't want anyone to find out before I was ready to tell them. I didn't want him to think I was only telling him because I needed his money."

"Well, if it's okay and I'm not overstepping, I think I'll make a couple of calls and see if I can get you in somewhere here as soon as possible. Especially after last time." He laid his hand on my knee. "Just so you know." It was at the dating scan that we had found out that our baby didn't have a heartbeat. It had been heartbreaking to go through.

"You are probably right. Thank you Adam."

"Advisor, relationship counsellor, appointment coordinator… think of all the things I can add to my business cards." He said with a smile.

"Know it all, big head and general lad about town?" I added and he narrowed his eyes at me.

"I might evict you from my sofa if you're going to be unkind!"

***

Towards the end of my third week in London, Nicole was on the phone nagging me. Not only was she concerned about the final dress measurements, and the last minute wedding arrangements but she seemed really concerned that I was actually coming back and would be there in time. I reassured her that I was, telling her that my flight was already booked for the Thursday before the Saturday wedding. I knew I was leaving it tight, but I was just grateful for the time and space to get my head together. I was also thankful for the style of dress Nicole had picked. I had tried it on once before I'd gone away and as it was a simple empire line dress, it had the flexibility and flow to hide my stomach. I didn't have a huge baby bump, but my shape was slowly changing, and I was suddenly afraid it would be noticeable to others like it had been to Adam.

Adam had been true to his word at getting me in for a scan, he seemed to have favours owed to him everywhere! While he had insisted he wouldn't come in, he felt he was stepping on Jackson's toes to do that, he had been supportive of me and waited outside until I was done. I'd reasoned it must have been hard for him too, and so went in alone, waiting apprehensively for news. I needn't have worried, and watching the monitor I saw my baby bouncing around the screen. I couldn't feel it yet, but seeing it move was amazing. Seeing it made it even more real, and I knew that I needed to tell Jackson he was going to be a dad, even though the thought of it terrified me. Coming away had worked in that I had been able to clear my mind, and work out what I wanted to do, but it hadn't fixed things between me and Jackson. I knew I'd have to go home to do that, and face up to things, rather than continuing to hide.

CHAPTER 21

"Imogen?" Jackson answered on the first ring, his voice full of hope.

"Hi Jackson." I stopped. I'd forgotten how good it was to hear his voice. Strong, safe and reassuring.

"How are you? Where? Can I ask that? Where are you?" His words tumbled out.

"I'm here. I'm back."

"Are you? When? Why didn't you call me?" I heard relief, followed by confusion in his voice.

"I'm calling you now." I smiled at his impatience. "Nicole and her plans are doing my head in. I'm going to be tied up here with her, but after the wedding, we should sit down and talk."

"Talk good or talk bad? Shit sweetheart you are making me so crazy. I have never felt so tied up in knots by a woman."

"I'm sorry, I don't mean to Jackson. I wouldn't have said anything, but I thought I should warn you that I'm back so it wasn't such a surprise at the wedding." I paused before adding, "I've missed you."

"That's good to hear." He stopped. "Look, I'm at Mason's now for his drinks thing, apparently he doesn't want a stag, but I could skip out and come to you now?"

"No don't, I'm with Nicole, for her not hen, hen party. We're at a hotel."

"You're not going to have strippers are you?" He asked.

"I hope not. Are you?" I said laughing.

"I haven't arranged any!"

"Good." I paused for a moment, "So, I'll see you on Saturday?"

"Do I really have to wait that long?"

"It's a day and a half."

"It's already been a month and a half."

"So another day is nothing."

"You're killing me."

"Stop being so dramatic."

"We could just stay on the phone all night?"

"Nicole will actually kill me, she wants my undivided attention to make up for me being away."

"So do I."

"I'll see you on Saturday." I told him more firmly, still smiling.

"Okay sweetheart, I'll see you then."

If I was honest with myself, I desperately wanted to see Jackson, but I felt more nervous than I had ever thought possible about seeing him, about telling him about the baby. I wanted more than anything to get it over with. It was all so confusing. The only good thing was how busy I was as it took my mind off thinking about anything other than the wedding. Nicole was an excitable ball of energy, and keeping her on track took all of my concentration. We spent the night in the hotel where the ceremony was going to take place. It gave us a chance to be spoiled and get ready slowly before the main event. The men however had spent the night at Mason's and were coming over by car in time for the ceremony, so I didn't easily have a chance to sneak out and see Jackson. I had hoped for a couple of minutes beforehand, but it didn't look like that would happen.

Before I knew it the morning of the wedding was upon us and professionals swept into the hotel room to do hair and makeup. Nicole looked amazing. She had her long hair curled, tumbling down her back like a princess, and a strapless simple white dress which fell to the floor. I, along with two much younger girls, members of Nicole's extended family, were wearing matching empire line dresses, all in a pale lilac colour. I couldn't believe how much my dress hid, and how flattering it was, it was almost like Nicole had known when she had chosen it. Which of course she hadn't, because I still hadn't told her. Nicole herself was preoccupied, but it reassured me that she hadn't noticed, and that meant I still had a chance to tell Jackson before he saw for himself.

"Ready?" Nicole's dad Phil had arrived and stood with them now, ready to escort his only daughter down the aisle. Nicole looked happy but ready to cry.

"Hold it in. It's going to be great. You look amazing." I told Nicole, straightening her veil for her, and giving her a delicate hug.

"So do you beautiful mummy." She said with a twinkle in her eye.

"How...?"

"Don't worry, it's not obvious, Mason told me. Why do you think I chose that dress? You look lovely babe, and he won't notice."

She smiled at me and we hugged once more. "You do need to tell him before it's born though."

"Thank you Nic." I squeezed her hands, "Okay, let's go get you married!"

From inside the function room music could be heard playing. The bridal party stood waiting for their cue and once more I found myself fussing with Nicole's train, making sure it was perfect, and trying to occupy myself. Then all at once it was time, the doors swung open and they were walking, all eyes on us as we made our way to the Minister standing at the end of the aisle with Mason and Jackson. My eyes met his and it was like there was no one else in the room. I could feel the smile growing on my face and his reflected it back.

Taking Nicole's flowers from her, I held them with my own, self-consciously trying to distract attention from my tummy, although I knew he couldn't see it, I felt suddenly uncomfortable about not telling him sooner. And then it was over, it had passed in a whirl, and the newly married couple were kissing, before making their way back down the aisle together. Jackson moved towards me, holding his arm out, which I took, smiling gratefully at him as I fell into step next to him. I needed to be led through this, I had no idea what was going on.

"Hi." He inclined his head slightly to mine as we walked.

"Hi."

"You look beautiful."

"Thank you. You look really lovely too."

We were outside then, being organised into groups and seating arrangements for photographs, and for a while I lost Jackson. He tried to catch me a couple of times, but then others got in the way, and both of them were needed for other things.

"After the speeches, I want to talk to you properly." He said, holding my chair out for me to sit down for the meal. It wasn't even as if we could sit together as we were on opposite sides of Nicole and Mason. I was beginning to wish I had come home sooner. It felt like the longest meal ever and I was frustrated at the amount of times I had to refuse wine, trying not to draw attention to myself. Then the speeches started and while I knew I was getting closer to seeing Jackson, they seemed to go on forever. I kicked myself for being so grumpy. I knew in reality that I was the one who had chosen to go away, and had stayed away for so long. It wasn't as if it was anyone else's fault. It had been easier at the time, but now I'd seen him, and been close to him again, I just didn't want to be away from him.

Finally, Mason stood and helped Nicole to her feet, leading her to the dance floor. They fit together perfectly, holding each other tightly, and I couldn't help but smile. I was happy that two of my best friends had found each other, and that I was able to be a part of it and share in their happiness. I felt eyes on me and looking along the table, I saw Jackson watching me, curiosity on his face.

"What?" I mouthed to him.

"You." He smiled and stood up, "I think we should join them."

"You're probably right." The first song was ending, and I remembered that Nicole had wanted us to encourage others onto the dance floor early on. Jackson held out his hand to me, and I placed mine in his so he could lead me to the dance floor. As we came to a stop he pulled me close to him and I slipped my arms up and across his shoulders, linking them behind his neck. I was so conscious of my tummy, I thought it would be the first thing he noticed but he didn't say anything about it, even as he held me.

"It is so good to see you." He murmured into my ear after a while. "I was beginning to wonder if you were just a dream I had."

"Or a nightmare?" I grinned up at him.

"The only nightmare I had was when I lost you." He said softly. "I don't want to push you for decisions, I just want to tell you that I love you. I'll always love you Imogen, even if you don't want to be with me, but I really hope you do." He lowered his head, kissing the side of my neck. I closed my eyes and breathed him in, savouring the moment as I stood with him, gently swaying together. For the first time in a long time it seemed we were both were completely oblivious to others being around us. I didn't say anything as I tried to work up the courage to share my news with him. Before I did he spoke again. "So, I was wondering, Imogen, will you marry me?" I froze and looked up at him.

"Are you joking?" I asked him.

"No sweetheart, I'm serious. Let's get married. I'm all in. I don't want to let you go again." He looked nervous, "I'd drive straight to Vegas right now if you said you'd marry me." I just stared at him, although it was exactly what I wanted to hear it made the fact I hadn't told him the truth even harder.

"Jackson," I started but he interrupted me.

"I'm selling the house too. It's not official yet, but I have a serious buyer interested. I want to buy something with you, something that is ours rather than mine." Taking a step backwards, I took his hand.

"Can we go outside for a minute?" He looked warily at me but nodded, allowing himself to be led by the hand out through the foyer and into the grounds. Walking down into the garden I looked for somewhere quiet and out of the way, finally settling on a bench, but when I reached it I was too nervous to sit still.

"What's wrong Imogen? I thought you were pleased to see me? Is this it? Are we over?"

"You've got such a bad habit of jumping the gun, and getting things wrong." I said still holding his hand. With my other one, I rubbed my forehead, trying to relieve the tension as I thought about how best to handle this situation.

"Sorry." Letting go of my hand he took a step towards the bench and sat down, resting his chin on his hands, elbows on his knees. "Go ahead."

"Thank you." I took a deep breath. "Okay, so you asking me in there to marry you, do you mean it?" He nodded.

"Of course I did. I don't tend to go around throwing proposals out when I don't mean it."

"That means the world to me, that you'd ask me, and I want to say yes…" He cut me off,

"You do?" He looked surprised,

"But, there's something I need to tell you first, because you might not feel the same way when you know." I bit my lip, holding his gaze.

"What is it?"

"I've been so scared. I wanted to tell you, and I put it off, and I shouldn't have done, and it's been too long… And now it's so much harder." I stopped speaking as he rose to stand before me, gently taking my hands to stop me pacing about. It must have been obvious that I was working myself up.

"You can tell me anything Imogen. We'll work it out." He said softly. "Is there someone else?"

"No, it's nothing like that. Please don't be angry with me. I don't expect anything from you and I get it if you don't want to be part of it, but please don't be angry." I was so nervous, and that seemed to be rubbing off on him.

"Part of what sweetheart? Tell me."

"I'm…" I took another deep breath and looking up at him I softly let it out, "I'm pregnant." The look of shock on his face was almost immediately replaced with a huge smile.

"Oh my God, that is amazing." He said beaming, wrapping his arms around me and gently lifting me up, planting a kiss on my lips as he set me back down again.

"You really think so?" I asked looking up at him. He was taking this so much better than I thought he would have done.

"Yes." He was still holding me tightly, as if I couldn't stand on my own.

"I wasn't sure how to tell you. I didn't know if you'd be happy or not. I want to keep it Jackson. You don't have to be involved if you don't want to, but I know I want it."

"Do you really think I'd walk away from you both? Do you think I even could?" He leaned back looking into my eyes. "There's no chance." He gently placed his hand on my tummy. "This is our fresh start sweetheart. You, me and our baby."

"You didn't even ask if it was yours." I said with a smile.

"It didn't even occur to me that it wouldn't be mine." He said with a little frown. "But why didn't you tell me? Is that why you went away?"

"Can we sit down? I said gesturing to the bench.

"Of course." He followed me, sitting down beside me.

"I guess I was afraid that either you wouldn't want it, or that you might think it was intentional to trap you or something. I just wanted to work out if what we had was enough before we added anymore confusion to it."

"If what we have is enough?" He looked shocked, "I've been telling you for months that I love you."

"I know. I just wasn't sure."

"What changed?"

"I was going to tell you tonight anyway, but then you asked me to marry you, and whether that still stands or not, you said it without knowing, and it didn't feel like you had to, if you see what I mean?"

"I do see, but yes it still stands." He moved from the bench, getting down onto one knee in front of me, "So Imogen, love of my life and mother of my child, will you please marry me?"

"Yes." Once again his arms were around me spinning me around with him.

Suddenly a loud whooping noise followed by whistling and clapping filled the air and Jackson and I looked back to the hotel to see Mason and Nicole and some of their guests watching them with huge smiles on their faces.

"Congratulations!" Nicole called loudly blowing them kisses before rounding the crowd up and returning back indoors.

"How embarrassing!" I said dropping my head against Jackson's shoulder.

"They're happy for us. It's nice." He said with a grin, "Maybe I should have sent you off to London sooner if this is what happens?"

"All I did was swim and sleep."

"And go to restaurants with your ex, looking sexy as hell. You're lucky I'm not a jealous man." He drew me into him again. I'd been worried about how he would react to those photos but he didn't seem bothered, quickly moving on. "We'll make it work. I promise, I'll do anything for you, and for this little one." He splayed his hand on my tummy again. "God, it's amazing."

"Oh, I have something to show you." I sat back down and picked up my small purse from the bench, pulling out an envelope I had been treasuring before passing it to Jackson. "Here." He looked puzzled, but carefully opened the envelope, pulling a black and white photo from it.

"Oh, wow." He looked at it in awe.

"I'm almost twenty weeks." I said biting my lip. "Further than I thought before I had the scan. I think it must have been that first time we were together after we split up. I am sorry it's such a surprise."

"It's a fantastic surprise." He was still holding the picture. "You don't look pregnant."

"I think this dress is particularly flattering. I'll look like a whale when I take it off. It must be noticeable because Adam guessed, I didn't tell him. I wouldn't have told him before you."

"It's okay, I mean, of course I'd prefer to have been the first person you told, but it's not like it's been normal between us. Does anyone else know?"

"Mason does. He heard me being sick before I went away. I had awful morning sickness, I'm surprised you didn't notice too, I couldn't really hide it. Thank goodness that's gone now! Mason told Nicole, but that's it and I didn't know she knew until yesterday."

"So I'm the last one to know?" He said and I pursed my lips feeling uncomfortable. "It's okay, hey, this one isn't going to be an only child Imogen, so as long as I'm the first one you tell next time, it's all good." He grinned at me, lowering his head to mine, and I knew he was right, together we could work everything out.

ABOUT THE AUTHOR

Hattie Wells is an author and blogger based in the South West of England.

As a lifelong avid reader, Hattie is a firm believer in reading for escapism and enjoyment, writing books that readers will enjoy.

You can find Hattie online at https://www.facebook.com/hattie.wells.author - she'd love to hear from you.

Printed in Great Britain
by Amazon

59135203R00166